Lost In Plain Sight

Alan Camrose

Lost in Plain Sight

Lost in Plain Sight

Lost in Plain Sight

Lost in Plain Sight

Lost in Plain Sight

Lost in Plain Sight

Lost in Plain Sight

Lost in Plain Sight

Lost in Plain Sight

Lost in Plain Sight

PART ONE

THURSDAY, AUGUST 5TH

1

2:00 pm
SAM

The "Security Suite" of the Beachcomber Hotel was cramped, dark and musty, like a coffin fitted with broadband.

It was where they housed the CCTV kit, in a dingy box-room next to reception. Just enough room to swing a cat; Pagoda had wedged herself into a gap under the table to avoid any such thing.

'Ready?' I said. Meyra was always ready, a hint of a nod.

I fiddled with the controls and hit play.

The large screen lit up and the video started, time-stamped *07:04:38*, showing the hotel's entrance earlier in the day. The receptionist stood behind the heavy desk in her ink-silk dress soaking up spare light. Her thin black hair was tied in a bun - if it had been any more severe, I'd have felt obliged to drop down and do a hundred push-ups. No-one else in shot. The picture was clear, sharp enough for me to admire each old local Brighton photo dotted on the walls in their non-matching frames. I could almost smell the thick carpet's mixed browns and oranges. No sound except a loud ticking clock.

The hotel doors opened and a figure stepped in.

Here we go.

Meyra hunched forwards. The shadows created by the screen's glow accentuated her Alpine cheekbones, her eyes glittered a different, darker shade of black.

The video showed just a guy, an old guy, walking into a tired Brighton hotel, could have been anywhere. But it spelled Dark *Ma gic*, the six-letter version, the one with a silent and invisible .

'No question. It's Walker. I'd recognise that hair anywhere.' I didn't need the built-in facial recognition software to tell me that.

I caught Meyra's furtive reflex glance at *my* hair, a similar shade of silver-white, for me a permanent reminder of the watchtower where Meyra and I had "met". She hadn't done enough to kill me, but plenty to remind me in no uncertain terms never to take *Ma gic* for granted. Or her. Who knew that I'd end up babysitting her?

'He is excessively active in the circumstances, Sam Franklin,' said Meyra. She'd never managed to grasp the name thing: if I told her my middle names, our conversations would last forever.

'It's the sea air', I said.

Endymion Walker's hair flopped over his thin, dry-riverbed face, a light blue linen suit buttoned up to his throat over his rope-thin body. Dapper, and at the same time weird bearing in mind the sweltering weather. Besides, I'd never seen him before in anything except Smart Funereal. He was carrying a small grey package and looked in an unseemly rush for someone who hadn't been alive at the time of the recording.

He strode through reception and headed for the medieval lift, upgraded from prehistoric no more than twenty-five years ago. He waved dismissively to the receptionist as he passed her, ignoring her polite greeting, leaving her with only the ticking of the clock.

Walker fought the lift's doors closed. It was one of those where you have to clank shut the inner cage and the outer door before it lurches into life, wheezing and grunting upwards every time as if that would be its final journey before it plummeted to tangled destruction.

As something of an anti-climax, the video cut to him getting out in one piece on the third floor.

He hesitated, looked to his right and left, then turned to his left. He walked briskly, checking the numbers on the doors as he went before reaching his. The only splashes of colour against the faded magnolia walls were his suit and the intense red flowers artfully placed in small alcoves along the way like smears of blood. Such a negligently arty look, I nearly lit a Gauloise.

At Number 319, Walker waved his electronic key at the lock and pushed the door. He stopped when it reached halfway open, pushed more. It didn't budge. He hunched his shoulders close to the door, placed both hands close together palm up in the centre and shoved hard. The door resisted for a moment longer then opened enough for him to squirm inside. I rewound and froze the frame with the door open but couldn't make out any details in the room beyond.

Another cut. The door opened – *09:04:37*.
Walker emerged carrying a large grey
canvas bag on his shoulder. He headed
slowly back to the lift, straining. The bag's
material was stretched tight and he
constantly shifted its position to support it
with his back and hip. He dropped the bag
at the lift door then dragged it inside.

The film jumped back to reception.
Walker emerged from the lift, carefully
picked up the bag and started making his
way over to the hotel doors. He briefly
paused a few times, clumsily hefting the bag
as he went, ignored the receptionist and
lurched out of the hotel. The doors swung
shut behind him.

The playback ended.

No sound in the darkened room. No
sense either – Walker had been murdered in
the early hours of that morning. Ambushed.
Killed more emphatically than I cared to
think about by a blue, horned demon. Yet
here he was.

I waited for a few moments, 'I checked. The system doesn't seem to have been tampered with. No glitches. Could it be Re-animation?' I rolled the name of the Hex around in my mouth, tasted acid. Just *saying* it gave the word power.

'I believe that would be a serious breach of the Lore, Sam Franklin?' I could see how agitated she was as she pushed a fractionally stray strand of her short black hair back into place.

'Yeah. All of them.'

'I would not expect it to have been Re-animation,' said Meyra. 'The hotel remains standing,'

Good point. No smouldering crater to explain.

The last thing we needed was outsiders taking an interest in our activities, better that we were left alone to handle any uncontrolled *Ma gic* outbreaks in our own way. Keep it in the Circle: that's the role of our *real* Magic Circle - not the other one with the website and open days. Especially not the open days. We're the practitioners – and guardians – of the real thing, not those make-flowers-come–out-of-your-sleeve jockeys, or even worse the ones who make funny balloon animals. Mind you, I *could*, if pressed, make a nifty blow-up sausage dog.

Meyra extracted her wafer-thinness from what I had come to think of as the security cupboard while I downloaded the video onto my phone. Some snuffling in the gloom reminded me not to close the door behind me. Pagoda was still asleep.

It felt like we were drawing a chalk line around a corpse that was still moving.

2

2:30 pm
MEYRA

Mother is Elvish minor royalty and Daddy is a Hong Kong investment banker, so what chance did I have to be restrained and patient? I pressed the service bell for a long time again at the currently unoccupied reception desk. And then once more, just to make absolutely sure.

I sensed Sam Franklin's lanky form loping up behind me from the extravagantly named 'Security Suite'; Pagoda would not be far behind. Wretched beast. If I ever Bonded with a familiar, it would without question not be a cat. Maybe a hawk. Mother would view that as tacky, so a bright red hawk would be deliciously tempting…

A figure emerged from the office behind reception as I loomed over the bell ready to stress-test it further. Margit. The seemingly ever-present receptionist. She scuttled over to us and arranged her face in a thin smile which she aimed between us.

I met her gaze, realising that she was still not sure what the arrangement was between Sam Franklin and me. Who was in charge? I endeavoured to put any doubts at rest and leaned forward.

'Do you have any idea what was in Endymion Walker's bag this morning when he left?'

She wrinkled her long nose and shook her head, jangling her earrings. She tip-toed around the jagged crags of the English language on her perilous journey, 'No. I not know. He no say. Mister Walker - he stay here ten days, always backing and forwarding. He very quiet, no trouble. Then I no see him after he leave yesterday. He only come back this morning, then *poof!* He go again with some of his stuff.' Her eyes darted between us questioningly, concerned; this was her watch. 'He alright?'

I held her gaze, 'We need to find out where he has gone. A spare key, if you would please.'

Margit nodded and gave me an electronic room key for 319. Her face was taut as she watched the three of us out of the corner of her eye. When she saw me looking, she busied herself tidying the immaculate desk.

Sam Franklin headed for the lift; Pagoda slunk in his wake with a lazy yawn. She had a long streak of pure white fur along her back, her echo from when I first met Sam Franklin. I felt her glare even though she was not looking at me. I perfectly understood: cats have long memories. I suggested to Sam Franklin at the time not to interfere with what I was doing there, and I was of course right. Accidents happen. It has been two years. A trickle into an hourglass for me. Time passes differently for me. Sam Franklin and I had made the best of it, I think, but Pagoda neither forgets nor forgives.

As we reached the lift, Margit cleared her throat nervously and called out to us, I thought mainly to me, 'Mister Walker, he *vary* untidy.' A warning and a marker. The jammed door in the video. I translated that as *Please do not blame me for the mess*, so I prepared myself for untold horrors, starting at clothing without a crisp fold and ending up in the realms of Nightmare (in the realms of Nightmare, unfolded shirts are the least of visitors' worries). Mother, bless her, has only ever employed cleaners who have been diagnosed with chronic OCD.

Pagoda broke away from us and pattered up the stairs rather than braving the lift. She was protecting her remaining lives. That seemed reasonable, she was at least one down.

In the event, her suspicion was understandable. My journey proved to be considerably more alarming than I had anticipated. I opened the inner door at the third floor when we jolted to a halt. Pagoda was waiting for us, her head cocked to one side with an *I told you so* expression. I avoided eye contact with her, wrestled with the outer door and quickly slipped out. Sam Franklin sauntered out behind me.

We were at the end of a long corridor, pale walls leading off to our left. I saw Pagoda hunt some crimson geraniums arranged in small vases in alcoves along the corridor. In the way that cats do, she retreated from them, then advanced, then

back ready to pounce. Shortly after, I heard a
fierce volley of whispers and hisses between
her and Sam Franklin as he firmly instructed
her not to eat any flowers.

We arrived at Number 319. I almost
expected Walker to shoulder past us, rude as
ever, and barge in. I reached into my
cashmere hoodie, pulled out a pair of white
latex gloves and a face mask and slipped
them on. I never leave home without them.
Humans can be so *unwholesome*, and in
situations like this I could not be too careful
down here even after all this time.

I unlocked the door. Sam Franklin
stepped in front of me and filled the
doorway, his Shield ready, just in case. He
moved smoothly to his left as he went in and
I stepped to the right, that cat behind us, tail
bristling.

I took in the scene.

No gore was smeared across the carpet,
no sinister Pagan symbols, no slithering
tentacles. I flinched, nonethcless. The textiles
and colours clashed horribly. What were
they *thinking*?

'It's OK. Chronic naffness isn't catching.'

'That is of course very fortunate for you,
Sam Franklin,' I said, looking up and down

at his crumpled check shirt and highly unsuitable cords.

He grinned lopsidedly at me, 'Funny. Let's get started.'

3

2:45 pm
CURTIS

'The programme has been accelerating,' said the greasy-haired man. He ran his fingers through the long black strands as he fidgeted in the vinyl chair. He was on the receiving side of the desk.

He fought to keep still; this was embarrassing enough as it was without any tell-tale squeaks of guilt. He ensured no eye contact with the tall figure on the other side of the desk in the large white office. 'It's because we've taken on more clients. Like you said to. Sir.' A hint of, if not defiance -

that would not have been wise - an assertion of his side of the story.

The other man nodded, ruffling his neatly trimmed beard, lucky not to lacerate his fingers on the razor tips. He leaned forward, 'While laudable endeavour on your part, Curtis, to increase…participation, due diligence is *key* in situations like this. You should know that. There is infinite difference between "no close family contacts" and her being the daughter of a senior Circle man.' A pause. 'One we have now had to silence. Most regrettable. He and I sometimes used to play chess.'

'It wasn't my fault', said the man trying to sink unnoticeably into the chair, away from the broken glass of the other's voice.

'But nonetheless it *was* your responsibility.' He gestured to the corner of the office which had a curved picture window looking out over the expanse of the site. 'I would like you to come over here. I want you to see something.' The man went over, dabbing at his forehead with his sleeve 'No need to worry. I do not bite. Indeed, I have noted many advantages of having you on the team. Your performance aside from this blemish has been exemplary.' A smile which, if he'd seen it, Dracula would have sued for image rights infringement. He waved at the scene below the window, a flash of silver under the bright lights, 'You have been a cornerstone of this venture, and I thank you. I would like that to continue.'

The man inwardly sighed with relief as he looked out over the operation. He reflected that he *had* been instrumental in its construction, well at least the design. While the girl had been an administrative cock-up, it happens to everyone. He began to feel a little better. More confident. So why did he still feel rivulets of sweat under his arms and his forehead was damp again despite the cool air in the office. At least, he hoped it was sweat, and not blood from the earlier surgical cuts of his boss's words. He took comfort from there not being a covering of plastic sheeting on the floor in which to wrap his dead body, haha.

He looked round and saw the other man gesturing to him again. No, not to him this time, to the floor. Strange.

The floor lurched beneath him, destabilising him. It seemed to sweep away from him on all sides at dizzying speed; he was at the centre. The world was suddenly a Venus fly-trap with him a panicked fly. The ground did not touch, even less damage, the other man's desk or his leather chair, as if it were alive and knew what was off-limits. A yawning gap blossomed under the man's feet and he completely lost his balance at the sharp shock, falling prone, arms outstretched, the edges of the growing pit tantalisingly out of reach as the rock seemed to swirl and deform around him.

He scrabbled for a handhold on the side of the pit to pull himself up but his hand was batted away by the rock. *Batted away?* The pit deepened. He needed help: none came.

His view of the office started to contract as the floor began to close over his head. He screamed and shouted, 'Is it an earthquake? Help me!' No response for several seconds.

'No, I can assure you everything is fine, dear boy,' came the other's voice, partially muffled by the sound of scratching and creaking rock drawing together above the man. 'You need to think of this as a transfer to the shop floor.'

A final scream as the ground knitted back together seamlessly over the man, his boss pleased that there was no ugly join. He had become so much more adept with the Dig Hex.

As for the girl, the show must go on. At least she was a fine specimen, a perfect match. And there was no backing out now, even though he would expect them to come, if they could find him. Let them come.

His thoughts were interrupted by a polite knock on his door and a man's head appeared. A polite cough. 'Sorry, sir, I wondered if someone was still with you.' A late lunch.

'No, no, that's quite alright, dear boy' He flashed a barracuda smile, in an unusually good mood, unprecedentedly so. 'I have been re-organising my office.'

4

3:15 pm
SAM

I've never had a moment's doubt that I'd
follow in my dad's footsteps at the Circle.
And his father's, and his, and on and on way
back, an unbroken chain of service spanning
the centuries. Unsung and unknown to the
general populace. Which has always been a
Good Thing – much less dangerous for them.
Wearing a pitchfork via its sharp points or
acting as an over-sized firelighter had never
been an ambition for any of us. It's always
been about the service.

All that history seemed to have led to this glorious moment in this traditional British seaside hotel room.

Faded red-and-brown-striped curtains, with a touch of algae-green lovingly mixed in to create a decomposing and rusty palette. They showcased wide open sash windows that looked out over the sea under clear skies. A few tired flags drooped on nearby buildings; the net curtains hung immobile, all undisturbed by any hint of a breeze. Mind you, the panoramic sea view view was disconcerting given that the hotel stands in a quiet, leafy square up a side street off the main drag, but that's *Ma gic* for you.

Ma gic: a word that needs to be handled carefully like you would handle a Ming vase filled with scorpions. Particularly if you say it out loud, because words like that have real power. Verbalising it in full or writing it down too often or at the wrong time is a dangerous business, immediately inviting attention - unwanted attention in a sanity-threatening, eviscerating kind of way - from things that are best left to stalk ancient ruins or isolated cabins in the woods. I noted that

Walker's room showed no trace of *Ma gic* in it at all, completely scrubbed. Not magical in any way whatsoever, even if candles, sprinkled rose petals and champagne had been included in the room charge.

What it did have was an enormous wardrobe, and next to that a deeply inset marble fireplace with a fire basket lightly coated with ash. A mirrored, over-ornate overmantel sat brooding over the fireplace showboating cutting edge design flair from when indoor plumbing was going to be the Next Big Thing. Under the window was a mini-bar with a glass front, filled with indifferent bottled beers and sad one-person bottles of unmemorable rosé. There was a writing desk served by an ergonomically challenged chair. A full-length mirror stood in the corner next to the fireplace with a distressed – in this environment, probably suicidal – gold frame.

The king-size bed boasted a triumphantly vile tartan headboard and had accompanying rickety bedside tables with tatty lamps. No TV. Walker would have had it removed, otherwise he would've put it flat and used it as a tea tray.

Everything stood on a dark orange seashell-patterned carpet; a threadbare black-and-white chequered rug had been artfully thrown in a heap under the window. Small touches like that added a sophisticated feel.

I smiled to myself. Meyra had needed to brace herself for the harrowing prospect of no suite at the Beachcomber. At least all the rooms were en suite. She's accustomed to at least five-star; a communal bathroom would've given her brainfreeze. I could tell she was steeling herself for a rough time down in Brighton and I hoped for her sake that if we ever met the murderous demon it had nice manners.

'If Margit considers *this* to be untidy, Mother would employ her on the dot,' said Meyra. I kept my mouth shut; it was not the time to be finicky.

Meyra stripped off her face mask, relieved at the lack of physical threat, wary of the existential one posed by the furnishings.

Not *vary untidy* at all. More *cleaned out.*

It looked to me like Little Miss Tidy and Mary Poppins had had a full-contact Clearing-up Contest here that had gone to extra time and penalties.

'Let's see if Walker left us anything helpful.' I put on my best Fred Jones voice for her as a test, 'We should split up, gang, and search for clues.'

Meyra had definitely been practising her cultural assimilation, and she played along for once, 'Jinkies!'

5

3:45 pm
SAM

Nothing yet.

I was head-first in the depths of the enormous oak wardrobe, fighting my way through Walker's dingy black suits, the jackets lined up like the cloakroom at a Blues Brothers party; Meyra was delving under the double bed. Sunlight streamed through the windows in the blazing August afternoon as we tore the room apart hunting for something – anything – to help us.

'Why am I in a dead wizard's wardrobe on a nice sunny day at the seaside?' I stretched out to make myself a bit more comfortable. 'Not even a gateway to Narnia in here.' That said, if I was the lion, that made Meyra the witch. Perfect. I sensed Pagoda's glower at my miscasting of the feline; she had no complaints otherwise.

There was plenty of empty space. Enough even for the contents of Meyra's two huge Louis Vuittons that she'd brought with her to test Jezebel's suspension. Cue the choir of angels at the mention of my beloved Jezebel, the Supreme Goddess of Campervans, divine apart from her dodgy starter motor.

Meyra shuffled out from under the double bed for some air, albeit neither cool nor fresh. The air in the room immediately felt chilly rather than super-heated. She nodded behind her, 'I prefer not to flounder around in the dark. That is what dwarves are for.' She took a few deep breaths to emphasise her point, then smoothed down her immaculate clothes and slid back under the bed to carry on searching.

'Enough already with the quaint minority thing. You're not Welsh.'

I heard her silence from under the bed in response. Her rather more complicated than usual background meant that she had smooth edges that needed roughing out. That was how our dubious team-up had been sold to me by the powers that be. We were never going to make a smooth blend. Brought up within a diamond's throw of South Kensington, she once told me that her mother was proud that Meyra's first words had been *au pair,* closely followed by *canapé.*

She re-emerged and drew herself upright and unruffled as I gave up on the wardrobe and headed over to the fireplace. It was adorned with a few desultory specks of ash. Meyra turned to rifling through the bedding scattered untidily on the bed.

'Nothing?'

She shook her head.

'Think of all this as part of your training,' I said.

Her nostrils flared slightly, 'I prefer to think of it as information exchange rather than training but, however we describe it, you do count as a hardship posting, Sam Franklin.'

Pagoda interrupted us with a growl from across the room – cats shouldn't growl – as she fruitlessly hunted around the mini-bar for snacks. She soon got the message that none were to be had and trudged over to the rug for a lie down and a sulk under those hooded eyes.

Meyra started to examine the mini-bar and poked around among the bottles, finding nothing but more bottles. Pagoda looked up with narrowed eyes at Meyra in case she came up with any missed snacks. Still no luck, so she bared her teeth as if she were originally from Cheshire. Point made, she settled back down contentedly in the sun on the rug.

Meyra and I converged on the battered writing desk. The adjustable wooden chair that went with it promised heinous discomfort. An ornate five-pronged candlestick on the desk held spent and dirty cream-coloured candles that had oozed down to the desktop, mingling with a dried coffee stain. This was our last chance saloon in the room, our hopes clinging on by their bitten and ragged fingernails.

A vivid image popped into my head of Endymion Walker at the office hunched over his desk, fiddling with some executive toy. He was wearing his customary forbiddingly black suit, his untidy long strands of white hair bobbing dangerously around a mass of flickering candles. He always preferred to rely on them to light his work; absolutely no electric lights for him which, as with most modern technology, he regarded as the Devil's work. He had had a wide-ranging view of what would constitute *modern*.

Meyra took the in-room dining menu out of the small, otherwise empty, drawer and passed it over to me deadpan; I spotted her minute change of expression. 'Look at this, Sam Franklin.' *Tinned fruit salad*, almost certainly in a small round metal bowl; and *gammon steak with a pineapple ring on top*. Not to mention *crinkle-cut chips.* And *petit pois* for a bit of foreign glamour.

'Wow. This menu catapults the Beachcomber forward to 1975.'

'Soon after I arrived here,' said Meyra.

'And still a teenager, right?'

'Since human beings first walked on the Moon.' Meyra moved towards the door. 'We have found nothing,' her voice lower than normal. In thirty degrees heat, her cool was fracturing a touch.

She glanced back over her shoulder at me, expecting me to follow, but she'd have to wait. I gestured that I wasn't finished yet, and Meyra displayed no reaction. She knew that rushing me never – ever - works. I wanted to try one remaining thing before we gave up here. Sometimes a different perspective works. I levered myself into the desk chair and gingerly pivoted on it to take a final look around the room.

I could feel two sets off eyes on me, Pagoda's dismissive, Meyra's unreadable.

'There is just some spilt coffee, used candles and a dead end in this room, Sam Franklin,' she said.

I ignored her. The creaking desk chair was as unfit for purpose as I had expected. I tuned out and let my thoughts wander as I tilted it back. Apart from inspiration, I was hunting an angle that might improve my sitting experience all the way up to excruciatingly uncomfortable. I reached a position where it felt natural to put my feet up on the desk.

There were two small brown smudges next to each other where my boots came to rest; they fitted over the smudges perfectly. Not just part of the dowdy wear-and-tear, but landing markers for generations of idly musing guests – including Walker? - gazing out over the view, maybe nursing a thin Aussie beer, or in his case a tankard of mead.

I looked around me.

To my right, the view from the window hadn't markedly changed; to my left, the wardrobe seemed to be too far over to crane my neck without my risking some unplanned acrobatics. That meant that the fire basket in the fireplace was now squarely in my line of sight.

I saw that I could crumple pieces of paper and toss them into the fire basket and Burn them. That would account for the ash in the fire basket – not much other reason in the middle of August. It's like a *Ma gic* version of another of Walker's executive toys. Probably the most fun Walker ever had in this room. Or anywhere else; he hadn't really done fun. Too vulgar. Even his toys were more like puzzles or tests of skill. I stood up, risking life and limb, and padded over to the fireplace and the scorched fire basket again.

Meyra stood in the doorway. She never fidgeted. On principle. But she was really close to starting, 'What are you doing? We need to move on.'

I didn't answer.

As before, there was nothing to the left behind the fire basket in the corner of the grate.

Then I spotted it.

'Gotcha.' To the right, wedged right at the back, was a small scrunched up piece of paper. It had been thrown at the fire basket, ricocheted off the top and landed in the far corner. Jammed in the shadows from the window. So well embedded that the clean-up exercise had missed it, and so had I the first time round. Here's to bloody-mindedness, but I imagined Meyra would not let the chance pass to make a point.

I used some Focus and fished it out of the corner with the end of a pen. A floorboard creaked behind me as Meyra stepped back into the room, interested again. I stole a glance at Pagoda and even she didn't automatically opt for disdainful.

I restrained myself from starting a victory dance yet, and Meyra looked like she was biding her time before bursting into song.

Pagoda pondered for a few seconds, then decided to lie back down.

Almost inaudible from Meyra, just enough for me to hear, 'Groovy,' and for the moment unspoken, but not very far away: 'better late than never'.

I gently unfurled the ball of paper and smoothed it out on the desk.

6

4:45 pm
MEYRA

The piece of paper was darkly stained.
Coffee. It had been torn from a notebook.
Written at the top in spidery handwriting
was the word '*HAVEN*?', thickly underlined.
Immediately below it were two lines of text
in the same handwriting:

Mirror of Galadriel?
Tree of Life? Casa of Life?

Painstakingly transcribed under those
words or names was a long string of letters
and numbers, asterisks, question marks and

hash-tags, seemingly random, finishing in a soaked, crumpled mess of illegibility.

'Does that mean something to you?' I said.

'Only the Tolkien reference, and I know how you feel about that sort of thing.' It was true. Humans' cultural portrayals of my people veered between haughty and ethereal to "cute" and "hilarious" to cruel and cat-like. I do not approve of such representations, particularly where I am compared somehow unfavourably to a feline. Sam Franklin is well aware of this but appears to derive amusement from the distress these false portrayals cause me. I merely concentrated on remaining calm and slowly stripped off my gloves; Sam Franklin had removed his earlier. Reckless.

'I believe it is your howl,' I said in revenge, angling my head towards the fireplace without expression.

'Shout,' said Sam Franklin, distracted. I presumed it was his correction of my argot rather than a suggestion. 'Good plan.'

Pagoda's ears pricked up at the possibility of food to match the promise of drink. She waited attentively until we reached the door before uncoiling herself upright. There was no point in her wasting her energy if it had been a feint from Sam Franklin.

Rather than being seen to agree with a cat, I took my life in my hands by using the creaky lift again; Pagoda ostentatiously kept to the stairs. At reception, I asked Margit if she recognised the names on the list, but she shook her head sorrowfully. *It ring no bells.* Sam Franklin stepped away pulling out his telephone, muttering something about speaking to Virginia, his personal assistant.

'While we are out, Margit,' I said, 'please can you send a message to River Smith? In case we need to meet.' River Smith was the police's Circle-liaison liaison officer for this region.

Sam Franklin pocketed his phone. 'No luck. The daughter's not around. Virginia's going to keep trying and let us know.'

Olivia Walker was the victim's closest relative, Endymion Walker's only offspring. Such a tiny family. I decided to leave it to Sam Franklin to break the news to her about her father's death.

We left the cat behind, her expression as close as felines can get to a wounded pout. Her eyes narrowed and I could sense the sub-titles to her low grumble to Sam Franklin, *Yes I will stand guard here while you go off gallivanting. But tonight my dinner had better be smoked salmon.* Sometimes, it was not clear to me which of them was whose familiar. Their Bond seemed strong enough, although I did not want to contemplate what she would do if intruders offered her some dried liver treats. Her temptation to strew – albeit half-chewed – roses at their feet in welcome would have been a challenge for her to resist.

In the meantime, Pagoda, stiff-backed, pupils vertical like arrow slits, took up a sentry post part way up the stairs.

The Angel tavern was six doors up among elegant white and cream buildings. An old-fashioned drinking house according to Sam Franklin. It was dusky inside even on such a sunny afternoon. A parade of ale pumps gleamed proudly under the lights like sentinels at home guarding our Queen. We each had a flagon of beer. That was fine: I had long ago become used to descending to his level drinking beer in places like this, chilled Chablis apparently being out of the question. I no longer even ask about the beer's vintage, except when I wish to provoke him. Bitterness flooded my throat as I allowed the burbling of the other patrons to trickle over me. Tendrils of an idea began to mesh into a pattern before me.

'I believe I have one answer at least to this tangle,' I said, leaning forward. 'We are agreed that Endymion Walker was already dead before we saw him this morning. What we saw on the video was something else, Sam Franklin, and I wager that I can prove it.'

7

Time: Unknown
SANCTUARY

*My body surely needs to breathe, to perform
the physical act of filling my lungs and exhaling,
again and again and again, but then I remember:
there's no need in here, in my perfect bubble. I am
and have always been safe, cossetted in its perfect
symmetry, drifting in luscious translucent gel
without me getting wet, walking without ground
beneath me, floating and spinning at the centre of
the world. Totally safe.*

*A brooding song breaks in on my
concentration, the low, soft song of a choir of*

*colours throbbing in a rainbow rhythm, getting
louder and louder, not unpleasant but alien.*

*I tumble in place, moving without going
anywhere, serene, weightless, untethered: my
arms and my legs will flail in the ooze, my hair
clumps and breaks and streams against the fluid,
like floating in the Dead Sea but louder, walking
in Space but coarser...a susurration of smells
around me, a blaze of coloured textures. All
mingling a thousand years ago with the sharp
taste at the edges of my tongue of shattered pale
stalactites.*

*My mind has fractured but I must be fine if I
know it has fractured. All I need is some help.
Some guidance.*

*And the rhythm, now loud but not jarring, I
sway in its embrace.*

*I can see white all around my bubble, pierced
with fierce points of cold light, a glitter of silver
rotating in front of my eyes like a compass needle,
or is that me?*

*Disorientated and cowed, frightened and free
all at once, I float in my spherical world,*

separated from Outside by the diaphanous, steely membrane, trying to remember in a straight line, but it was and will be so difficult.

The crescendo of melody teases images from inside me, drags them into my mind where we look at them, stunned. They creep out from under my eyelids into the white gloom, none of them coherent or ordered; I used to be so ordered, didn't I? Until I stopped, until I moved on, escaped from the bonds of the world, found something new. This. I ended up here. Or was it before? My memories are huge boulders resisting being moved into their proper place.

Now it will come back to me. There was a man in a murky cave; a den. He was my lifeline with his fiery hair? I talked to him among his flickering candles for what seemed like days, noisy and filled with tactile promise, tinged with cinnamon and copper. So relaxing. So comforting. So heavy.

When I had nowhere to go, no hope. He was my saviour.

And then I am here among the silver angels who stare at me facelessly, waiting, waiting for what? They must know the dark man and his fires. Will he tell them? Is he an angel, too?

I reached out with my sugary mind for any answers that will brush my skin and soothe my taste buds, feed my memory with pungent landscapes.

Before they can tell me things with their secret fragrance, there is something close by: streams of whiter light in the white space beyond my bubble. It startles me as the reek of white fire reflects off my sanctuary, creates fat threads of after-image in my eyes.

Muffled screams breaking over me. Just one or many? Not me. All Outside my bubble. I cannot see what is making them, but I can feel reverberations of pain from Outside, not here, not in my safe bubble. They shimmer in my skin as the screams continue and continue and continue, pouring like a waterfall on barbed wire.

The screamers are constructed with pain and despair; they are being dis-assembled piece by piece.

Then the screams stop. No more pain for now.

Until I start screaming too. I was safe and now it has dawned on me: there is no hope. None of it will ever stop, I will hear the screams in my head forever, those screams are my future.

My mind shatters around me once more as my memories grapple with an elusive taste of reality and the cathedral's blue clock dissolves back into the white, its time running out as if from a cracked hourglass. Then blackness. Then nothing more. White becomes black. There is nothing more than the screaming deep inside me which drains away like the time, and I am calm.

My body surely needs to breathe, to perform the physical act of filling my lungs and exhaling, again and again and again, but then I remember: there's no need in here, in my perfect bubble. I am and have always been safe enveloped in its perfect symmetry, drifting in luscious translucent gel without me getting wet, walking without ground beneath me, floating and spinning at the centre of the world. Totally safe.

8

5:30 pm
SAM

I saw the gold sovereign had dropped –
pennies don't do it for Meyra. Hope
flickered.

'Show me the video again. Quickly,' she
demanded. I pulled out my phone and put it
on the table between us. I played through the
clip. 'That's it, further…further…stop.' She
was tense, excited, obvious because she very
slightly adjusted one of the buttons on her
shirt. She pointed at the screen. 'Now play it,
Sam. You must remember this.' A black-and-

white image of fog at an airport came fleetingly into my mind.

We watched – again. Walker exited the lift on the third floor and began walking to his room; by now I knew the footage as well as some episodes of *Friends*.

'Stop!' said Meyra. I froze Walker in mid-step. 'There! Did you see that?'

'What?'

'His hesitation when he got out of the lift. He looked round to see where he needed to go.' A brief pause. 'He stayed here for *ten days*. There is *one* lift. The corridor only goes in *one* direction.'

'I think you have something.' He was 120 but could still recite Pi to fifty decimal places without blinking.

'This is someone trying to work out *for the first time* where he is going,' said Meyra, her face so close to the screen that I could see Walker's image mirrored on her face. 'An impostor.'

'There's something else,' I said. 'How Walker got to and from his room.'

'What do you mean? He simply walked along the corridor and opened the door.'

'Before that. He *used the lift*. There's no way that a Luddite like Walker would have used that death-trap. No chance. The intruder used *Ma gic* to get past Reception disguised as Walker.'

'The facial recognition software confirmed that it *was* Walker. I hazard that the *Ma gic* was performed *after* Walker died or it would have shown up at his exit séance. An earlier substitution would have been too easy to detect.'

I felt my jaw tighten. 'This may have been a Snakeskin, then.' I drained my glass in one. 'That's why he kept quiet in reception, though Walker always was an unfriendly bastard.'

There was an uncomfortable silence, punctuated by the surrounding pub chatter.

Snakeskin would've been like putting on a
fancy-dress costume but using real skin and
hair, borrowing – or taking - someone else's.
Here, it was worse, shrugging on a dead
man's body like a purple velvet tuxedo with
very wide lapels – obscene.

I retrieved the scrap of paper and rolled it
out on our table. Nothing under the surface
when I Focused, no imprints of other words
when I held it up to the light, no Princess
Leia hologram triggered. Meyra fiddled with
her phone as we sat. 'There is nothing for
'Haven',' she said, 'with or without a
question mark. It is too generic.' A pause. 'I
do not know bout the Tree or Casa - House?
- of Life. However, there *is* a shop in this city
named *'Mirror of Galadriel'*. It claims to sell
'genuine magical artifacts' and 'New Age'
products. The name cannot be a
coincidence.'

We were on a roll: we'd found some litter
with ideas above its station; and we'd
worked out that hard-core banned *Ma gic*
might have been used by someone unknown
to trick their way into Walker's room, clear
out all his kit to hide something unknown

and take it away to somewhere unknown for an unknown purpose.

Impressive.

'Sam Franklin, I believe we must go shopping,' said Meyra, finishing her beer and dabbing her lips with a silk handkerchief.

'Absolutely. I'm thinking I might need a new kaftan.' I tuned out Meyra's delicate but pointedly unmissable groan.

9

6:15 pm
MEYRA

As we walked, I heard words from Sam Franklin that should never be uttered by a man in his forties, 'I could wear a bandana. To blend in.' I am strong, but not that strong: this felt as if it were akin to him incanting a forbidden Soul Crush. I mentally made offerings to various deities and endeavoured to convey to him complete indifference and *over my dead, resurrected and killed-again body,* all rolled into one.

I noted with satisfaction that we now fully understood each other on this subject, in case he had been merely amusing himself at my expense – all this time here and it remained difficult to tell.

In the crush of shoppers, we avoided bumping into a living statue, silver-painted from his top hat down to his spats, holding a silver-sprayed rose and walking cane. A man with a long ponytail was playing 'Don't Cry for me, Argentina' on steel pans, sunlight flashing from the polished drums like solar panels. A newspaper vendor was giving away free copies of the *Brighton Star* under the headline, 'VAGRANT PLAGUE'.

All of this was in truth far too *urban* for me. I still crave meadows and woods (and, I concede, Harvey Nichols). The Parents sent me here to 'broaden my horizons' and it has always been unwise to disagree with Mother. Daddy has always been more biddable, but Mother holds every trump card in their discussions (except sometimes the deuce: to make Daddy feel empowered). I have learned to love parts of my new home, but my broadened horizons presently incorporated a disgusting 'kebab' shop – what I presumed would be a wild boar on

the upright steel spit was like none I had
ever seen - and a disreputable-looking
nightclub lying in wait for the night.

My favourite leafy glade with its dappled
sunlight felt a very long way away,
exceedingly elsewhere.

We moved on. Dragon sculptures spilled
out into the street from one shop in a
muddle of burnished teeth, claws and wings
– nothing like the ones to be found near my
home. Balinese wood carvings. An electric
sitar. Eye of Horus tote bags – not Chanel.
Purple polyester altar cloths – totally not
Chanel. Candy-pink mystic crystals placed
in precise rows in one window, each with a
genuine hand-signed certificate
guaranteeing enhanced esoteric power.
Available for the discerning and
undiscerning alike, the dreamers and the
jokers, the curious and the misguided. A
mountain of detritus. Humans have so many
words for *rubbish; w*e have two, and one of
those is seldom used in polite conversation.

Endymion Walker's interest in all this was
puzzling to me, New Age suiting those

easily led, at the bargain-basement end of
our world, alongside palm-reading and
horoscopes. Endymion Walker absolutely
did *not* fit that profile. I was confident that
he would not have been browsing for cut-
price spell mixes.

Sam Franklin was set to enter that dingy
place with that cat; I craved and would track
down a chai latte, a benefit of delegation.

10

6:45 pm
PAGODA

The rooftops. He asked me to keep up with Him and the other one and stay out of sight. He must have been missing me. That was only natural. This was also my chance to hunt: there might be a grounded seagull up here to discipline. Birds rather than small, furry things. More challenging, more satisfying. Sometimes I've felt Him wanting to join a hunt. Sooo glad he's restrained himself so far. He has no rhythm, no elegance. Tragic. He was lucky to have me, but at the end of my forepaw of course. Was I lucky to have Him as my familiar? 'Familiar not friend', that's the mantra I had been taught, the golden rule. Back to the chase given the disappointing seagull availability. Below me, He was ready to enter a human hut which, even from here, looked to me like a covered litter tray. And I was about to follow Him. Because, on a whim of course, I wanted to keep an eye on Him, as all good owners of familiars are wont to do. To make sure he was not mis-behaving. Nothing more.

11

6:50 pm
SAM

I stopped outside *Mirror of Galadriel*. It had the air of a charity shop run by messy druids.

A tiny candle emporium was on one side weaving tantalising scents of bergamot, nutmeg and jasmine into the still, dusty air; a Native Americana shop on the other, showcasing a home-assembly Totem pole on special offer; I wasn't tempted.

The lower parts of *Mirror of Galadriel's* windows were crammed with Voodoo dolls, pentagrams and crystal pyramids. All of them looked the part, none of them generated any aura. No surprises there.

The rest of the frontage was a tip. Posters were plastered in layers over the door and the windows, with details of a local Kasabian tribute band's gig that we'd missed by two months; blue posters with offers of tea and biscuits for homeless waifs and strays, *Do you need a refuge, a place to call safe?*; psychic readings advertised by Yolanda the All-Seeing (*no appointments required: she expects you*); and a multitude of other pinned up posters, notices, circulars and flyers, from tempting to tacky, often both. It would keep archaeologists going for decades.

I glanced over my shoulder before I went in and saw that Meyra had installed herself in a Turkish coffee shop opposite. A small shadow streaked with white detached itself from a drainpipe above me.

I pushed the door. There was a harsh jangle of doorbell as I stepped in. I left it slightly ajar; a silken presence insinuated itself into the shop. The impromptu collage

Lost in Plain Sight

on the windows accentuated the stygian interior despite the sunny day. A few dim white lights fought the gloom like escape-path lighting.

I didn't need them. I opened my eyes wide, glad of Pagoda's proximity, my pupils feeling the size of golf balls using her Nightsight. I padded confidently through the murk, glad there was nothing that looked like car headlights, otherwise I might have felt an urge to lie still on the floor staring fixedly upwards with those big eyes.

I eased past some barricades of trestle tables and open trunks, cluttered with displays of candles, gnarled baskets of mandrake roots beckoning like deformed hands, lava lamps (set to viscous), toy wands. I was careful not to tread on any rabbits' feet that might be lying around (best not to tempt fate), and I made sure not to accidentally topple over the full-size skeleton wearing an 'authentic wizard's cloak' and little round glasses. Appropriately, silver water bowls were displayed, jumbled on a central stand. The smell of incense was cloying, thick enough almost to rest my hand on. Chaos.

The shop was so bogus that it would be safe to chant '*Ma gic*' in there all day long without attracting anything hungry and tentacled.

A figure lurked ahead of me. Standing behind a battered black-painted counter. Watching me. I killed my Nightsight. He was illuminated by several coloured candles in cartoonish human and animal shapes. His black dreads had fiery orange tips like the embers of matches. His quick eyes were set into pale, sharp features, appraising me. He could see that I wasn't in the market for a light-up witch hat.

There was a sign behind him:

Mirror of Galadriel
Seen anything you like?
Derek Taylor, Manager.
If you break anything in the shop, We Will
curse you forever
(Just kidding : no more than 50,000 years)

There was a rustle close by, Pagoda
batting a rabbit's foot across the floor.
Concentrate! Derek seemed not to have
noticed, so I smiled at him and got right to
the point. I pulled out my phone and
proffered it to him. Its screen lit up the harsh
contours of his face like a spotlight on a
walnut.

'Can you help me, please?' When he saw
the picture of Endymion Walker, his eyes
pinballed onto me, the phone, behind me
and back to the phone. He took his time: I
knew that he knew that I knew that he knew
Walker.

'I've seen him here,' he said. 'A few days
ago...I remember the hair. Like yours.' He
paused and then spoke quickly, 'He was
after a necklace.'

'Necklace?' my voice level, politely
interested.

'Yeah. A necklace. He saw it on our web-
page. As a present, but we'd already sold it.
Shame.' He paused. 'He didn't stay long, just

poked around for a bit in the shop, then took off without buying anything.' A shrug. 'Doubt I'll see him again but if he comes in, I'll tell him you're after him.' His eyes flitted around then fastened on me, his aura cranked up to nervous. 'Who shall I tell him was looking?'

'Just a friend.' He quickly glanced behind him, then slowly reached down behind the counter. Alert, I watched for his hands. 'I lost track of him and heard he was down here. Just doing the rounds.'

Derek straightened up. His hands darted from under the counter.

He handed me his business card, 'Just in case.' I didn't reciprocate: a card with my official title - *Grand Inquisitor* – might have alarmed him, harking back to simpler times, before corporate-speak and compliance manuals. When *relevant stakeholder outcomes* involved real stakes going through real hearts - some colleagues call those *the good old days*. Derek seemed stressed enough already.

73

I nodded thanks and picked my way through the clutter back to the door. I heard the quick rasp of a match and I sensed him watching me. I glanced back and a lazy coil of smoke rose from his roll-up. It refracted dim light from his phone on its way to join the rest of the murk, a will o'the wisp in his busy fingers.

I joined Meyra in the coffee shop at a small mosaic table; she was hunched over a decaf chai latte with extra cinnamon, seemingly lost in her own thoughts but in reality taking in every detail across the street. Pagoda was somehow already *there,* like cats do. I ordered some industrial strength caffeine and it came quickly, satisfyingly heart-pounding and sweet. Stirring it counted as a cardio workout.

Cats can't clear their throats; Pagoda's application of a pin-shaped claw to my leg worked just as well. Treats – or, as she calls them, tribute – made their way down to her. I looked down at her, front paws half-covering a liberated rabbit's foot: a spoil of war. That's my girl. *No burglar alarms in the main part of the shop, nothing suspicious, no access to the back. You're welcome.* I filled Meyra in and she listened without comment.

'Either Derek's got a very bad memory, or he speak with forked tongue,' I said.

Meyra gave me a faint smile, 'I suspect his memory is fine.'

'More tellingly, their web-pages are not written with a quill pen...'

'Indeed. It is a matter of regret that Yolanda was absent today,' said Meyra, glancing at the window. 'Some mind-reading might have proved instructive.'

'We need a closer look. There's more to Derek than meets the third eye.'

12

7:00 pm
BETHANY & ANDREWS

The ring-tone on Bethany's phone went off: Jangling techno synthesisers in a low but rising metallic throb. His love for the Terminator movies knew very few bounds and he let the brooding theme play for a few seconds to build up its sombre refrain before answering. He wasn't frustrated or angered-by the interruption, even though the two of them had been getting into the groove. That was not his or Andrews's place.

Bethany didn't ask who the caller was, he didn't need to. Both of them knew; there was

only one number stored in the phone. He
and Andrews only needed one number, it
was like a passcode that activated them
when it was punched in, special access to
their particular brand of man management.
That was what the boss demanded from his
team. Unquestioning obedience was the
price they paid for a free hand; more a free
fist.

Bethany put down the large wrench, slow
and sure, to avoid spilling any residue from
it on his suit. He had carefully chosen it for
this personnel appraisal; drip-dry, just in
case. He reached into his pocket to retrieve
his mobile. He didn't speak much, and what
he did say was softly spoken. Normally he
was only required to listen. And execute.
Execution was his thing.

Andrews looked across at the other man in
the room, the balding man tied to the
skeleton metal chair. There was no need for
anything comfortable, that was kind of the
point. It was also drip-dry. The man was
wild-eyed, his fully black pupils marooned
in two egg-white eyeballs, terrified and
disbelieving at the same time.

'If you don't mind, we'll take a break,' said Andrews in his funeral director voice, taking infinite care to enunciate each word, infinite care to reach the end of each sentence as if it were a rumbling glacier. He smoothed his neatly parted short black hair. It glistened under the naked light bulb. Butler school had not been wasted, he was able to polish a night stick to a dazzling sheen before applying it vigorously to whichever human or other body needed corrective action.

The balding man whimpered. Andrews chuckled to hide some embarrassment, 'I'm terribly sorry, that was insensitive of me, Mr Foden.' The right thumb, index and middle fingers of the man flopped against the duct tape binding him firmly to the chair. His arm was in an unnatural position, so he was at risk of giving away a handball in a football game. He whimpered again.

Andrews said to Foden in a discreet voice, 'I should be most grateful if you would be so kind as to remain silent while our employer is talking with Mr. Bethany. Much obliged.' Andrews had perfect manners, at least no-one had ever picked him up on any lapses of taste or politeness. *I hope you don't mind, your victimness, I am about to destroy your left knee-cap.*

Bethany put the phone on speaker.

'Is it finished?' The voice was more jagged than a combat knife, capable of disembowelling an Alsatian at ten paces. Despite their controlled ultra-violence and despite their resemblance to vertical cliff faces seen from a long way below the summit, Bethany and Andrews were wary of, cautious about, and if truth be told frightened by, their rasping boss. He had the Knack and he knew exactly how to use it, he had done for decades. Bethany and Andrews knew very well that they were simply the latest model of junkyard crushers that he had acquired for any housekeeping that he found distasteful.

'This is Andrews, sir. We're not quite finished yet, sir. But we are very close. Mr Foden stupidly paid too much attention to some Circle email traffic that he accidentally saw, which may compromise the operation.

We are tolerably sure that there has been no leakage.' He ignored the puddle under Foden's chair.

'Tolerably sure is not good enough.'

'Indeed sir,' said Andrews. 'Hence our slight tardiness. A little more endeavour will get us there.'

'I have another urgent job for you gentlemen, so don't waste my time.'

'We will be sure to get cracking, then,' said Andrews.

'I want you to go to Franklin's house. See his wife. He has two teenagers. You're to protect them under your usual authority. When I say "protect", you know what I mean, but do not kill them yet. Monitor for contacts with Franklin. He and his fleabag and that tree-hugger have gone to ground, and I need to know where he is, what he's doing and what he finds. He won't be able to get to us, but his family will be useful insurance if I am wrong. Watch her, she's a wizard, too. Don't underestimate her if you need to act.'

'Right you are, sir, we will make sure it's fine,' said Bethany quietly.

'It will be our pleasure to look after a valued colleague and her beautiful children,' said Andrews.

'They are teenagers, a girl and a boy.'

'We will be sure to take extra ammunition,' said Andrews.

'You are fools. Just get it done.' He broke off from the call.

'Charming,' breathed Bethany.

'His personnel files are like a sniper's alley,' said Andrews. 'We'd better get on.' He looked over at the slumped Foden and pulled his thoughts back to the matter in hand.

'What happens when we're finished?' He cocked his head in Foden's direction. 'We were on speaker. He knows who we were talking to,' whispered Bethany.

'That really does not matter. From the close of this meeting, Mr Foden is going on gardening leave.' Andrews hefted a large shovel from the huge canvas bag, the head gleamed with a beautifully polished finish. He beamed with no small amount of pride.

Bethany said nothing but nodded in understanding.

These things *matter*.

13

7:30 pm
MEYRA

An anxious looking young woman walked past *Mirror of Galadriel.* She stopped and stared for a long time in the window. Her face was lined with worry, an overlay to delicate features that were trying to make a break for freedom. She had the air of someone who was at the end of the line. Whatever happened next would be the difference between salvation and terrifying failure. The woman's long copper hair was tied in a hurried ponytail falling below her shoulders. Her calf length tie-dye linen dress was a swirl of muted purples and pinks

lending a theatrical air to her costume. She
had an olive-green rucksack from which
more coloured linen peeked. If her target
was an eclectic patchwork style, then
between her hair and her clothes she had
over-achieved. I thought that overall she
looked too much like one of Mother's
favourite jesters.

She shaped to go into the shop, then
hesitated. She pulled back and walked on up
the street, frowning, uncertain. *Make your
mind up.*

I lost interest and looked across at Sam
Franklin, 'I think it is time to go.'

'Yeah. Let me just finish this, it's like
chewing tobacco,' he said. His expression
was the same as the one he usually used to
display satisfaction. Unfathomable.

As we were getting up from the table, he
nudged me. 'Heads up.'

Two men appeared and went directly into
the shop: no hesitation, business-like, like
they belonged. Military-style. Both were

wearing jeans, black T-shirts and gaudy
training shoes; one had a black baseball cap
over black bristly hair; the other short,
startlingly yellow, hair. We sat back down.
Sam Franklin took the opportunity to order
another coffee from the harassed waitress.
Much more coffee for him and he would be
able to keep up with them even if they had a
car.

'Those men seem to be on some sort of
mission.'

'Not to buy a lava lamp,' he said.

Shortly afterwards, the woman in the tie-
dye dress re-appeared for a second stare into
the shop. She shook her head and drew
herself fully upright, I could almost see her
individually unwinding the knots in her
neck and back. It looked like now or never
for her.

She ventured inside. Her internal battle
won. She looked like the veteran of many
such battles.

I attempted to Focus through the shop window but it was too dark, and the windows were too smeared and covered with posters and leaflets.

I watched her dissolve into the gloom, her hair leaving something of an afterglow, 'She is different from those men. Although she knew about the place in advance, she did not seem very sure about going in. She was concerned what she would find in there.'

'I don't blame her, I needed a good reason to go in there.'

'The men look like they have been summoned for a meeting, whereas she looks like she has nowhere else to go.'

After ten minutes, the door opened. The woman came back into the street and blinked a few times to re-adjust her eyes. She clutched a handful of sky blue papers, creasing them into sharp peaks, her brow creased with what she had heard. She strode back in the direction from which she had originally appeared and merged into the crowd.

I sipped some latte, Sam Franklin made his throat beg for mercy with more of his revolting drink.

'I could not see the papers that she was carrying. Could you?'

'No, but they're the same colour as the posters in the window: she's either homeless or a volunteer. I'm betting not a volunteer. I wonder how they promised to help her.'

The door opened again, and the two men left the shop. They made their way along the street in the same direction as the woman but wrapped up in their own business. One of them was carrying something thin and flat, shiny, different from what the woman had carried. The other man peered at it and said something inaudible.

I concentrated on it: a photograph.

'He has a picture of you, Sam Franklin. Taken in that shop. Not a flattering angle, I must confess.'

Sam Franklin used the remainder of his Focus to replicate my superior vision, 'Taken by the security camera. My turning up seems to have thrown a cat into a pigeon loft.'

At that, I heard Pagoda's ears prick up with interest. It was only momentary when she realised it was just a metaphor. It receded, disappointed; she lifted her head in my direction inviting me not to waste her valuable time.

'I do not understand why your visit was so controversial.'

'It stirred him up enough to bring in the cavalry.'

'Do they not have telephones?'

'Face to face. No audit trail. Looks like I triggered a protocol for people who ask awkward questions beyond *does my aura look big in this*?'

'In a busy tourist location like Brighton, I would not have expected your questions to be viewed as awkward.'

'I specialise in awkward.'

I found it impossible to disagree with that statement.

14

7:50 PM
SAM

'Time for you to earn your keep,' I concentrated on our Bond and I momentarily felt Pagoda's warmth from hanging around on a nearby roof. And her irritation at the interruption. I commanded her – who am I kidding, I asked her nicely with a promise of a hit of catnip later – to track the men and see where they ended up. They were probably already en route to a picture framer to frame my rugged portrait.

I felt her stretch out and I caught myself getting ready to reach out across our table

and arch my back. I stopped just in time. For
a few seconds, an image of a waddling
pigeon sat in front of my eyes and I
reluctantly shook my head to clear it.

One moment Pagoda was there, the next
she wasn't. Meyra and I slipped away from
the café before we drew unwelcome
attention to what felt like my rapidly
escalating caffeine and sugar addictions.

'We need a closer look at that shop,'
suggested Meyra as we walked. The silver
statue had gone home, the shadows had
lengthened.

'I want to know why he was so keen to
circulate a picture of me.' The quick meeting
with the two men suggested a high level of
organisation being aimed at what, however
you look at it, looked pretty inconsequential.
It might have been the power of my
mesmerising interrogation.

Pagoda sidled back looking cute. That
could only mean she'd lost the two men in
the crush of late afternoon tourists in the
area. I looked disappointed, and she rallied

strongly to hint that it had been totally my fault. Sometimes, our 17-year-old Beth and Pagoda might as well be our twins, rather than her and Jamie. I could visualise her mother's rather fixed grin at that thought. Emma often complains about them and me counting as her triplets, let alone That Cat amounting to quads.

I indicated to Pagoda another job for her in advance of our infiltration later, which she interpreted as me finding her an interesting diversion. Whatever. Her mission? Scout around Derek's shop and find out stuff. I described it as *reconnoitring*, so she was pleased with how important it sounded. She padded off into the shadows while Meyra and I returned to the hotel.

I was holding out for bacon sandwiches and brown sauce, with a large mug of builders' tea, if the Beachcomber's menu could stretch as far as *haute cuisine*. I waited until Pagoda was comfortably out of range before letting those thoughts escape, hoping she didn't pick up on them from our Bond. Otherwise there would be trouble.

I was looking forward to a spot of smash-and-grab later. It's fair to say that being a loreyer (and for that matter a lawyer) feels at cocktail parties like it has the same level of cool as being an estate agent who trained as an actuary and now moonlights as a traffic warden. It's at times like this that our Lore Department's broader skill-sets came into play. *We got all types of crime here: breaking and entering.* For a better work-life balance.

The Beachcomber was a perfect base of operations from which to launch our foray. I'd fallen in love with it from the moment I went inside, immediately regretting all those years of staying somewhere else down here with the family, not having wanted to mix business with pleasure. It's the Magic Circle's representative office in Brighton; we have at least one like it in most major places. Our London HQ's in – well, under, if you're being picky and not very estate agent-friendly - Hyde Park. At Number 1, Hyde Park; the Duke of Wellington narrowly pipped us to the Number One, London address.

The Beachcomber's close to Brighton's
split-level seafront: Marine Parade is raised,
looking directly out over the sea. Below is
the parallel, wonderfully named, Madeira
Drive. It runs alongside Brighton's pebble
beaches boasting shops built into the sea
wall which separate the two levels, enclosed
by Victorian arches. The top level boasts a
regiment of hotels, including the
Beachcomber, bed-and-breakfast places and
up-market houses, all standing stiffly to
attention, difficult to tell apart from each
other at first glance, all craning to take
advantage of the uninterrupted sea views.

The Beachcomber's a four-storey, built in
the standard Regency style; has double-
rounded bays in calming pale grey-blue,
blending in with the other buildings. Little
else about it is standard. It is *very* discreet:
you'll never see the Beachcomber pop up in
any Internet search, yet it's situated in one of
the prime locations in Brighton, outwardly
in harmony with its surroundings.
Aggressively unobtrusive.

You need a Knack even to *see* it properly.
Normally, if you approach it, even when you

walk right past it and have a glimmer of
interest in looking more closely - or, even
more controversially, wanting to go in -
you'll feel increasingly uncomfortable and
disinclined to venture in. Or you'll simply
forget about it and walk on by without
further thought. It slips and slides away
from your consciousness.

When we eased ourselves through the
barriers into reception, we found that Margit
was *still* on duty. She beamed at us
beatifically, steering us past the solid dark
wood desk to the small, dark wood bar next
to reception. It had strings of small, tacky
coloured lights on the walls, and looped
Elvis Presley on the muffled sound system
wafting through much of the ground floor.

Sandwiches and coffee appeared like
magic as we waited for Pagoda, our Bond
not stretching as far as the shop. I contented
myself with the thought of a Commune on
her return.

As we sat and waited, Elvis was crooning
Suspicious minds, suiting the overall mood.

In the circumstances, *Devil in disguise* might have worked better.

15

11:00pm
SAM

A faint breeze wafted through my hotel room window, enough to stir the greying net curtains in the urban dark, not enough to displace the sickly scent of Lily of the Valley.

Where was Pagoda? She must have finished checking out the shop by now.

I shivered. Any damage to one of us would mean *pain* to the other: from what felt like a wasp sting to the excruciating agony of being delicately skinned while showered with sea water. Or worse. That made us highly attuned to the other's health and wellbeing, me keen not to show that I cared; her...she's a cat. Don't ask.

Before we finalised our Bond, I had raised with her, couched in diplomatic terms, Burmese cats' well documented and disturbing penchant for the suicidal. Not a great trait in a familiar. She initially had a crazily elevated, and mis-placed, level of trust in other creatures not to eat her. And a worrying impulse to investigate whether she could fit seamlessly into the treads of any available fast-moving car tyres. Her DNA was a 99.99% match with reckless lemmings.

She'd pointedly ignored me, then went away and quietly adjusted her operating parameters for predator-avoidance and the Highway Code. We hadn't spoken about that since. Not one word. She's now, purely on her own initiative of course, more streetwise, manipulative and cunning. Like every other cat.

We'd struck the terms of the Bond four years ago. I'd requested a new familiar (so had Pagoda, according to her).

Tense negotiations had followed. Burmese cats are often known as "bricks wrapped in silk". In Pagoda's case, the "brick" part refers to what she might hit you with if you cross her. That's exactly how the negotiations had felt.

In our back and forth on the Bond, as a sweetener I'd let her hunt my fur hat for a bit. And she demanded the insertion of special conditions in the Bond: no collar, particularly no bell, and *absolutely no Twinkle Tush. Ever.* No problem. I wouldn't have been stupid enough to try the collar, let alone a jewelled feline butt cover.

Pagoda had taken over from Toady the toad as my familiar, Toady's name conclusively proving that asking younger children to help name a familiar, a pet, or anything else really, never - ever - ends well. Thanks, Jamie. There was also some nonsense about me taking the place of a human called Gerald.

The Bond had been stress-tested at the beginning when I foolishly – briefly - entertained the notion of attempting to Train her. *There's of course absolutely no chance. At all. Of training a cat.* None. Nada. Rien. Throw in a cat evolved to be even more opinionated than the standard moggy, *and Ma gic*-capable, and the flaws in my plan positively *vibrated*.

Her predecessor had been more willing, although somewhat more limited. The opportunity for me to gain the ability to catch bluebottles in mid-air and periodically feel a compulsion to sit halfway up my stair did not make Toady terribly useful. That's not really fair, Toady had allowed me to make extended Hops as well, so the Bond had proved useful at times. As a slight throwback, I sometimes have to stop myself from referring to Beth and Jamie as my tadpoles. Bonds run deep.

That aside, my relationship with Pagoda has developed probably as well as it could between cats and humans: unintentionally impressed on my side, contemptuous on hers. But not *utterly* contemptuous.

Pagoda awarded me brownie points for not letting my offspring – well, Beth, in fairness to Jamie – ever try to dress Pagoda in a violent pink Little Coochy Cat outfit.

A soft thump announced her return at the window. Relief. A dramatic entrance, hurling herself onto her back on the worn sheepskin rug. Formalities needed to be observed. I supplied the commensurate level of tummy rub for this type of mission. Aircraft engine level, feline heavy metal purring ensued: in that respect, she had Trained me well.

She paused mid-stretch and casually licked a paw. It didn't matter to her which one. I signalled to her that it was time and we found a plump armchair in a corner of the hotel lounge. I noticed that it was unscratched. *Unscratched.* What a waste.

Soft and warm, Pagoda gripped me with barbed claws, her eyes narrowing to slits, an involuntary purr escaping her. I pretended not to notice; I was busy suppressing my own. And then our Commune engulfed me with her memories of the afternoon. I found myself *held in the moment*. Where cats always are.

16

11:01 pm
PAGODA

A sigh from Him. The Commune begins.

*The alleyway running behind the target.
Sweep along it. Take in the oozing bin smells and
the acrid spilt beer and ammonia.*

*A Dog. Careers from behind a rubbish bag,
comes to a halt, teeth bared, low growl. Jack
Russel? Terrier? More like a Pickandmix. Only
one ear. Seriously? Do you want to keep that
one? Thought so. Yes, that's it: run away, little
boy. A hiss. Just to make sure.*

Back of the target building. No sound.

Switch into the embrace of Cat-time, each moment luxurious and plush.

Risk assessment. Tail setting: Cautious.

Squirm through a tight hole to get in. Take care not to ruffle any fur. The human cage...office...is cramped for humans, cavernous for me, the main shop visible through the connecting door. No humans in this room. No guard dogs. Perfect.

And close by?

The black-haired one with the orange split ends: Derek. In the front of the shop talking to an adult human devoid of fur. Humans all look the same, the only way to tell them apart is usually their fur. And how they smell. Derek now exudes spilled korma, adding to his earlier sandalwood; the other human a mixture of sweat and golden retriever. Nothing sinister about him, apart from the Reek of Dog.

No immediate danger. Ignore both.

Look around. Prioritise.

In the corner: there's something. Food or potential food? Everything is one or the other. Tuna...skipjack..."Seriously Special" brand...Sniff. No more than six hours and seventeen minutes on the floor. Stored between two brown triangles. Must be a clue. Yum. It's food. Not a clue. Glad that's resolved. No need for fingerprint evidence.

Video camera mounted on the ceiling. Slowly whirring from side to side covering the front of the shop. Sit and watch it. Side to side, side to side, side to side, side to side...

Concentrate!

No sign of a burglar alarm.

What's that?

Something on the desk. A screen. Alert! There's another smaller *Derek. Here! Trapped in the screen! Talking to another furless human! Tail to Medium since they are only small. Why are there* two *Dereks and* two *furless humans? Why is one pair smaller? Is there no end to human trickery? The small ones copy the big ones. Better keep watch on all four. Tail back down to Cautious.*

What else?

A dull grey tower against the wall with evenly spaced bars for humans to grip and pull so they will slide out. Intriguing, but human thumbs are required. Ignore.

A human litterbox in a small separate room. Marking their territory: a faint trace of something trying to be lemon, but mostly pure human den. Enough layers to keep feline historians busy for a loooong *time. Fascinating but distracting: my pedigree etiquette would demand way too much self-grooming afterwards. I don't have enough tongues…*

Oooh! A roll of tape. All shiny and pretty. Potential food? Better chase it around, and - there you go - toss it up and attack it. Hah! Now, leave it alone. Leave it. Leave it. Wait for it. Wait…Re-trace steps up to it From A Completely Different Direction and then: Hah again! Victory!

Hold on, the front door is closing. The big and small shinyhead humans have both *gone. Two Dereks left. Where's that tape gone?*

Uh-oh. Big Derek is coming. Getting bigger with every step. And the little one, also getting bigger. Seems to be climbing out of that screen.

Alert!

Be even *cuter, in case either notices. Prepare to widen eyes to Very Big Indeed. That usually works. And, as a precaution, set tail to Bushy and Menacing. Maybe leave the tape alone for now.*

Time to go. Can't fight both Dereks. Sidle away in orderly retreat. Out through that gap in the back wall. Into the alleyway. Stop and catch breath. Reset. Time to look unruffled and immaculate…Outstanding.

Has the Pickandmix come back for more? No? Splendid. (And slightly disappointing.)

Hungry now. Sleepy, too. So: all systems normal.

But must wait until back with Him. Us? It's the deal.

17

11:20 pm
SAM

The Commune broke. Relief: my brain felt furry. I resisted an urge to yowl - there's a time and a place. Confusingly, my cheeks were alarmingly smooth when I rubbed them with the backs of my hands. Then I remembered: no fur, no whiskers. I yawned. Ravenously and urgently hungry. For sashimi and lashings of cream. No intention of moving, though.

In my peripheral vision, Meyra was looking in, fractionally wrinkling her nose at

us. I yawned again and stretched out;
Pagoda adopted the same languid pose.

Fish and chips appeared from the hotel
restaurant. Meyra watched us from the door,
and I nodded thanks.

I didn't think it was unalloyed altruism on
Meyra's part, more her not wanting to carry
out our burglary by herself later, but we
were grateful anyway. Meyra repaired to her
fruits de mer and crisp chardonnay in the
restaurant; I could smell them. Pagoda and I
bickered over a final piece of battered cod
then we slunk off to my room, both keeping
a close eye out en route for rolls of tape.

I checked my phone before crashing. Three
messages: from Emma, a wifely 'Call me,
xxx' text (no need to add the word
"immediately"); my PA Virginia – still no
luck in tracking down Walker's daughter; a
demand from my colleague – he contends
superior – Winterbourne – universally
known at the Circle as That Bastard Gideon
Winterbourne - for a progress report. Delete.

I called Emma.

'Hi Sweetie,' she said. 'You OK? What's going on? And *why* are Tweedledum and Tweedledee in our house?'

'Who?'

'From the office, Bethany and Andrews. Know them? They block out the sunlight. Apparently, Winterbourne sent them over to "protect" the kids and me while you're away.'

'I know them. I hope they're on their leashes. We use them for Corporeal Integrity duty. That all seems a bit OTT.'

'No kidding, I'm a practising wizard not a Mafia witness. We don't need "protection". I told them "thanks, but no thanks, I can look after myself and the kids" but they just kept on chewing their gum and smiling politely.

According to them, this is purely routine for this kind of thing. I suppose they would say that but it's news to me…Do tell, though. What kind of thing *are* they talking about? What have you got us into? Are hordes of

Orkish slave raiders coming round tonight? I can defrost some pizza.'

'I don't think you need to worry; for once, Winterbourne's just trying to do the right thing.'

'Do you think I need to send the kids to stay with Justin, or go along with this?'

'Maybe stick with the Tweedles for now. Justin's the all-fangs-on-deck option, right? It shouldn't be for long, and Bethany and Andrews are more or less house-trained; you'll get used to them.'

'I got used to you. OK…For now. Tell me more about Walker, then.'

'His death wasn't an accident.'

'Get out of town.'

'I did. I'm in Brighton.' Perhaps this wasn't the ideal time for banter.

'*Brighton?*'

'Yeah, the last place Walker was seen alive.'

'That was quick. The lengths you'll take to avoid putting the bins out.'

'Harry told me about Walker's exit séance,' I said.

Harry. Dirty Harriet. Our in-house medium, Harriet Eastwood. Her voice was gravelly enough to peel a poltergeist; her office, 'The Precinct', was based under the Serpentine in Hyde Park on the Very Lower Ground Floor of the Circle's main offices. Even now, in hot, sticky Brighton on the phone to Emma, I could feel the deep chill of the Precinct reaching out to me from this morning, not solely from the temperature.

Being a medium can be a surprisingly violent trade, occasionally the odd punk-ass spirit needs to be roughed up, even a minor god every now and again: *Go ahead, make my Deity.*

'You know what Harry's like,' I said. 'She posted Walker's death as a stabbing – but it was more than that. She didn't want to face the truth.' Silence. 'She said that what Walker had told her was "creepy"'.

Emma and I said nothing for several long – what felt like very long – seconds: plenty of time during which to pick a large amount of cotton and finish sewing a shirt out of it.

'I haven't heard her say anything like that in all the time I've known her,' said Emma, 'and she's faced things that would make your brain dribble from your ears.'

'Walker communicated to her that the last thing he remembered seeing before he Departed was a blue, horned demon,'

'A blue…horned…demon?' said Emma, her attention focused like a laser sight on those words (probably not so much on "blue"). Potential encounters with a murderous demonic entity – my teenage daughter doesn't count – tend to be a sensitive topic of marital conversation.

'Walker said it took him by surprise, ripped out his heart while he watched. Like a Post-mortem on him while he was still alive.'

The line went very still.

'And, since this morning, it's become a tiny bit more complicated.'

'I'm so glad there's more.'

When I'd finished, she said 'A demon *and* Necromancy. This is getting better all the time.'

'The good news is we think we've found something. A lead. A dodgy magic shop. We're going to pay them an after-hours visit tonight to see what we can find out.'

'Ah, burglary too. Great,' said Emma. 'The kids will be so proud.' Emma switched to Practical mode to rescue her composure from its burning building. 'I'll tell the kids you're going to be at a work offsite for a while. That usually does the trick.'

'Do you think they'll notice?'

'Not unless we stop paying their mobile bills.'

Beth and Jamie know my job periodically involves long business trips. Even now they have a hazy notion of what I actually *do*, not wanting to get caught up in frivolous details irrelevant to their uninterrupted broadband service. I'm *a lawyer or something*; they remain blissfully unaware of me also being a *loreyer*. They know their mother's a tutor, just not what she teaches.

My parents are sorcerers would probably raise awkward questions with the school's pastoral care people.

Nevertheless, it was a shame the kids were going to miss out on any *Ma gic* action down at the seaside: if I ever needed reinforcements, they'd attitude any demon into small pieces. No trouble.

'You have a nice trespass later, darling,' said Emma. 'Watch yourselves. The main risk in Brighton should be alcohol poisoning.'

'I may need your help if things get out of hand.'

'Just call. Justin can manage the kids, I wouldn't unleash them on the Tweedles – Bethany and Andrews haven't been trained for that… I'll be just fine up here in the meantime, simmering gently.' Her dangerously calm voice.

'Try not to take it out too much on your students tomorrow, eh?' It looked likely to be a more challenging Levitation 3 class for them than usual. 'Maybe run it somewhere with a roof?'

'We'll see. Get some rest, you've got some ransacking and pillaging to do.'

After exchanging goodnights, I unwound. Time for a nap before our sortie. I lay down, caught myself licking the back of my forearm and rubbing my nose with it. Pagoda insinuated herself in beside me.

We both dreamed of vast flocks of juicy turkeys laden down with heavy wooden wings.

PART TWO
FRIDAY, AUGUST 6TH

18

2:00 am
SAM

I woke up in my room, refreshed after my cat-nap. The main after-effects of the Commune with Pagoda had - mostly - drifted away.

I'd stretched out on my bed and Pagoda had managed to sneak onto my chest while I was asleep. Like many Burmese, she's perfectly at home clamped to a human chest. She periodically feels compelled to sit on my shoulder - like a furry parrot - while I'm walking around. She saw that this was not the time for any of that and removed herself to my pillow and waited in a state of hair-trigger irritation, idly wondering why she was suddenly trying to remember the lyrics to the third verse of *American Pie*. Our Bond works in mysterious ways.

It was past two. The darkness was relieved by the soft glow of a street lamp seeping into my room. I knocked on the wall separating my room from Meyra's, and a couple of minutes later she tapped on my door and came in.

She switched on the main light and, when my eyes adjusted, I saw that she was dressed ready for action. Black hoodie, black jeans and black designer pumps, with a black cashmere scarf lightly tied around her neck.

'More Vogue Ninja than Rogue Ninja,' I said, between a couple of throaty coughs.

'I am not sure that I need to take fashion advice from someone who is having hairballs.' Rude.

I pulled on a dark jacket over my black T-shirt, dark jeans and trusty trainers. There was no special pocket in the jacket for a magic wand. Wands are for Sooty.

We looked like we were heading for a funeral rave.

I asked Pagoda to come along with us and act as a look-out. She looked pleased at the prospect of a possible return match with the Pickandmix - I found myself oddly up for that, too. Pagoda arched her back and stretched to limber up: the equivalent of cracking her knuckles.

It was quiet in the city, a late Thursday night, early Friday morning straining towards the weekend. A man sat slumped in the doorway of a side street with a bottle of something, wearing a Brighton and Hove Albion FC bobble hat embroidered with a jolly seagull. Not much else going on. As we homed in on North Laine again, we saw the lights, and heard the sounds, of a sprinkling of late-night bars, enticingly carrying into the cloying night air.

We reluctantly avoided them, even though they looked a lot more fun than breaking into a shop full of random toot. We checked the front to make sure that the main shop was closed and locked, as were its neighbours. No late-night activity.

We walked casually into the empty alleyway behind and peered through the windows, re-assuring ourselves that there were no lights on inside, no movement. We spotted a small glowing blue light on the ceiling. The security camera continued its tireless sweep. Muscle memory - not mine - made my head go to one side and back. No more.

The alleyway was empty. I cautiously approached the back door. There was no *Ma gic* around the door and I did a KnockKnock on the lock and it obligingly clicked open. I gingerly pushed the door. Meyra made ready with a Dampen in case any alarm sounded. There was no sign of that.

We made sure the metal blinds on the windows were all closed, leaving a small gap for Pagoda to keep watch. Pagoda's style is like a Beefeater, lots of fur and zero movement. I conjured up a small Lantern to float next to me as I looked around; Meyra did the same. I tried to see any major differences from earlier in the day. The laptop had been removed, but otherwise it was pretty much as I'd seen it through Pagoda's eyes. I pocketed my favourite roll of sticky tape which was still lying where I – Pagoda – had pummelled it into submission. Result!

'Better be careful, the security camera's probably remotely linked to the laptop,' I whispered. Meyra nodded.

'If there is anything here, Sam Franklin, I would expect it to be in this part rather than the front.'

Meyra opened the unlocked filing cabinet. Inside, there were two layers of untidy hanging files. There were tabs on the files covering utilities, invoices, shipping dates, refunds and other fun stuff. There were also various catalogues advertising the dubious, but to be fair not illegal, range of merchandise for this sort of business. Meyra and I took a layer each and sieved through them. Nothing of interest and nothing hidden in the rest of the cabinet.

'Criminal bad taste and not much else.'

'Perhaps there is less to Derek than we thought?'

'Maybe. Doesn't sound right to me, though,' I said. 'What about the two guys with my picture?'

'You did mention criminal bad taste.' If cats ever snigger, that's what I heard from across the room.

As I looked around, I saw a gleam of metal under the desk. I crouched and saw a combination lock built into the floor. The light from my Lantern had bounced off the faces of its number wheel. Meyra and I slid the desk across the floor, revealing the outline of a hatch protected by the lock.

It took quite some effort with another KnockKnock, but the lock eventually succumbed. I levered up the hatch. More files stored in the space below the floor.

Unhackably private, presumed safely hidden under the coating of squalor.

There were around a hundred coloured files, arranged on hanging racks, black at the front, just three; then three yellow. Behind them, a large swathe of blue files.

'They've taken a lot of trouble to hide all this. Probs not the arrangements for their office Christmas party.'

We unloaded the files and stacked them on the floor. We divided the files between us, both of us poised with our phones. We took pictures of the contents as we leafed through them and replaced them exactly as we'd found them. Even down to making sure that any mistakes were replicated when we put them back. Just in case.

There was a photo at the front of each file, most having been screen-grabbed from the camera feed in the shop. There was the picture of me from yesterday and one of Endymion Walker looking irascible, so he'd been fine at the time of his visit.

Both of us were in black files. Ginger-haired Vanessa Grant was in a blue file. In a yellow file, another Walker: Olivia. Not surprising that she hadn't been returning Virginia's calls.

There was no time for any of that now. *Just get the documents copied.*

When we'd finished, Meyra and I replaced the desk in its original position on its footmarks and re-set the lock to its original combination. Pagoda was looking sullen, clearly unimpressed by the alleyway's pitifully low level of food, comfort or violence.

Before we left, I saw Meyra taking a final look round in case she could find something I'd missed.

It was the time of night when it is early morning; it had stopped being late. There would be problems if Derek or any other over-enthusiastic early starter opened the shop while we were finishing off.

I pointed at my watch: 'Tick, tock.'

19

4:00 am
MEYRA

Margit was still on duty at the Beachcomber. She looked like she had freshened up at an undertaker's, hair secured more tightly than before as if anchored by barbed wire. She bustled downstairs to get the hotel's large conference room ready in the 'Business and Communications Centre' located next to a door marked 'Scrying'.

Sam Franklin and I followed her. By the time we walked into the room, there were neat, crisp piles of printed pages stacked at the end of the black mirrored glass boardroom table. High quality enlarged prints of the pictures had been extracted from our cameras. I poured myself some of the peppermint tea that she had left me, while Sam Franklin filled his mug with scalding coffee. We settled down to examine the fruits of our larceny.

'Let's do this methodically. Black first,' said Sam Franklin.

I reached down and plucked out the front black folder, not Endymion Walker or Sam Franklin yet. I opened the flap.

A man's face stared up at us, non-descript in a drifter sort of way. Dark hair, grey eyes, a thin mouth. A thick red cross had been drawn over his features in permanent marker. A deletion, metaphorical or literal?

'Insolent eyes,' I said.

Sam Franklin pointed to the man's faded sweatshirt, 'Led Zeppelin.'

'How do you know?'

'The burning airship, from their album cover. 1969. Iconic.' The year that I arrived here.

'It looks like the picture was taken with a zoom lens,' I said. 'Outside, late evening? Perhaps early morning.' The background was blurred, possibly trees and tall plants. A pale tent lurked in the background, behind the foliage. 'A tent with chimneys. Very odd.'

What did it mean? I could not say. What did the red crosses mean? I could not say.

'Why the different files? The Walkers are different colours,' said Sam Franklin. I could not say that either.

'I'm looking forward to your new career as a mime artist,' said Sam Franklin.

There was nothing else in the man's file except a doodled smiley face next to the red cross.

I opened the other two black files, knowing their subjects, Endymion Walker and Sam Franklin. The picture of Sam Franklin was the one that had been printed for the reference of the two military types at the shop.

'I think they caught my good side,' he said.

'And no red cross. Yet.'

'It feels like the telescopic sight on a sniper rifle. If I didn't know better, I'd feel Officially Paranoid.'

'You are always paranoid, Sam Franklin.'

'It's your effect on me.'

We looked at Walker's file and his daughter's side by side. For both, their picture had been taken in the shop in more or less the same place. The same as for Sam Franklin. Although their features were similar - Olivia Walker's less sour - his unruly white hair would have thrown them off their family resemblance without more.

Endymion Walker's full name had been incorrectly noted in the file, his first name mis-recorded as Damien. There would have been consternation when the two files had finally been brought together.

'How sloppy,' I said, pointing to the name error.

'Endymion's not exactly on any list of popular boys' names.'

I detected that Endymion Walker's image had unnerved Sam Franklin. Their identical poses, similar hair colourings and serious expressions seemed to overlay each other. The difference was that there was a red cross scrawled over Endymion Walker's face. And the other one. Two out of the three.

Walker's picture had *'Olivia W!! WTF!! Too late. CURTIS FAULT!'* scrawled next to it. The connecting dots seemed not to have been drawn together until some milestone had been reached with the girl.

'I am convinced that the black files denote individuals who are or might be troublesome. Who could possibly have thought that?' I said, looking pointedly at Sam Franklin. 'Perhaps even targets.' I gestured to the red cross, to make him feel even better.

'Uh-huh, how about the three yellow files?' Sam Franklin laid out the three files, placing Olivia's documents next to a young woman with long brown hair and a dark-skinned man, probably of Middle Eastern origin. All around their mid-twenties in human time.

'In this light, the files look shiny. Golden,' I said.

On each woman's file was written the words: *homeless - no close relatives – FAST TRACK!* On Olivia's, those words had been crossed out and _WALKER!_ had been written beneath them and underlined. The tone married up with the scrawls on her father's file, after he had come along and the filing error had been noticed.

Walker Senior's appearance asking about his daughter had stirred up a rich blend of confusion and anger, in the same way as too much Red Bull and vodka. And then Sam Franklin had come along to make it worse.

'Endymion Walker did not ask us for assistance. Why not?' I asked out loud. 'It was perverse of him not to come to us to help to find her. All of the Magic Circle's resources would have been available to him, instead he chose to keep it a private family matter. Stupid.' *He keep himself to himself.* As a result, Olivia Walker remained missing and Endymion Walker was dead. Very stupid.

The other two yellow files contained details of a man and a woman. The man was named Asim Hussain. *KEEP* READY was written next to his picture. For what? He certainly looked ready for whatever came along, an easy smile and a confident expression framed by short black hair. A man who radiated invincibility from the picture.

The woman - whose features looked faintly familiar to me, but I could not say why - had been caught in mid-sentence, her hand raking through her long mousey hair. Her name was recorded as Becky Carpenter.

We laid out the blue files. The scene conjured up by all the files in the conference room looked like frenzied preparations to make the seating plan for a maniac's wedding; in my experience for most weddings. They also contained screen-shots. Like the rest, apart from the Led Zepellin man, the only identifiable background was *Mirror of Galadriel*, taken with the security camera.

The pictures of the men and women were across a broad age range, at the younger end of the spectrum. No older than thirty or forty, sadly fitting the profile of the streets. We did not have this sort of thing at home.

All had 'homeless' written next to their pictures, all were people you might otherwise find on any normal day walking along the high street, waiting at a railway station, shopping in a supermarket. Except that these had no home and were more likely to be found wrapped in cardboard in a doorway.

'Here is the shabby woman,' I said , holding up one of the blue files with a picture of a ginger-haired woman in bright clothes that defied the gloom of the shop.

'Vanessa Grant. Where does she fit in?'

By the time we had worked through all the files, even peppermint tea was not enough. I was sorely tempted by some of the dark liquid in front of Sam Franklin. Sam Franklin, if anything, looked worse than I felt, reminiscent of a car crash in pounding rain. Suddenly it did not feel quite so bad.

It was 5am by the conference room clock, which also usefully told me the time in Hong Kong and New York so that I could be exhausted across multiple time zones.

Dawn was imminent.

20

10:00 am
SAM

I had immediately plummeted into a deep
sleep in my room. I hadn't even taken the
time to undress. I had some fogged
recollections of disturbed dreams, a swirl of
blue and yellow faces angrily jostling me,
with random faces periodically turning
black, their hungry eyes slashed with deep
red crosses by the other figures. The
morning had bizarrely not come quickly
enough.

When I awoke, I found Pagoda wrapped
around my feet snuggled in with her

favourite velociraptor cuddly toy. She was snoring noisily on her special tasselled velvet cushion. I was still exhausted; I seemed to be as nocturnal at the moment as Pagoda but was getting less sleep during the day.

I went through a shortened yoga programme to put my head in a row and my ducks in order, or something like that. The yoga would help me focus and sustain me for what lay ahead. Sometimes, going into a trance for a while accompanied by the gentle ringing of a small tinkly bell, and a cloud of pungent incense, was the only way to get back on track.

Pagoda kept well away from me, not wanting her fur contaminated by the foul-smelling smoke that hung in the air around me.

I came out of my trance. Fifteen minutes would have to suffice. I roused Pagoda from her cushion and she followed venomously.

Shortly after, I knocked on Meyra's door and she opened it after a few seconds, looking annoyingly chipper.

She retreated to her bed, sat down and picked up her phone again. She gestured that this wouldn't take long.

I divined from her half of the conversation that she was speaking to one of our London trainees.

'Yes, I am sending the files through now, Felix. For your eyes only at the moment, all of it is highly sensitive material.' I could hear the tension crackling at the other end as the trainee scribbled rapidly. Meyra played with the phone and pinged the files over to him.

'This is urgent,' she said. 'Very urgent. I want the answers by close of business today. Preferably sooner. Top priority.' I could almost feel the nervous nodding at the other end; Meyra is not one to be messed around, and the trainee was well aware of that.

'Good plan,' I mouthed to her as she ended her call.

We left her room. Strong coffee had appeared for me, and some sort of herbal gloop for her, as well as some freshly baked croissants. They arrived on a tray outside Meyra's door as if by magic, but in fact by Margit. Pagoda immediately pounced on an outlier croissant before I could scoop them all up. She ignored my pained growl at her as she dragged it away in triumph out of my reach.

I know, I know. No pet shop in history has sold French bakery products as cat food, but what can I tell you? *Everything's food or potential food.*

I put it down to our Bond. Pagoda periodically picked up traces of human traits in our two-way street. Pagoda was firmly of the view that I get all the useful stuff. Every now and again she tried to get a flash of insight into the offside rule. VAR? Not even a Bonded familiar could be expected to make sense of that.

I picked up and drank some coffee and guarded the other croissants, offering one to Meyra. By the time we had finished, Meyra's phone rang, and she answered it with a *go on, impress me* expression that she deftly

managed to transmit through the telecoms.
The trainee had sensibly decided to report
when he found something important, rather
than waiting to hand it over all at once.
Good move.

She put her phone away. 'Felix confirmed
that none of the blue stars in the files marked
'homeless' has a fixed address. Apart from
Olivia Walker. They were all last seen in the
Brighton area or close by and have since
dropped off the official records.'

I drained my coffee mug. 'If all Derek's
doing is acting like some sort of Guardian
Angel helping people to find their feet, and
it's all purely on the level, then he'd be a
local hero. They'd probably name a street
after him. Trouble is, I don't believe in fairy
godmothers.'

'Derek is not a demon-conjuror either,'
said Meyra as we headed out of the hotel.
'He does not have the skills. There is
something else at play here.'

'Right. From what I saw, he might just
about be able to do a few card tricks.' I

paused at the door. 'Derek looks more like a cog to me, a public face for something.'

'There may be more like him in the area,' said Meyra. 'Not merely that rancid shop.'

Meyra and I - with Pagoda's glowering presence reluctantly shadowing us - headed in the direction of the Pier.

21

2:00 pm
SAM

The severe red-and-cream-bricked
Brighton Star newspaper building lurked in a
narrow side street near the Pier: turn left at
the 1890's. I could almost feel the printing
presses in its crumbling basement gleaming
in semi-darkness, straining for the next
edition.

Meyra and I Stealthed from the brightly lit
public area into its darker newsroom.
Meyra's lean inner darkness gave her a head
start blending in; for Pagoda, it came

naturally; I needed to concentrate on my Hex.

I'd expected jangling phones and hubbub, what I found was open plan and murmuring. Eight desks partitioned into cubicles, arranged two by four, four occupied, three people on mobiles. The clean desk policy memo had been lost in the piles of files and papers scattered on the floor around each desk.

'It's not *The Times*', Meyra sniffed.

Meyra and I eased our way through the strictly beige, angle-poised room, the blinds shut to crank up the journalistic tension. One seemed as if it had been skewed artfully, allowing a thin shaft of natural light to give some dust motes their day in the sun. The feeling of intense journalistic endeavour was lessened by a man with his feet on his desk cleaning his fingernails and checking his lottery numbers; Citizen Kane was nowhere in sight.

The public area's atmosphere had been as quiet as a confessional: scattered old editions

- I insisted on Pagoda not shredding them -
and smooth walls densely clad with ranks of
framed front pages, pinning local history in
front of us like a kaleidoscope of butterflies
in a nature museum. The newsroom was a
throwback to the Seventies, I half-expected
Robert Redford and Dustin Hoffman to
wander in and compare Pulitzers.

A sharp-featured woman with alarming
cherry lipstick looked as if she were about to
direct her gaze towards me. She leaned
forward, distracted just in time by her phone
conversation with her own Deep Throat
about the recent spate of cat-mutilations in
the area. Pagoda's angry hiss almost broke
through our Stealth when she'd absorbed the
story from me. I passed close by the
woman's desk, careful not to disturb her.

At the grandly named 'Research Block'
Pagoda waited for us testily, drumming one
set of claws rhythmically in exasperation,
one of the things I could proudly say she had
picked up from me through our Bond.

The Stealth held out.

Low profile was the goal here – there'd been no press stories that summer about youths on broomsticks playing weird rugby or London streams getting uppity, and we wanted to keep our dead wizard out of any headlines.

The Research Block seemed the beating heart and collective memory of the building, but it was also where the budget had run out. Rows of half-empty filing cabinets lined rosewood-panelled walls of a double-height chamber excavated from the centre of the original building.

I hoped no gargoyles had been knocked off the roof and hurt in the making of this mausoleum. It reminded me of my training with the Circle and the fun searches around shadowy book cemeteries for annotated pages from the Kabbalah and the original manuscript-amended Circle mission statement. Happy times.

Meyra seemed more agitated by the number of trees that had been sacrificed for this by us irresponsible humans – her left eyebrow arched with her outrage.

A spiral staircase up to the next floor of the chamber cast bands of shadow from the harsh, impersonal overhead strip-lights onto the bank of filing cabinets and scattered desks. A woman in a yellow dress loud enough to get her banned from any public library was nearby, reading intently, the shadows striping her like a bee. She didn't look up, we were like ghosts.

On the upper level, a man was working through a pile of books and articles spread out on a nearby desk. Old school. Oblivious of us.

'It feels like we have fallen through a crack in time,' whispered Meyra dubiously. She sat down at a desk in the corner and breathed a small sigh when she assessed the computer, 'Wow, they have keyboards and everything.'

This was the centre of the peeling wallpaper and battered paintwork in the building, crumbling from its core, reaching out towards the modern world, eventually reaching the chrome and light wood at the entrance. It contrasted with the Beachcomber which at least embraces its lot, achieving, throughout its majestic tawdriness, rundown and out-dated; aspiring to grim.

Endymion Walker would have felt right at home here with a candlestick and his long quill pen. Its cobbled together tech and carved flowers framing the dark bookcases created an awkward impression of a steampunk Charles Dickens.

I checked on Pagoda. She was lounging on top of a filing cabinet, her talents not needed here unless a giant mouse decided to go on the rampage. An enormous furred shadow loomed for a moment in my peripheral vision and then disappeared.

I stood next to Meyra's chair and noticed something that had been nagging me for a while. One of the main lights above intermittently blinked. In exasperation, I crumpled a piece of paper into a ball and took aim, firing it at the misbehaving light with a nifty Push.

The crisp concussion from the stored energy fixed the problem. Violence is, it's fair to say, my tried and tested – and indeed only - DIY maintenance tactic. The other denizens of the Research Block carried on with their work, undisturbed.

'Cool beans,' whispered Meyra, approvingly. She'd been nineteen since the Seventies, so the decades blurred for her. She switched on the computer and logged in.

When I'd insisted, the scruffy guy with the wooden ear tunnels and hunched insolence manning the 'helpdesk' in the lobby had stopped worrying about missing his mate Georgia's daily posting of a photo of her morning cappuccino. He'd suddenly fully appreciated the urgency of my request. Username? System password? Cup of Earl Grey with a spoonful of Tibetan honey? Certainly. Jedi-whatever had worked for Alec Guinness - *These aren't the droids you're looking for.* And my Nudge had worked for me.

The computer rumbled into life. Slowly. Meyra made impatient whip-cracking sounds. It allowed access to archived internal research information for the previous two years, interviews, background pieces, official documents. Meyra settled down to play while I trawled the filing cabinets for hard copy materials. Pincer movement.

Some back issues were filed in broadly date order, the records more haphazard as they went further back. The physical files covering homelessness regrettably took up a whole large filing cabinet, a crusade of the newspaper. I took some promising files and planted myself next to the busily tapping Meyra.

We seemed to generate a gradually widening radius of tension and despair as we ploughed through the nightmare.

22

3:30 pm
MEYRA

'More than 300,000 'homeless' people in
Great Britain?' I enunciated each word
slowly and separately, scarcely able to
believe that they came together in that order.
A nice round number, one that rolls off the
tongue, one that at that moment felt
meaningless.

'People fall through the gaps.'

'That is a *lot* of gaps, Sam Franklin. A *lot* of
individuals. I find it difficult to imagine
them all standing in front of me. Even just in

Brighton, nearly 4,000 'sleep rough'. One in 70, the size of ten of our villages. I am shocked.' I shielded my eyes from the sun and glared down at the beach, disturbing the large pebbles underfoot, each one seeming to wear a worn-down face with despairing, hungry eyes looking up at me.

Why could we not have gone to a forest instead? Bark and leaves would not have toyed with my thoughts like that. I noticed I was fiddling with my hair between my thumb and forefinger and hastily smoothed it down.

'There's plenty of information but no answers. No-one knows the full figures.'

'No-one has looked hard enough, Sam Franklin. Human beings have a strange talent for ignoring misery. At home, we would not let it stand.'

'I'm guessing you're talking about your home-home, rather than Knightsbridge.'

I had the grace to smile. A little. I was not in the mood for his 'banter', and I was chastened by the thought of my five-bedroomed apartment with the modest wood surrounding it in that quiet cul-de-sac. Half home, half here, a short walk in nine-inch heels from Harrods.

We looked out from the shoreline, trying to focus in the blazing sunshine. Ink-black clouds would have been more appropriate, looming over a shattered oak smote by a jagged slash of lightning.

I broke the silence, 'It is a huge animal trap, a pit. People have a crisis, lose their home and then Shapechange into meaningless black-and-white shapes on a page.' A giggling small child ran by with a bright pink bucket and spade, heedless of the brooding adults; she did not lighten my mood. 'People living on the beach and in doorways are just the start: The obvious ones. 'Street dwellers' and 'squatters' and 'sofa-surfers' and others. We have fewer names for 'tree'.'

'It means they can split it into smaller chunks. Make it vanish.'

'Whether someone has lost their job or something else, it matters not what it is called when they have no place to live and the cold is coming. If anyone abuses the system, no-one would know? It seems broken already.'

I caught my fingers reaching for my hair again and restrained myself. Settling my hair *twice in an hour*, human frailties have moved me beyond imagining. Never could Sam Franklin have seen such emotion from me. How very native of me.

Mother would be livid.

That at least made me smile fleetingly. Evidently, it is possible to find positive outcomes in any situation. Sam Franklin shared a surprised look with Pagoda, who was further up the beach sunning herself on the hot stones (as removed from the water as possible without looking intimidated).

'A lot is left to the charities to sort out.'

'Sadly, Sam Franklin, mobile food kitchens and night walks on the beach are not enough.' I felt anger but resisted any further unseemly displays.

We found a bench and spread out between us a list of the organisations in the area that provided succour for the homeless, however those people were labelled and filed away. The big names were there, they were always there: the public authorities, the major charities, church organisations, and other people without whom the creaking system would collapse.

I pointed at an entry on one of the pages: An understated logo of a house fashioned in four rough brushstrokes by the name 'Havenward Foundation'.

'Haven.'

The tracks of Walker's footsteps felt close. If we were going to walk in them, I was uncomfortably aware that they had been made by a dead man.

23

5:00 pm
MEYRA

Felix had worked miracles in such a short time. I decided to shower him with praise, 'Good.'

Many of the individuals in the files had dropped off society's radar completely.

Olivia Walker: Head of house at her private school, county chess player, marathon runner. An excellent student until the end of her second year at university and then she dropped out. The pressure had overwhelmed her. Having a senior-ranking wizard as a father would not have helped.

She had moved back home, struggled to hold on to any employment and a few months ago disappeared completely. No note. Nothing. A breakdown?

She covered her tracks to avoid her father, or perhaps someone else did. Regardless, Endymion Walker persevered and tracked her down here, but the trail had ended for him in a starkly permanent way.

Olivia Walker in a yellow file, Asim Hussain in another, the brown-haired woman, all had drifted down here; how had they drifted into the hidden files?

The blue files told fragmented stories of people who had fallen away from society, either by happenstance or by choice, through hardship or in some cases mere disillusionment. Felix had not been able to track down all of them, some had given false names, some had vanished off the grid.

I pointed to the black files, 'I believe that there is more to it, Sam Franklin. Something darker. All of the individuals in the files seem somehow graded, from exceptional for whatever reason to run-of-the-mill to vexatious – and that includes you,' I said, pointing at Sam Franklin's picture. 'You represent some sort of danger to them and need to be dealt with, like the men with the crossed-out faces. Personally, I also tend to view you as vexatious.'

'Thanks. They did jump on my case like they'd just sat on a live wire.'

'That suggests that they are under time pressure, and we would benefit from some assistance, Sam Franklin.'

'I know just the goblin.'

24

6:30 pm
SAM

I texted River Smith to ask for a meeting and got a reply back within five minutes to say: *Usual place, one hour. XXX*

I figured out what I needed to say to River, then I beckoned to Pagoda to come with me to see her. Pagoda raised her head up and back and showed me her tonsils and fangs with an expressive yawn, then languidly appeared at her standard fuck-you pace. *If we must.* Suffice to say that their relationship can be somewhat tense at times, but Pagoda needed to hear what River might have to say.

We struck out from the city centre along the seafront towards the dis-used pedestrian subway that was the site of our usual catch-ups. *Ma gically* Hidden behind various Illusions and Wards, it was not one of Brighton's famous landmarks, in fact the exact opposite, shrouded in secrecy.

I was well aware that her police colleagues had fixed views on the type of matters that we discussed, keen to ensure that *that sort of thing* was minimised at the station; it was bad enough that River had an office there in the first place.

We were in plenty of time - River would pout if we were late.

We skirted the Bandstand. Past the skeletal marooned pier. Pagoda kept close to me, not too close.

As we walked, my thoughts on where we were on the Walker thing strayed to my 'quick chat' about it at the office yesterday

159

with Gideon Winterbourne, our Special
Operations Director. His full name is as far
as I'm concerned *That Bastard Gideon
Winterbourne.* All of him always bristles at
me, from his pointed shiny shoes to his spiky
beard and sharp suit. Even his pin-stripes
make me bleed.

The 'quick chat' had touched upon the
Circle's coordinated communications
approach for this matter. He'd given me a
prickly warning: *no police, no press, make sure
we keep a lid on this,* and I'd already ignored
half of it; I was just about to ignore the other
half. I get it with the Circle's obvious need
for rabid secrecy – sorry, careful discretion -
but I didn't need him to give me orders
about it, thank you very much. As the
Circle's Lore Director, this was *my* case.

Winterbourne's attitude to me? A
nightmare. I don't take *all* of it personally.
He's a pain to everyone except maybe
Napoleon, his objectionable crow familiar,
but familiars shouldn't count. If you can't get
on with your familiar, then you're in *real*
trouble. Winterbourne and I did have a great
deal of previous to add to his disagreeable

nature, and Winterbourne reserved his
special vitriol for me. It's mainly because of
our difference of views over Hilary all those
years ago.

No, not a spat over a woman.

Over a goblin.

That goblin's claims against
Winterbourne's Special Projects Group made
our relationship toxic for decades. A species-
ism claim *and* a sex discrimination claim (it's
hard enough to tell with goblins at the best
of times), all rolled into one. For my part, I
blame it all on HOR.

The Human/Other Resources team at the
time had wanted to defend the claims, and
Winterbourne had weighed in on their side
demanding blood.

I'd like to say he was being metaphorical,
but I'm pretty sure he wasn't. I'd pressed
hard for a settlement because it was the right
thing to do.

The settlement with Hilary was on fair
terms for Hilary – after all these years, I'm
still playing it safe about pronouns for
Hilary. Best of all, it avoided all of us having
to turn up at the Lore Courts, where the fine
art of cross-examination has been known to
involve crucifixes.

That outcome was the catalyst for decades
of mutual loathing between Winterbourne
and me, and I can't see it ever improving.

Sharing nicely with him was a no-go. It
was never going to happen.

We reached Brunswick Lawns, a parched
buffer between Brighton and the sea,
overlooked by creamy yellow mansion
blocks across the main road.

Pagoda prowled like a lioness on the
mown Savannah; Meyra would have ripped
off her shoes to dance on it if she'd been
there   that's Elves for you in the big city.

I just walked.

Not many people at this end of town under the late sun. Except three men ahead of us, occupying a wooden bench. A surreptitious glance, a flash of recognition. They aimed for nonchalant but missed; Pagoda slunk low, sensing trouble.

The right-hand one had been at Derek's shop - the same black t-shirt, black jeans, DMs. All Black. The middle one's dark grey, baggy t-shirt had '*Karnage*' defiantly printed in huge jagged yellow letters on the front. The other had a fiery dragon tattoo coiling up his right arm: he was *The Boy with the Dragon Tattoo*. I guessed he was clueless about computers unless he was hitting you with a keyboard.

Their black panel van, a long Peugeot, its nearside door open, was parked nearby. On double yellows: must be desperadoes. Its wipe-clean floor looked ready for me in one or more pieces, with or without a black cloth bag pulled over my head and cable ties around my wrists and ankles.

They detached themselves from the bench and moved towards me, well-drilled.

River might have to practice her pout. This was not in the schedule.

All-Black unsheathed a serrated knife that gleamed in the sunlight, slowly weaving patterns with it in front of him with easy skill. Karnage and Dragon Tattoo slid on some knuckledusters. Pagoda hissed, arching her back, her face stretched downwards into the grass, ears flattened backwards. My ears tried to do the same.

'You bin pushin' your face in our business. Not cool,' rumbled Karnage. He spat on the grass between us.

'We're gonna pull you inside out, an' ask you what we wanna know', said Dragon Tattoo. His eyes narrowed.

'If you manage that, I'll talk louder. In case my voice gets muffled,' I said, standing my ground. I Puffed Myself Up, courtesy of Pagoda, but in truth it wasn't as effective without a tail. My 6ft 2' and 200 lbs now presented a more substantial target.

Something to be approached with caution,
but a target all the same. Pagoda growled.

'Let's get this over with,' I breathed.

They were upon me, blocking my escape; I
had no intention of escaping. Not right then
anyway.

The world truncated: a patch of dry grass,
a bench, a van, three thugs and us: nothing
else. No seagulls, no traffic noise, no surf,
just this.

Contact.

Time slowed down, like it always does.

Glints of reflected light from the evening
sun on a knuckleduster; Brutalist
performance art.

I felt rather than saw the knife start on a
vicious low arc towards me.

I bellowed. Was I calling for help? Didn't
matter: All-Black didn't stop.

I thrust both hands out in front of me, palms up, pointing directly at Karnage then rotated them to widen my field of fire.

Energy coalesced and burst through my hands; I felt a scalpel of pain in my side just as my Push hit them.

Karnage's face changed from cocky and expectant to startled as the Push lifted him and Dragon Tattoo, hurling them into the bench with a satisfying crunch. All-Black twisted with military precision, nearly dodging the Push but was still momentarily stunned.

Sometimes, *Ma gic* needs a little help. A lunge punch into his solar plexus. Sorted.

Now three of them in a row. Sprawled, untidy figures, draped over the bench like a dripping Salvador Dali still life; one from his Hoodlum Period.

Or maybe more like the Ugly Sisters because I really needed a Fairy Godmother to appear at that moment, sinking to my

knees from the inferno in my side courtesy
of All-Black's knife.

'Bibbidi-Bobbidi-Boo', I mumbled, and
collapsed face forward on the grass.

25

6:40 pm
SAM

I woke up. Seconds later? Maybe hours? It felt like days.

The three thugs were where I'd left them; there was no crowd. So, not very long. Pagoda was beside me, alternately licking my and her sides, mewling. A comforting glow warmed me as her Healing kicked in, enough at least to close the wound properly. I ruffled her chin gratefully. My side still hurt like a bastard.

A few minutes edged by, even the time felt sharp.

We – I'm being collegiate: Pagoda isn't designed for heavy lifting; she was standing guard - manoeuvred the three men over to the van and dumped them in the back. The effort and the pain that it triggered made me hiss like a black mamba with a hernia. I clambered in, Pagoda behind me. I pulled the door shut.

The interior was bathed in a dim light and there was a hot smell of acrid sweat, rusty blood (some of it mine) and leaking oil. The van was kitted out like Torquemada's holiday home. I grabbed some stylish matching handcuffs for each of the thugs, attaching each of them to a handy bar on the side of the van like crumpled ballerinas ready to practise some pliés.

Each had a copy of my photo. Touching, but not yet a fan club. Karnage also had a cheap mobile phone, password-protected: there are some things *Ma gic* simply can't get around. No wallets or any form of ID. Master criminals. Karnage had a keyring sporting a clenched fist with its middle finger upraised. On it: one van key. I pocketed a handy knuckleduster.

Start with the leader. I pulled Karnage upright. Shook him awake, his eyes out of focus.

He groaned, 'What was that?'

'Ju-jitsu,' Right then, I could have said 'Lapsang Souchong' and he would have nodded thoughtfully.

Serrations of pain in my side, then sweat coating my face. I shook my head to clear it and waved the photos of me at him. 'Why were you trying to jump me? Who sent you?' He rattled his handcuffs on the bar and said nothing.

I reached forward. Time to speed things up. I whispered in his ear that I had a friend who would *really* like to meet him, and I pointed into the gloom at the end of the van, implanting in his head an Apparition of my children's favourite godparent, Justin.

In his werewolf form, not in his Liverpool away shirt.

Justin and I had hit it off when we met, after we'd reached an accommodation on the teeth and claws issue (his, not mine). The Apparition slavered hungrily at Karnage – I reproduced Justin's image from when Emma and I got him round for dinner on a full Moon, when the kids were at their mates: that crazed look when he saw the tethered goat. It's always nice to spoil guests. Karnage's yelp of fear in response was gratifying.

Pagoda hissed in alarm as some of the Apparition seeped into her head. Cats and werewolves have a tense relationship, not surprising with their respective family trees. Some time ago, when things were threatening to get out of hand, I had A Talk with both of them and they know to play nicely.

I kept my voice low, matter-of-fact, 'I want your phone code and some answers. Or I'll make my friend think you're Little Red

Riding Hood's Grandma. In a bun with fries. Understand?'

'OK. OK…OK.' He slumped, defeated, more frightened of Justin and me for now than someone – anyone - else later.

All-Black had provided the pictures. They'd had orders to give me 'a good shoeing' and find out where I'd come from, what I was after. Nothing about Meyra or Pagoda.

'Code,' I prompted.

The teeth did it, Justin's gleaming – and, it must be said, very well flossed - incisors. Justin in a public-spirited way always ensured that his trips to the dentist fell in the middle of the lunar month, working out better for everyone at the surgery. Particularly for the hygienist, whose limbs remained intact after each appointment.

Karnage saw no escape routes, no clever wheezes, just a hungry werewolf with his flavour in its nostrils.

He gave me the code.

All the time, he stared at the corner of the van where Justin's Apparition lurked viewing Karnage as the werewolf version of 'Meals-on-Wheels'. If I gave the word. He'd always been a fan of meat pies, preferably human. Without pastry or gravy.

He was fine with human tartare.

The phone had a brutally short Contacts list:

< DT >
< NO NAME >

'DT?' I knew what was coming.

'Derek Taylor. He runs a shop in town. *Mirror* something. In Gardner Street. He knows more about this stuff than me,' he ventured, hopeful. 'He's spreading your picture round town. Like we always do when anyone's sniffing around.'

'Anyone else been 'sniffing around'?'

He looked hunted. Not so much as if I texted Justin his address, but hunted nonetheless.

'No-one lately. There was a guy a while ago. Asked loads of questions. We got a tip-off. Sorted him out,' sounding pleased.

Walker?

'What did he look like?'

'Like a crap headbanger. I hate LedFuckingZeppelin.'

I showed him the photo from the shop.

'Yeah, him'. I cocked my head towards the back of the van, and he carried on, pre-occupied with Justin, not noticing my wince of pain, 'We knew he was in the gardens. By the Pavilion. He often hung out there. We got him, gave him a good seeing-to. Left him messed up on a bench. Went and had some beers. Never seen him again. That's what we was going to do tonight with you.' Wistful. Disappointed.

Brighton Pavilion: the big fuzzy 'tent' with 'chimneys' in the photo background.

'When we got it out of him, what he was interested in, turns out it was nothing to do with us. No point missing out on the fun, though, right?' His grin twisted as he shifted position, a brief grimace, then that twisted grin again. 'Then we found out he was a Five-0…Party time…'

Pain scalded me, like someone feeding my spleen through a mincer. Keep going, keep control. While I still could.

Karnage visibly shrank back when I made Apparition-Justin roar back into his head to give me a breather.

'Tell me about the Haven.'

'Looks after deadbeats. At Belvedere Farm. On the Downs. All the deadbeats know about it – some get put off – too many rules.'

'Anyone turn up there with money?'

A puzzled look. 'Dunno. Doubt it…They're deadbeats.' His aura remained rock solid, unwavering. 'Above my pay grade. I just collect my wages; they just want to be left alone. End of. We only do what we're told. We just know it's private. Real private. They want it to stay that way.'

'So, you're the military wing of a homeless charity. Seriously?' I was running out of steam; coloured blotches in my vision...Just a bit longer. 'What's the 'no-name' contact?'

'A burner. Changes all the time. For instructions.'

I released Justin into the three men's subconscious to keep them busy. They drooled and writhed: I may have overdone it, but I can't say I regretted it. I locked the van, a Ward concealing it in plain sight. How it was parked, passers-by would think it was a Nigerian diplomatic vehicle.

River was waiting for us a short stagger away.

26

11:00 pm
SAM

Feathery bed, lurid pink duvet and pillows, soft lighting. Unsettling aroma of rotting cabbage. Heavily snoring cat. We'd evidently somehow managed to drag ourselves to the subway on the main road. I didn't remember anything about getting there or what had happened next.

'It isn't polite to keep a lady waiting, sugar,' her breathless voice made my ears tingle. 'Not as bad as collapsing when you arrived, though. No stamina. *I* had to carry

you up to my boudoir.' A smiling face was
pushed into mine as she knelt on the bed.

Inspector River Smith: bright yellow skin,
red eyes, three-and-a-half feet tall, short legs,
long gangly arms. Goblin. She looked pretty
good to me.

The police height requirement hadn't been
so much relaxed for her as shot with
elephant-stopping tranquiliser darts. She
flicked her pink boa over the shoulder of her
purple velvet trouser-suit. Whatever else,
she wasn't a plain clothes officer.

A suspicious look at Pagoda stretching at
my feet. 'Still no muzzle?' Pagoda knew she
was mostly joshing; Pagoda mostly found it
amusing.

'Shall we get down to it?' she enticed. I
pulled myself together. It's how River
operates - after internal conference calls, I
imagined the participants hurrying for a cold
shower.

The Circle-Police relationship is
complicated, fragile. We agreed long ago

that keeping it off the books was best. Coppers have a fixed, manic expression if any crazy person talks about demons, ending in a Taser discharge or an urgent straitjacket fitting. Identity parades for a blue demon are a non-starter unless a cooperative Smurf parade's passing through.

I showed her the pictures of Walker and the policeman. She squeaked, making Pagoda sit up, wide-eyed. River pointed at the headbanger. 'I don't know the other one, but *he's* one of ours,' no trace of come hither now. 'DS Kieran Hastings. Disappeared two months ago.'

'What was he doing?'

'Routine surveillance. Some punters did a bank job in Essex that went dwarf-shaped. We heard they'd come down here. Hiding among the homeless crowd. Hastings went in undercover with a full surveillance package. Then he vanished.'

'Any intel before he disappeared?'

'Enough to collar the gang. They admitted the robbery…swore blind they had nothing to do with Hastings. No shaking them on that…' A sly look, that voice again, 'Now, precious, where did you get that picture, or shall I get my handcuffs?' Teasing, insistent.

'One of our Governors' - I tapped Walker's picture – 'was killed last night. A demon…it was messy. He'd been down here looking for his daughter and your guy's face turned up'.

'Bank robberies and demons don't normally go well together, liebchen.' A pause. 'Sam: losing one of our own is a huge deal for us.' Each pupil individually narrowed. 'The picture?'

'River, we need some slack. I don't know if Hastings is alive or where he is, but we'll find him and call you in with the cavalry.' We both knew the obligatory official dance; with River it was a raunched-up Argentine Tango. 'In the meantime, you'll find three guys handcuffed inside a van five minutes' walk away. I'm sure they'll be happy to chat once they've recovered from my little Punch and Judy show.'

She slowly folded her long, thin arms, parting her luscious yellow lips. She pointed one of her nostrils at me, inhaling deeply. 'Three men in the back of a van. Sounds a little risqué, how can I resist?' She was silent for a few seconds, 'Sam, darling, I can't just leave you to get on with this, it's too close to home for us.' A pause, then an exhalation. 'But, as you're *so adorable*…Let's see how my little dangerous liaison goes with the boys. You can have 48 hours to come up with more. After that, we'll take over. And we won't play nicely.'

If that offer ever needed to be officially documented, I knew it would be written in a small grey notebook and filed in a locked underground room in the Orkneys. Under 'Supplemental'.

'Fair enough,' I said.

River sashayed out of her office, a glimpse of watercooler and filing cabinets in the corridor beyond, in the less flamboyant part of Police HQ. 'When you've got something, *do* come up and see me, Sam' she said, one ruby eye fixed on me fondly, a carefree wave over her shoulder, 'And please don't forget the mobile fur gloves when you leave.' An answering grumble from Pagoda.

As the door closed, River's husky voice, laden with promise, '48 hours, my dear...Missing you already...'

A perfumed silken rope slowly started to tighten around my neck from the slack.

27

12:10 am
MEYRA

I lit some incense at the hotel. Sam
Franklin and I set to work.

The Havenward Foundation is a not-for-
profit organisation established in the British
Virgin Islands. It had been registered as a
charity since 2005. Of modest size. Modest to
the point of being painfully shy and retiring.

There was nothing obviously
incriminating on show. People behind this
type of organisation tend to be keen to
remain very private, under the public radar.

Without more, there was nothing suspicious here. On the face of it quite the opposite, with its extremely generous annual donation to Brighton's official coffers, completely in line with its charitable purpose which included *providing help and support to homeless people in the Brighton area.*

That all seemed beyond reproach.

Of more interest was the fact that the Havenward Foundation had one significant real estate asset in the public records. An old farmhouse that most people simply called the Haven.

The Haven had a public-facing, albeit low profile, presence and clearly did more than simply donate money. The farm was close by, tucked away in the South Downs National Park, east of the city, an area of undulating chalk hills, covered by a rich mixture of pasture and woodland; quintessential British countryside.

'It's in Central Nowhere,' said Sam Franklin. 'The only witnesses are hikers and sheep. And more sheep.'

It appeared to be an ideal base for a charity to get on with its charitable works without disturbance in a peaceful and secluded location.

'If they've got a dark side, it's perfect to hide away any mischief until the Death Star's fully operational,' said Sam Franklin.

'I agree,' I said. 'If it stopped at them giving shelter to the homeless and putting people back on track, I would not have a thing to say against them. But of the three people who have actively asked questions concerning their activities,' I checked off my fingers, 'one is dead, one is missing…'

'And I've decided not to wear my bulls-eye patterned T-shirt for a while.'

'But there is nothing *illegal* if all they do is help to straighten people out in their remote farmhouse,' I said, looking up from the scattered papers. *Remote farmhouse* sounded a lot more palatable than *isolated lair*.

'A large piece of this puzzle is the missing policeman,' said Sam Franklin. 'Hastings seems to have been working on something completely different but managed to ask the wrong questions in the wrong place. He got caught in the middle.'

'None of this gets us any closer to what happened to the Walkers.'

'Indeed. We can pick this up in the morning – I want to take a proper look at that farm,' said Sam Franklin.

'Are we going to drive there tomorrow?'

'Not straightaway. Before we pay them any personal visit, we'll need to put the kettle on.'

PART THREE

SATURDAY, AUGUST 7TH

28

8:00 am
SAM

I called Emma.

'How did Levitation 3 go?' I asked.

'I think we need to put some padding on the gym ceiling,' she said with grim satisfaction. 'Don't worry, it's Burn for Beginners next.'

'Is that some sort of cardio workout thing?'

'Are you suggesting I need that?'

'Of course not, darling,' I said, complimenting myself for having nerves of steel. 'How are the kids?'

'Not sure,' Emma replied. 'Same old same old. The kids surfaced at the crack of 3 yesterday afternoon, ransacked the fridge then disappeared. In other words, They're fine. They're very skilfully keeping out of the Tweedles' way, fed up with them, and I'm sure the feeling's mutual. The kids grunted hello and sent Their mild affection to you.'

'I'm deeply touched, at least Beth didn't say she hated me.'

'It's because you're in a different county at the moment.' Emma's voice then switched to Serious, 'How much longer? The novelty of Mr. Bethany and Mr. Andrews has rather worn off. Where are you at, my little chickadee?'

'We *know* someone down here's preying on homeless people. We *think* it's a fake charity - the Haven - but we don't have enough to officially raid it. Walker seems to have got in the way looking for his daughter. She's still missing, and he's walking dead. Add a missing undercover plod, and the main thing we're doing at the moment is generating loose ends.'

'Awesome. I of course have total confidence in all of you,' she said, and I heard in those words Emma trying to convince herself that everything really was in hand.

'I need to make things right down here,' I said, knowing that she understood. She and I had worked this sort of stuff out over the years. 'Wherever it leads.'

I promised I'd call her again when I could.

Room service – satisfyingly terrible: lukewarm and greasy, no idea what it was supposed to be – provided fuel. I carefully spread out on the floor the maps and plan of the area and the farmhouse, and methodically went through them to familiarise myself with the route and the layout as far as I could.

Figuratively as well as literally, all roads seemed to be leading there, one way or another.

29

9:45 am
VANESSA GRANT

They had been efficient, she had to give them that, on the weekend.

Slightly unsettling, for reasons that she could not quite articulate at the moment, but unsettling nonetheless. Vanessa Grant looked around her room. Dormitory-style, uncomfortably similar to a hospital ward in some ways but clean and with that hint of the smell of strong pine at the edges of her nostrils.

There were eight beds, empty at the moment. All female thank God. She had been put in the corner, the newbie in here, processed fast enough for a late breakfast. The others were presumably finishing theirs; she settled in, made plans.

She hadn't wanted breakfast anyway. Not hungry. She'd only been thinking about one thing. Becky. And there had been no sign of Becky so far.

She thought about her route here. She'd just been processed without them realising that she had given a false last name (she'd given her favourite aunt's surname, easy fo r her to remember). Her background information was false, everything that she had told them was a lie.

All for Becky's sake, her headstrong super-annoying sister who had run away from home on Thursday after the latest blazing row with M and D. There had been *plenty* of yelling, plenty of slamming of tables and rattling of breakfast crockery - by D as usual: when will he learn that it does no good whatsoever?

It had all been over the lively, too lively, debate about (Becky) *how we need to become vegan and save the planet,* and (D) *if you want to save the planet why do you always leave all the lights on around the house and don't bother to recycle,* and (Becky) *I hate you, like you just don't get it, it's the end of my life and everyone else's.*

As always, the underlying cause of the flare-up had been about something quite different: Becky's recent rather acrimonious break-up with Aidan, and the fine art of transference of the issue. Vanessa congratulated herself on having spotted what was wrong, she had simply assumed that - like always - it would blow over and they could get back to some serious family seething that evening. It didn't this time.

Vanessa was a redhead, taking after D, Becky's looked like she'd skinned a long-haired vole and stuck it on her head, no offence, whereas Becky had inherited D's explosive temperament, Vanessa was much calmer. Vanessa felt she'd had the better part of that deal overall, although her self-inflicted role of painstaking Nobel-level peacemaker had always felt that it was a strain.

This time, crazily, it had gone a *lot* further. Becky's rumpled bedroom on the face of it had everything in the world crammed into it in sedimentary layers on the floor, except one particular thing: Becky. Her open wardrobe with the myriad clothes strewn out like multi-coloured lava, combined with the absence of her favourite toy bear from its permanent position on her pillows (holding the secret stash of cash that Vanessa knew about and which Becky kept in its plush tummy), told the tale. Becky had gone.

It was Vanessa who was the family member supposed to be good at drama; her Leeds Uni Theatre and Performance finals were coming up next year to prove it. The other three were streets ahead, though, this time around. For a seventeen year old, Becky's exit had been a command performance, demanding a standing ovation, flowers, the lot.

She had stalked off a few times in the past, quite a few when it came down to it, so there had been no sense of panic, just annoyance. Just the absolute certainty that she would be back in due course, the front door would slam shut behind her when she flounced back in and another vase would know that its time had come for a percussion demonstration.

By the end of Thursday evening, there had been no sign of Becky. *Still sulking,* D said. Probably smouldering with the injustice of it all in some rank part of Burgess Hill, the metropolis of Vanessa's and Becky's dreams, alluringly placed on the borders of West Sussex and East Sussex. The World's End district of Burgess Hill said it all for Vanessa.

M had once said something about the name coming from the arrival of the railway but Vanessa knew it was really a description of its cultural credentials: too far from the relentless cosmopolitan razzmatazz of London to the North, too far from the attraction of the tourist magnet of Brighton to the South, too far from anywhere, really. M, in tears, had wanted to call the police, D

had said it was a lot of nonsense and Becky
would come crawling back soon enough,
staying at one of her no-good friends for the
night until she grew up. M and D had at
least agreed on one thing: they disapproved
of the catalyst in al this, Aidan. *Good riddance
to bad rubbish.*

Vanessa had known exactly where Becky
had gone, down to Brighton to see Tabatha
at her squat. That grubby squat, all countless
layers of peeling wallpaper and rising damp-
flavoured air freshener. Vanessa reflected on
the folly of having introduced Becky to her
dazzlingly exotic friend all those months
ago.

She was pretty sure that's where Becky
had sloped off to a few times previously, to
the fug of weed and the pounding old-
fashioned UK Garage, not *too* loud so as not
to annoy the neighbours in the terrace and
stir up the eviction of her and whatever
mates were staying there that week.

Tabatha didn't allow phones, too easy to
be spied on by the Feds, so the discovery of
Becky's phone in a drawer of her bedside

table had somewhat oddly tended to proved where she had gone. M and D would have hit ballistic, definitely called the police. That would have been a disaster when Vanessa *knew* that she would be able to fix this. She just needed to talk to her sister, make her see sense for once, before it all spiralled out of control.

Vanessa had packed a few things for a couple of days, M and D would know she was not as flaky as her sister. She left them a scribbled note saying *Its k. Getting her now. Don't worry. Vx* No point texting. M and D didn't "do" what they cutely called "social media".

Tabatha had greeted her with an airy wave and told her that Becky had already gone, and that she'd seemed really serious about *some time away from it all*. When she'd heard what had happened, Tabatha had suggested to Becky that she should tell her family where she was.

That had saddened Becky, made her realise that no-one - not even Tabatha - understood, no-one could see what she could see, and she had made her excuses and left, toy bear and all, with a determined, non-committal *I'll see, but I need to take a break from all this shit.*

Before she went, Tabatha had mentioned that Derek - at one of the local New Age shops - was someone that she knew and trusted should Becky need any more help. It was the least she could do.

Vanessa looked out of the window at the compound and sipped some water.

She had left Tabatha to it and headed off into town. Vanessa believed that Becky had somehow wound up here, by virtue of a dose of sisterly intuition, and where else would she have gone except on Tabatha's recommendation? Becky had no phone, no other people that she knew down here, her resolve would surely be faltering by now.

Vanessa hadn't liked to think of Becky as a missing person; that was too scary. Nor a homeless person; people from Burgess Hill didn't become homeless.

Her memories of the shop were a blur. She remembered that it had been dark with an undercurrent of spices in the air, but the main thing that filled her thoughts with a mixture of confusion and fear had been the sight of her sister's pin-sharp photo left face up in a filing tray on the counter with a word scrawled across it: *FAST TRACK.* She restrained herself with a huge effort. *FAST TRACK?* What the hell was that?

Should she trust this guy and his secret camera? Was he merely being thorough with the picture and a note that this was an urgent case needing help, or was he a creep, or perhaps something worse?

She had not confronted him, wanted to let him give himself enough rope to hang himself. *Don't let on.* Vanessa had asked the owner whether he recognised the name Becky Carpenter, a friend of hers down on her luck in the area. Instinct told Vanessa not to admit any family connection at this stage.

She'd kept her voice level, drawing on the hours of performance theory and practice to keep her features under absolute control, kept her tone casual, pleased that the two of them didn't look very much like each other.

No mention of the photo, eyes front, full-on eye contact with the audience. She pretended that she hadn't seen it, even when the man's eyes had inadvertently darted over to the filing tray while she described Becky. His eyes had changed when she mentioned the long light brown hair.

He said, 'Sure, she came in yesterday, all over the place. I reckon she was on something. Typical runaway, we see them all the time. I pointed her to the Haven.' He had pulled out a shiny piece of paper from a drawer, a printed leaflet. 'I gave her one of these. Any port in a storm, eh? Give her a chance to get her shit together. Might help you, too?'

As she'd thanked him, Vanessa had kept her features impassive, managing to leave the shop and maintain an iron, purposeful grip on her expression until she had turned the corner out of sight of the front door. She had immediately started shaking. She didn't trust the man in the shop, there was something about the photograph and the reference to *FAST TRACK* that bothered her. A lot. Like Becky had passed some sort of selection process, not been given a helping hand.

A thought forced its way into her head that the printer was probably even now chugging her image out into that tray on top of her sister's picture. Perhaps she was going to be "fast tracked" as well.

Everything would work out.

She'd decided to crash with Tabetha for the night and make an early start.

She was sure that she would find Becky at the Haven, then the two of them could go home after the end of Becky's silly little adventure. And if that still wasn't the end of it, she would call in M and D. One way or the other, how she and Becky would laugh about this one day.

When the man in the shop had been satisfied that she was out of sight, he pressed a button on the underside of his counter.

There were too many questions at the moment, the blonde girl, the two white haired guys, the latest two girls. This one had seemed to be by herself, not connected to the white-haired guys, less of a problem, he thought. Less of a threat.

That said, he needed to get this one off his desk and onto the guys at the commune. They could find out what she knew, and he should maybe keep a low profile for a while. It was the Haven needed to sort things out. And keep them sorted. Not his responsibility.

He had done his bit. He had heard on the grapevine that Foden had vanished and he didn't want to find out up close and personal what had happened, he didn't think it was a secondment to their offices in the Caribbean.

30

10:09 am
SAM

Not many hotels have a Scrying Room among the amenities that they offer: trouser-press, pillow menu, huge copper cauldron for Scryings and Readings; and Herbal Infusions in the hotel gift shop.

I went through the sign-posted door and found myself at the top of rickety wooden steps that descended precipitously into a double height cube Dug out of the hotel's foundations. It was once used as a panic room for hunted *Ma gic* practitioners who had nowhere else to go.

I could see the indentations in the walls around the room hinting at cots for a lengthy stay. The hotel had once been a discreet place of Questionable Morals, a useful source of misdirection and distraction before building-sized Wards had been developed. This was like burrowing back in time.

In the centre of the room, a gleaming copper cauldron, classical shape, the size of an Essex hot tub, hung from a hook in the ceiling anchored by three thick iron chains equally spaced around the rim. It was like a confused bell. As facilities go, easier to operate than a trouser-press, same room rate.

The cauldron was suspended over what was essentially a giant fire basket. Meyra was currently coaxing its contents into life with a Burn. It was like a scene from the Sorcerer's Apprentice, not that Meyra would be thrilled with that comparison, and I trusted it would not end up the same way.

The only nods to modernity in the room were a large extractor fan fixed to the ceiling directly above to reduce the lethal choking

205

hazard. Practical *and* thoughtful. And a hosepipe plumbed into the wall.

'Did you bring the bat wool, Sam Franklin?'

I retrieved it from my pocket and handed the gauze bag to her to add to the pile of logs.

I ran my hand over the smooth cauldron, catching our reflections in the curves of the cauldron, hoping that the visions that we'd see would be less like a hall of mirrors in a funhouse.

I picked up the hose, unravelled it and went over to the cauldron, reached over the rim and triggered the water to fill it up to the *MAX* line. A bit like making a giant pot noodle.

While it steadily filled, we added other ingredients, including some eye of newt and toe of frog – Shakespeare's source materials were impeccable. His end-product wasn't just great literature, it was a recipe book for high quality Hexes.

The flames curled around the base of the cauldron and the liquid started to bubble. I could feel that Pagoda had picked up the warmth while she stretched out upstairs on a rug, and there was the peculiar feeling of her luxuriating in the warmth of a fire in a room where she wasn't.

'I brought some Camomile,' I said. Secret *Ma gic* ingredient? No, it was for when a cuppa became essential, my concession to weird beverages. I filled a small flask and dropped it into the cauldron on a short chain where it floated upright in the frothing liquid.

The bubbles and the murk started to part in the centre as we combined to start the Scrying.

We projected the various site plans onto the white walls and a Google Maps image: it's important not to feel obliged to stick to the old ways of smeared pig entrails when there's an iPhone to hand.

The plans showed an enormous farmhouse with two large shaded-in boxes to the side, representing outbuildings which were described as 'approved for conversion to residential accommodation'. The digital images showed no buildings other than a farmhouse, there were large gardens and some fields for pasture and woods stretching over 10 or so rolling acres. The planning permission had been granted around three years ago, but the Google Maps image seemed out of date, and the plans hinted at possibilities and potential, not reality.

'The farmhouse wouldn't be able to handle all the people in the files,' I said, nodding towards the surface of the liquid. 'We'll see when the image comes fully online.'

The heat of the fire was intense. The muddy water cleared from the centre of the cauldron and an image of a large house appeared, grey rendered, gleaming white wooden sash windows, a large front porch supported by fish-out-of-water Corinthian columns with their tell-tale leafy patterns at the top. We set our viewpoint in its cluster of ornate chimney stacks to minimise the risk of anyone seeing the rippling in the air.

The image flickered as we panned around the site, sharpening when we stopped and focused. People strolled around the gardens next to the house, going in and out of the two outbuildings built close by, fleshing out the plans. Men to the left; women to the right, all dressed in overalls like some sort of uniform. Clean and simple.

The outbuildings had been turned into residential accommodation with a large hut in front of the two buildings kitted out as a communal eating area. Extensive shower and bathroom suites were nearby. Some residents were working on an allotment. Meyra nodded with wary approval. More comfortable and spacious than the Beachcomber.

There was another hut close by, square, massive with tinted windows, not on the plans. Based on the rest of this place, it was probably a spa.

A narrow, rough road led up to the front of the farmhouse, from the main gate according to the plans. A well-kept gravel track headed away from the house at right angles to the entrance road. Several small, squat four-wheeled vehicles were parked on a large patch of more gravel a short way away, a brief walk from the house.

They resolved into six-seater golf carts, ready to buzz to and from the main gate, and towards a low fence in the distance that looked like it was marking the boundary of the property; there were no buildings at the boundary. Beyond it were trees, lots of trees. The gravelled track was not marked on the plans.

All consistent enough with the plans and the usage of the property as a haven. All peaceful, ordered, no signs of duress, no signs of any residents wanting to be somewhere else. No sign of any problems at all.

The Haven was so squeaky clean that I had no doubt that even the rats at the property used strong mouthwash.

31

10:11 am
SAM

We recognised a number of people from
the files - the blue files - wandering around
in a seriously not sinister or alarming way.
Their body language was calm and relaxed,
as if they had recently finished having a
head massage.

Meyra and I needed a break, and we set
the Scrying on the equivalent of pause.

Ma gic is *hard* work. Its use requires
training, technique, experience and

concentration. And a readily available energy source. Especially the energy source.

The energy can come from pretty much anywhere – *Ma gic* isn't fussy: motion, sound, heat, all of them work. But most of all it really likes it to come from you. The personal touch. For a richer experience. You can re-direct energy from somewhere or something else, or - for dark *Ma gic* - from some*one* else. The plain fact is that it will always prefer to take it from you if you can't provide enough from elsewhere. You need to make sure not to give it too much from yourself.

When you have conjured it and moulded it and fed it, *Ma gic* is ready to be channelled and directed; controlled. Any carelessness or faltering when, say, you try to conjure a Lantern can result in a flurry of coloured ribbons popping out of your sleeve or a large smoking crater.

We returned to the Scrying and identified fifteen of the people in the blue files out of the hundred or so people staying at the site.

No non-blues though, just the vulnerable homeless ones.

The Haven had been described in the Council papers as making a *significant contribution* to cutting down homelessness in the area, and this Scrying could have been used for a publicity video for them. The Haven commune neatly stripped the farmhouse residents out of most categorisations of 'homeless', substantially improving the official figures.

People magically vanished from the books, no longer treated as victims in the system.

The residents had an ongoing roof over their heads, security and a degree of belonging, to allow them to re-focus and re-start their lives. It looked like a perfect arrangement. The organisers deserved a medal, right?

Here's the thing: the hidden files, the black files, my interaction with Derek. It all looked too good to be true.

Meyra pointed into the cauldron, 'What is going on?'

Three women emerged from the women's outbuilding, close together, two of them in red-and-white jackets, one with a desperate need to say no to more Botox, The other was dressed in creased blue overalls, with long, untidy auburn hair. I recognised her straightaway: Vanessa Green? Grant? Grant. From the files.

They looked like they were supporting her weight. Was she ill or high? They manoeuvred her down the steps and towards the golf carts. Botox was holding something near the small of Vanessa Grant's back.

The two women forced her to sit down hard on one of the golf cart seats and she flopped down, unresisting. I caught a glimpse of dull grey metal passing into Botox's pocket.

The other woman touched her right ear and her mouth moved. Some sort of communication device. Then she pressed a button and the cart accelerated towards the boundary fence carrying the three of them. It didn't stop at the medical centre, so something else was going on.

'Maybe they're late for a spa treatment,' I said.

Meyra ignored me, 'They were acting like enforcers with her.'

The golf cart reached the boundary fence and passed through a gap.and the scene reverted to serene and peaceful.

We broke off contact and I reached for my paracetemols and dry-swallowed two of them. Meyra took one. I *love* those headaches: too much *Ma gic* too quickly or for too long and they appear right on cue. Meyra rubbed her temples, 'It never gets easier, does it?'

'Never easier. More manageable, maybe,' I said, waiting for the painkillers to kick in. They were more of a precaution than anything, I told myself, but sustained *Ma gic* like that always came at a cost. A blasting headache's the easy bit.

'I think we may have just seen a glimpse of the dark side of Utopia.'

'You are most wise, Obi-Wan' said Meyra.

Suddenly there was a loud and piercing squeal from the cauldron.

'Your turn to make the tea, Padawan,' I said.

32

11:15 am
MEYRA

'Brighton seems to attract a steady supply of homeless people, people like Vanessa Grant, blown along with the wind. The Haven accommodates some of them,' I said. 'The newspapers leave them alone and the authorities manufacture medals in their name for their generous assistance.'

'But there's a missing piece: when they leave the Haven, where do they go?'

'No-one cares, Sam Franklin, It is deemed enough to remove them from the official statistics.' Pagoda insinuated herself between us, not wanting to be excluded.

'Thoughts on next steps?' said Sam Franklin.

'I shall become homeless,' I said. 'A target. I shall go underground.'

'Undercover. And are you sure about that? I've seen eight-foot fire elementals that look less like a target.'

'I shall take that as a compliment, Sam Franklin.' Grudgingly, I had to accept that he had a point. 'You do not think that I would be convincing as a vagrant?'

'Don't you have that five-bedroom apartment in Kensington?'

'It is not in Kensington Palace Gardens.'

'Life is so hard...You somehow live in a glade off Kensington Church Street, with two housekeepers. What can I say?'

'I shall adopt a pseudonym,' I said, changing the subject.

'That should do it.'

'I shall start at the train station and try to find a way in. If I fail, I shall attend the *Mirror of Galadriel*. They have not seen me yet.'

I was hopeful that, in a city like Brighton, there would be easy access to places like the Haven, places which were on the look-out for new blood, new opportunities to gather up vagrants who could be absorbed into the grey underbelly of the Haven. At home, travelling markets and bordellos served much the same function.

'Let's give it a try,' said Sam Franklin. 'I'll drop you and Pagoda outside the city near the main road in. Better if you thumb a lift. More natural. Make your way over to the station. See if there's a reception committee for people like you. Pagoda will come with you.' A venomous glare. From me and from the cat. 'While you do that, I'll take a closer look at the homeless crowd down here.

Shake the wasps' nest, see if there are any wasps.'

'You dress badly, how will I blend in with penniless vagrants?' I said, seeking some tips.

'I think we'll need to tone down your designer gear.'

'I shall make sure that my Nikes are properly scuffed.'

As a precaution, I handed Sam Franklin my mobile telephone. He put it with the thug's telephone and his own, 'This looks like a Hong Kong taxi driver's phone collection.' I did not understand; I do not approve of public transport.

He saw my confusion, pointed at the three phones, 'Broker, mistress, wife - in that order. Remember, this is just fact-finding, not the Normandy landings. No need for stupid risks.'

'I shall leave those to you, Sam Franklin.'

We drove in silence until we reached a quiet lay-by just outside the city and I retrieved my small bag from the back of Sam Franklin's vehicle. I opened the passenger door and stepped down onto the tarmac. He nodded to me, I suppose in encouragement, as Pagoda sprang down from the van and made herself scarce but close enough.

Sam Franklin leaned over and shut the door, no further words were necessary. He indicated and started to drive away. I watched him leave, confident that I would be able to unlock the Haven.

In my peripheral vision, I saw that Pagoda had merged into an accommodating shadow nearby so that only her green eyes with arrow-slit pupils were visible. She was hungry or sleepy. Potentially both. Nothing about her brought the word *useful* into my mind.

I needed to perform a conjuring trick: find a way into the homeless scene in Brighton and determine whether the Haven was indeed the opposite of charitable. But unobtrusively. And with that cat.

33

12:01 pm
SAM

I found a table in the hotel restaurant for a quick sandwich and some strong coffee. It would have felt wrong to have a roast and two veg given where I was off to next.

I was going to find Beattie.

My research at the *Star* had highlighted Beattie as one of the well-loved prongs of the local community's assault on the homelessness problem. I was struck by the

energy and resourcefulness on show. It was
time to investigate first-hand.

Beattie's current site was the Saint
Matthews car park. There may have been
space for twenty cars. but it was empty when
I arrived except for a large and battered
white van with a side door that opened
upwards, propped open to act as a canopy
for shade. Dozens of people of all shapes,
sizes, nationalities and clothing were either
queuing at the small counter or milling
around with sandwiches and polystyrene
cups of soup and coffee even on such a
warm day, some stood alone lost in their
thoughts, some in small groups quietly
chatting.

I sought out one of the volunteers who
seemed to be on a break, a plump middle-
aged lady with kind but watchful eyes, with
a plastic badge on which her name had been
printed: Sarah Grantham. 'I can see you're
not here for a cuppa-soup. You're not press
or cops, right?' she said quickly, with an
edge to her voice. 'Here is a correct answer
to that question.' The kind eyes evidently
only went so far.

'No, I'm not, my name's Sam Franklin and I'm looking for a friend and his daughter who've gone missing. They disappeared. I think they came down here.'

She looked at me for thirty seconds, top to bottom and back, without hesitation or embarrassment. I felt like I had just been given an MRI. 'OK, I believe you,' she said, finally, 'we have to start somewhere each day with trusting others, don't you think? You're today's choice. I can't be too careful with those press vultures, always looking for a sex angle or a double-suicide to spice up their rags.' Those kind, watchful eyes were showing a lot of strain at the edges.

Neither of my pictures of Olivia and Endymion Walker seemed to jog Sarah's memory. She shook her head and said ruefully, 'Around 100 people a day come here, some we see again some just come for food and a hot drink and move on. I can't remember either of these people, I'm sorry, but I know someone who might.' Her eyes darted across the car park and fastened on a group of three men in the corner.

I followed her eyes and saw a man in his fifties with a stooped posture and greasy, greying hair, wearing a battered trench coat. His lined face was so lived in that it could work as a block of flats. He was talking to a man dressed in torn cut-off jeans and a dirty sweatshirt, sporting a flattened nose broken several times in previous battles; the other man was listening intently, winding his threadbare football scarf around busy fingers. Sarah took me by the arm and led me over to the group. They all tensed when they saw me coming towards them.

'It's OK boys, sorry to interrupt,' she said to them, 'I *think* we can trust this one I'd like you to meet Sam Franklin. He's lost some people down here and is asking for some help to find them.' Even then two out of the three mumbled half-hearted apologies and left, leaving the man in the trench coat behind with us.

'Mr Franklin, this is 'Casablanca' Brown, he's one of our best customers,' she said with a warm smile at him. 'The waiting list hasn't worked out for him yet, but we're still trying as hard as we can.'

'Just call me Sam, Mr Brown,' I said reaching out to shake his hand. He drew back and then he caught Sarah's eye and relaxed a little. He still didn't shake my hand. 'I'm sorry to hear that things haven't worked out for you yet. I hope it gets better. I'd appreciate it if you'd look at these and see if you recognise them, they're lost on the streets.' I showed him the pictures of the two Walkers and DS Hastings.

He didn't recognise Endymion Walker or Hastings but, when he saw Olivia's face, he overcame his reticence and urgently grabbed my phone from me pulling it closer to his face. I noticed that up close he was a lot younger than I had first thought; that was the heavy wear and tear on people from this type of life, the face of someone with experience way beyond their years.

'Yes, yes. Sure. I seen her,' he said, excitedly in a cracked voice. 'A few weeks ago. She was only here once, but she's difficult to forget, isn't she?' He took a nip from a scratched and battered hip flask under his too-big trench coat, and Sarah held her gaze on his face, trying to ignore the flask.

Casablanca carried on talking, fuelled by nerves and another swig from the flask which made him wince. 'I could tell that girl was out of her depth down here. She sounded to me too posh to be homeless – it was obvious she was new, and I didn't know what to say to her, but I knew Fezzer would. I told her he'd be able to help,' he said, smiling with the satisfaction, all too briefly felt in his present circumstances, of having been helpful and suddenly relevant in a world that had left him behind.

'Fezzer?'

'That's right, his name's Fezzer.'

'Is that his first or last name?'

'Yes,' said Sarah.

'He's a legend,' said Casablanca, holding out his arms to encompass the crowd.

227

'Everyone loves him. Mad as a hatter but knows everything there is to know about surviving on the streets.'

'He's never here,' said Sarah. 'You'll normally find him on the beach. The new ones tend to go to him for advice. I tried to recruit him once, but he wasn't interested.'

'He lives in his Bird Cage,' Casablanca chipped in, his eyes slightly glassy after another sip of whatever the heinous brew was from his stash.

I took a punt, 'The Bandstand?' He nodded. The intricate one on the main beach.

He offered Sarah and me a drink from his flask, and Sarah firmly and politely gestured *thanks, but no, I'm on duty and need to be all of next week* and gave me a pitying look. I took a cautious sip anyway and my head nearly sheared off. Whoa. That didn't so much hit the spot as batter it into the ground with a sledgehammer and then stomp it with steel toe-caps.

'Thanks for your help, Casablanca Brown,' I choked with feeling, handing the flask back to him. Quite a bit quicker than when I took it. Sarah smiled at him with genuine affection and came with me. Her face reverted to impassive apart from some crinkling at the corners of her eyes.

'Guaranteed no more than 60% ethanol,' she said with a laugh when we were out of his ear-shot. 'Your sight should return in a few weeks.'

I allowed myself the luxury of another choking cough, 'It's OK, I can see both of you clearly, Sarah *and* Sarah, so no worries.'

'I did try to warn you. He'll get through a few of those by tea-time.'

'Respect. Now, before I leave you alone, I must know: why is he called 'Casablanca'?'

'Because everyone who knows him says he's been in all the bars, in all the towns in all the world', she replied with a chuckle. She nodded to me and turned away, 'I hope you find what you're looking for'. She was already moving on to her next challenge.

One last look around here as I left. I took in the relaxed, peaceful scene as Sarah walked back to re-join the good fight. She brought an astonishing feeling of calm, energy and love to Beattie and her 'customers', and I saw that all of them reciprocated it. The atmosphere around the van gave some respite, however brief, from the troubles of the day. Now *that's* magic, conjuring up hope where otherwise there could be none. One step at a time.

Here's looking at you kid.

34

3:30 pm
SAM

Not much point looking up Fezzer online, that would just bring up a bunch of Tommy Cooper videos. Better to beard him in his lair.

I headed past the entrance to the Pier and dropped down to the meandering bricked path beside the beach. Nothing more from Meyra yet. There was a large merry-go-round playing enthusiastic oompah music and a couple of fairground stalls. I resisted the temptations of a quick game of Hook the

Duck, and wandered onto the beach proper, making a satisfying crunching beat as I strode over the densely packed pebbles.

I skirted families and couples lounging in deck chairs, looking pink and British regardless of where they were from, eating their fish and chips and drinking fizzy pop and beer, for the moment finding it enough simply to be sitting communing with the ocean as the world went by.

The sea and the sky danced on the horizon, impossible to tell apart, the view broken only by the brooding, spidery remains of the burnt-out West Pier, soaking up sparkles from the water with grim determination. Once the pride of British piers, its lustre had faded until it was shut down in the 1970s. Abandoned for decades, flames eventually devoured it, leaving only the skeletal cast iron supports holding on in the sea and piercing the paved walkway on the beach, sad and glowering memorials to a lost world.

The Artists' Quarter with its upmarket knick-knack shops and photography

232

galleries built into the sea wall were scant
compensation. I walked past the towering
'Needle', watching for a short time the
serene rise of its circular glass and metal
observation pod towards the panoramic
summit. A nearby Punch and Judy show
weaved its timeless nasty spell on a crowd of
small children, lured away from their
electronics for a short while by the slapstick -
and disturbing-when-you-think-through-it -
violence. I hoped the missing policeman had
fared better than his diminutive wooden
counterpart.

On the Bandstand deck, a brass band was
desecrating 'We will rock you', the sound
washed over the small crowd in the café
below perched on loudly striped deckchairs
on the beach; they lounged around, drinking
in sun, tea for most and beer for some, all
basking in the mid-afternoon sunshine
enjoying the music.

The Bird Cage had been re-constructed
and re-plumed several years ago back to its
former pomp. Its imperious Victorian beauty
stood proud next to the beach, harking back
to the days of Empire, the roof coated in

burnished copper like the Beachcomber's cauldron, glowing in the afternoon sun. Ironwork arches and balustrades meshed around its deck. I was hunting a particular bird in this pretty cage, taking shelter for the night when the parties, bands and weddings had packed up and gone home.

Polite applause greeted the end of the song and a leisurely packing up process began among the watchers, then an exodus. It was time for them to fret about souvenirs and an evening meal. I could see that the café was closing, and the tables were starting to empty: day's end, running into evening's end - and then night's beginning. The atmosphere had tangibly changed from baked jollity squeezing the maximum joy out of the sunshine and beach and music, to a more forlorn feel. The sun's rays shone through the latticed ironwork of the Bird Cage, adding a sense of fragmented melancholy to the scene. I carried on watching.

A bulky figure with a square head was loitering in the sharply defined shadows, biding its time, calm and unhurried, in contrast to the last, bustling concert-goers. The Bandstand had emptied, silence fell, the figure moved. It set off for the lower part of the Bandstand at a steady pace, still in the shadows, unhurried, seeming to become more solid as it grew into the vacated space, no longer invisible to anyone passing, reclaiming its domain.

The figure struggled over the short white iron fence marking the outside area of the Bandstand and began to work its way round, avoiding the small tables left out overnight, ready to claim a time-share of space until the morning. It was far removed from the light-heartedness of the earlier scene: a shift change. Two different worlds in one place neither with any tangible connection to the other.

The figure headed for the steps built into the sea wall. It climbed to the start of the ornate bridge leading to the top deck of the Bird Cage. I watched as it crossed, pausing halfway to check that the coast was clear. When it reached the top deck, it started to uncoil. I saw the figure shedding layers of thick skin in the lengthening shadows.

I headed for the steps. If it wasn't Fezzer, then someone who might know where he was. Best to be cautious either way. I ventured onto the bridge. It creaked underfoot as I slowly made my way across. No rash moves. No point spooking the figure, which was hunched over an opened out sleeping bag that it had been carrying on its back, the source of its sloughed 'skin'. The figure was unpacking some items that I couldn't see.

As I got closer, there was a fizz, and I stopped in my tracks. Hello.

The unmistakable tang of *Ma gic.*

A Ward. A crude pentagram blocking the way in. Crude but effective. A barrier between the figure and me. I readied a Shield of my own.

The figure unwound itself from the ground and peered out of the opening to where I was standing. It appeared in the failing light, ringed by a halo of late sun, hard to make out until it came closer.

A large man, very large, hungry blue eyes, hair that stuck out at ninety degrees from his head as if frozen in a gale. His square head resolved into a crimson fez, with a gold tassel over a wide forehead, and fleshy jowls; his nose had been broken a number of times. Black, studded leather jacket and a jaunty cravat, like he was about to go punting with Mad Max.

I stood my ground.

He looked me over warily, 'Unless you have nowhere to go, please leave. This is my place,' his voice low and even.

'I'm not trying to steal your place,' I said. 'In many ways, I do have nowhere else to go. I'm looking for Fezzer and I'm guessing that's you.'

'Brilliant,' he replied, his eyes flicking upwards and back to me, openly hostile.

'I'm not police or anything.' I said, 'I just want to talk. Sarah Grantham from the van said you might be able to help me.'

'Who are you? What do you want? It's been a long day.' Weary, slightly less belligerent at the mention of her name.

'Can I come through? Your Ward's making me itch.'

Those hungry eyes lit up. Hunger, but also more suspicion. Quickly, 'What do you mean, Ward?'

'A standard pentagram Ward, a protection Hex effective to seal off an area like this. Create a barrier. Very handy if you're worried about unwanted visitors.'

'Like you?' He paused. 'Night-time is when they come.'

'Sorry?'

'The demons, they come at night, I have seen them. No-one believes me about it, they all say I am mad. There, now you probably think so, too? Don't worry, like you, the street people still come to me for help, when there's no-one else to turn to.' He shifted his bulk and stared into my eyes; I stared back, unflinching. 'There's usually no-one else.'

'I *do* believe you, I'm hunting a demon, it killed one of my colleagues. It might have harmed more people: my colleague's daughter, and a policeman, maybe many more. I understand you keep an eye on people around here, the ones who can't look after themselves? They are like that, missing and in danger. Right now.'

'There are so many missing people,' he said. 'It's easy to lose track.'

'With these two, I've hit a dead end. Not sure what I'm dealing with, but it all seems to revolve around the Haven. I need your help.'

His mouth tightened when I mentioned the Haven, 'I'll see. Do you have pictures of them?'

As I reached into my jacket for my phone, he started to talk, looking as if he were, if only a little, dislodging some of that heavy burden that I'd seen, 'The Haven is not the answer. Most of the people who come to Brighton with no home and no hope aren't addicts or wastrels or drifters.' His tone was clear and measured, shot through with sadness. 'Most of them have been driven from their home by illness or abuse or some other terrible thing in their lives. Not some sort of gap year whim like many in the press make out. I know this because I have met hundreds of people on the streets who have real problems, real worries. I have made it my business to try to help as many as I can. But I need to be careful where I try to help; people aren't always what they seem.' He looked at me significantly. 'I hope that does not include you.'

There was no sign of a madman in those words, putting to one side his mains-voltage hair and funny hat. Here was simply a man who, for whatever reason, had found his path and was determined to stick to it. He didn't seem shackled by his appearance or his lot – he could be a philanthropic millionaire for all I knew. I could only judge him by his words and what I had heard earlier; I couldn't help thinking that he reminded me of Sarah from the mobile kitchen. Well, Sarah on a nightmare hair day. Two people doing their bit in different ways aiming for the same thing, along different paths.

'I'm running out of time before the police tear this area apart.' That got his attention. 'I can head them off with your help.'

I saw him calculating, figuring out the downsides of helping me. My knowing Sarah evidently counted for something. And recognising the Ward. And potential action from the police. He made his decision, 'I'm going to take a chance. I trust my instincts, I have to here, and I hope I won't regret it.'

35

4:15 pm
SAM

Fezzer gestured and let me through the
Ward. Nothing else could come through
without his permission as long as it wasn't
damaged; I trod carefully. The top deck of
the Bird Cage didn't look like either a venue
for bands and parties or a place to try to fend
off the eventual chill of the evening. Nor the
Ma gic-protected fortress of a local savant.
Just an observation post out to sea.

However, I *was* temporarily on his patch
and here on sufferance. I checked his aura:
troubled but sharp, some rudimentary

Knack, a man carrying a large piece of the burdens of the world on his shoulders. But keeping going where no help had been forthcoming from anywhere or anyone official, where people needed real world answers not platitudes. I made a mental note that River Smith might be good for some more down-to-earth help and behind-the-scenes support for his efforts, if he passed muster. And if I propositioned her nicely.

The Haven was everywhere in my thoughts, left alone by the authorities because they made homeless people fade from the official statistics like an accountant's sleight of hand. Gratitude and official approval was probably better protection than *Ma gic* could ever be.

Fezzer looked at me with narrow, tired eyes.

I hadn't marked him down as a practitioner, but someone had taught him how to set up a protective Ward.

'Do you practise?' I said.

'This is the only thing I can do,' he confessed. He told me that he'd learned it a few years ago from a Traveller further along the coast. 'I find it a comfort to be able to create a castle for myself, even with no roof.'

He gave me a hesitant smile, 'You know about this sort of thing, then?' he said, waving airily at the Ward. It looked like it might be something of a relief to him to speak to someone about it and not be immediately ridiculed or dismissed as a lunatic. I kept it short, deciding to take him part of the way into my confidence, to repay his trust in me by opening the barrier for me.

'Yes, I do practise,' I said, 'some of it's mumbo-jumbo, but some of it's the real thing.'

He seemed to sense from my words and voice that I was talking down what I could do; I could see that he was filled with the urge to flood me with questions. I needed to cut through all that, find out what he knew. 'I know you won't want anything in return for helping, but if you're interested, I'll come back here after all this is over and show you

some Hexes. I think they might help you
with your work here,' I said. 'Think of it as a
gesture of thanks.'

He wanted to bite my hand off at the
shoulder to take me up on my offer,
desperate to learn.

'Watch, I promise this won't hurt.' I
created a soft Lantern on the back of his
hand to illuminate the area around the
Ward. His eyes opened wide and he stepped
back, afraid of being burned. 'It's OK, it's a
Hex, like a lamp, no heat. It won't harm you.
Now *I'm* taking a chance on *you*.'

He passed his other hand through the
Lantern, thrilled by the theatre, impressed by
the power. I pressed my advantage. I
showed him the photos of Endymion
Walker, Olivia Walker and the missing
policeman.

After a moment of intense concentration,
he passed the phone back to me.

'I don't know the last one,' he said, 'but,
yes, I have come across the other two.'

Progress, a first concrete trace of Endymion Walker, dead or alive, outside the hotel since he'd been in Brighton. 'I came across the girl - Olivia Walker - a few weeks ago. Pretty and sharp. People at the mobile kitchen had sent her to me for advice. She was at a loss, no idea what to do next. She had been given everything on a plate by her father all through her life since her mother had died. It had damaged her, rotted away her drive, taken away her self-belief. She said she'd achieved nothing, that she was now worthless. She wanted to try to find her way down here.' He looked at me ruefully. 'I talked to her for several hours. At the beginning, I thought she was just another rich kid with a chip on her shoulder and bogus 'issues'. But that wasn't fair, this was deep psychological stuff.'

'Did she say what she was going to do?'

'She said the people at Beattie had suggested meeting me, and she'd tried one of the shops in North Laine. Do you know them? She was doing her homework. She spent a long time with them, talking; I've never trusted them, they seem like they've hitched a lift on a large bandwagon. She asked me about their pet project.'

'The Haven?' He nodded, a scowl coming over his face.

'The Haven.'

'Have you been there?'

'It's set up like a commune. Everyone's expected - required - to work together, to 'collaborate'; everyone can then have what they need as long as they toe the line with the work and the community. It's a brilliant system if you can hack it, backs to the land and all that. But it doesn't work for me. All a bit too Big Brother. I thought about it but I didn't like the rules. It wouldn't have suited me. I like my freedom and the Haven doesn't tolerate that sort of thing'.

He fiddled with one of the studs on his jacket. I gave him some space.

'I told the girl about the place, what I understood were the rules of its game. I tried to give her a fair picture. She was drawn to it as if a commune might be what she was looking for: a new family, maybe. A fresh start.' He stopped and looked at me searchingly, guilty. Had he led her into harm's way? 'Maybe it did work for her. She left here wanting to at least give it a try. I told her she's welcome to come back and talk more whenever she wanted; I haven't seen her since.'

'You said you'd seen her father too? When he came looking for her?' I asked, leaning forward.

'Yes. He'd done the rounds of some bars and shops. He went into *Mirror of Galadriel.* He was desperate, he knew she was in the area, but he couldn't figure out where. A needle in a haystack. I heard he was asking around and I got a message to him, met him at the Pier. I told him I'd seen his daughter and where I thought she'd gone: he was mad as hell that she'd wanted to dump her 'perfect' life for 'a bunch of hippies'. It got out of hand when I pointed out that she'd needed her life to change. He stormed off, yelling and swearing.' He took a moment to compose himself, remembering the angry scenes by the main amusement arcade, the shouting competing with the jingle and chatter of fruit machines and the thumping music.

'I hope he managed to make peace with her when he caught up.' He paused, looking sad and thoughtful at the same time. 'But I can't see it would have ended well – he was too steamed up. I'm not sure she would have welcomed the interference from him and he wasn't in the mood to listen to me. It was going to be a showdown.'

All paths led to the Haven again.

If he'd followed her there, when he got close he could have homed in on her with a Bloodtracker. That's not as gory as it sounds: Bloodtrackers allow practitioners to find close family members. A useful practical trick for people at the fringes of society branded as dangerous warlocks and witches, pursued with burning torches. 'Saving' the accused was often not enough, there was plenty of room on the fires or in the well. A clean sweep of family members was often rounded up and their souls 'rescued' in the same way. *Witch-finding: a game for all the family.* Knowing the location of your kith and kin would have been a high priority, an evolutionary driver for wizards.

An awkward, possibly explosive, reunion at the Haven with Olivia may have resulted in Endymion Walker's death. Preying on my mind was the question of Endymion Walker's blue, horned attacker. When Walker had arrived at the Haven hunting for Olivia, a blue, horned demon seemed to have been part of his reception committee. Had she actively brought about his death? Been part of the wider plan?

It was time to catch up with Meyra. Go deeper.

36

4:15 pm
VANESSA GRANT

Vanessa Grant's exposure to rendition was
a rendition of *Frozen* medleys, not being
roughed up with a cloth bag over her head.

Earlier in the day she had hitched a lift
very early to Rottingdean then walked the
rest of the way to the Haven. She hadn't
known what she was going to do when she
got there. She was relying on her ready smile
and a talent for improv.

She hadn't expected to be grabbed from
behind when she had been shown into a

white-panelled office for her details to be taken.

She had tried to scream but she had been jabbed in the stomach, all the wind knocked out of her, her nose and mouth covered by a rag with something sweet-smelling that made her feel relaxed.

Really relaxed, baby.

A voice said, 'We can't keep her here, too much traffic, too risky. We need to get her down to the hut, find out if anyone sent her.'

Someone else had said, 'Come along, my lovely, let's go for a little walk.'

She had been dragged out of the office, dragged and pushed and dragged more for a short distance then bundled into a small, uncomfortable seat. What pretty trees.

She slumped onto the seat of a little buggy thing, it was soooo comfortable, time to sleep.

She didn't know how many other people were traveling in the cart, nor where they were going, nothing really. Her seat was too comfortable to move, but she needed to find Becky. Were these nice people taking her to her naughty sister?

Something hard and metallic was jammed into her side. The force of it jarred her out of her cosy reverie. Trees and more trees filled her vision, the sturdy farmhouse receding.

She had huddled in the seat, trying to focus and was then roughly removed from her seat and pulled to her feet, her head a little clearer. She saw that she was being taken to a windowless hulk of a building. A door opened in front of her and hands hustled her through it, no idea where she was.

A voice muttered *nosy bitch*. A reply, *find out what we need to know, then get her over to the crypt for processing like her mate.* Crypt? Sounded like a nickname for a bad place. Mate? Were they talking about Becky? Then another door and an uncomfortable seat on which she was firmly planted and secured with cable ties.

She had been left in semi-darkness until now, alone, it seemed like forever.

A voice from behind her, 'Time for answers, Ms Grant, or whatever your name is. Who sent you? Why are you looking for Becky Carpemter? As a friendly warning, don't waste my time.' An excruciatingly bright light was shone into her face.

When would this end?

37

6:00 pm
MEYRA

Among the travellers at a train station, I perceive that not everyone is there to travel. It can be a place of possibilities and potential, a place to meet like-minded people, a place to find salvation in difficult times. A place to hunt.

I had spotted Peter immediately, marked him as a hunter: he was handsome with quick eyes, a ready smile, light blonde hair, and what appeared to be a shopping list of people.

If I looked in other places around here, the bus station, the main roads, I would find other Peters, all with the same eyes. He prowled the station, homed in on his prey, a quiet word, some sympathy where needed, some encouragement where necessary, painting a picture of hope with blinding colours.

One man in a grey beanie carrying just a satchel, a woman with a long pony tail. Two party girls, one with vivid green hair. Not homeless? Lost enough.

He approached each person with different body language and the same unmissable message: *I have what you need, whatever that may be.* He handed the man and woman blue pamphlets; he took the party girls out of the station and the three of them disappeared into the crowd before he returned and had a last look around for prospects.

That was when I hunted *him.*

I came out of the shadows, blending in with everyone else in the station on a late Saturday afternoon, helpless and fumbling, with no idea where to go, looking around in confusion that I was desperately trying not to display to the world. I had clearly just arrived at the station on foot, trying to work out my next move down in Brighton, a little, lost teenager, another victim for Peter in a long line of victims.

He noticed me and accidentally bumped into me with all the usual apologies and embarrassed hesitation that such an accident warranted, found out my plight: walking out on my family determined to make my way in the world by myself and now having to do that. Finding it easier said than done.

I Nudged him to pursue me as someone for him to help, but he was already there.

I hinted at not just help, but the best help. Nudge is only able to go so far. He had a script – an agenda- and he was programmed to keep to it with minor variations. I was a challenge to his box-ticking, but I helped him to work his way through.

A few kind words from him, an unspoken promise of safety, and fun, behind his twinkling eyes, and I found myself following him trustingly to a large black SUV that was parked close to the station. The person he had been meeting had according to him not shown up, but all was well. He regarded it as a happy accident, otherwise he would never have met me. Where we were going, I would have the time of my life.

Who is taken in by such nonsense?

I played along, sat in the front passenger seat next to him. We chatted, him mostly, his important work in the financial industry, about his flat, how lucky he felt to have met me.

More nonsense. Whenever he tried to probe more deeply into the details of my life, I Nudged him away, leaving him slightly puzzled but complacently not suspicious.

Just as I wanted him. Poor little boy.

Brighton swept by. I began to look out for the Haven farmhouse, we were heading in that direction. Why was he taking me there? I was not homeless, I had dropped enough hints about disillusionment rather than desperation, yet we carried on into the Downs.

Still no farmhouse. Maybe I had been wrong.

Peter smoothly guided the car through tall automated metal gates that led onto a well-maintained tarmacked road and a large, dark grey squared off car park.

'Here we are,' he said. We pulled to a stop on the hard standing next to another big black SUV and a long silken saloon car, also black: a Jaguar. Daddy has the more expensive model. Three golf carts were parked in a row on the other side of the car park. Would one take me to the farmhouse? That would be surprising: the farmhouse – and its residents - did not have the correct profiles. This was different.

The other roadways were gravelled, one continuing straight into the trees, one veering at a right angle to the right, one to the left, both eventually lost in the trees, a cross shape with the car park at the centre.

We had seen none of this in the earlier Scrying, it revealed a different part of the Haven grounds. Different but connected.

I opened the heavy door of the SUV and got out, shutting it with a solid thunk. I felt a surge of joy as I surveyed the large expanse of grass and woodland around us. I liked that very much after the dirty and claustrophobic concrete of Brighton.

Peter took my expression as one of excitement for what might be in store. 'Let's take one of these,' he said, striding over to a golf cart and switching it on, its engine generating a low hum. I followed him and sat down.

'What is this place?' I asked, injecting what I thought would be an appropriate hint of nervousness.

'Don't worry, in thirty seconds it will blow your mind. Everything that we talked about.'

I said nothing, held lightly onto the front bar of the cart as it skimmed along the gravel track.

Cutting through my confusion, the answer to where the golf carts went when they left the car park suddenly came directly into view. Not the farmhouse. Something else. Something quire different.

The trees fell away to reveal another building. A High Baroque mansion, stuccoed and sweeping, hidden behind the screen of trees, gleaming whitely.

The plans of the grounds had shown nothing beyond the farmhouse and its outbuildings. The trees and the dip of the hillside had obscured it from our view during our our Scrying. There were balconies and columns and grandeur. The overall effect was of a royal retreat nestling in the hills, far away from the concerns of mundane life, as far as it was possible to imagine from the troubles of the homeless population of Brighton.

Sweeping stone steps led upward to the mansion, past cascading crystal water pools that glistened with frolicking dolphins and cherubs. On the ceiling of the porch was a fresco made up of a central silver circle surrounded by a circle of eight silver stick figures and four pale pink circles, spaced out in a regular pattern. As I approached, I saw that in the silver circle was a word in dark red: *Ma gic.*

A man with blond spiky hair dressed in a smart red-and-white striped jacket with a luxurious velvet waistcoat came towards us. Did he have a lace collar an cuffs? Was that a cape of crimson velvet? How charming. A hint of a bow:

'I'm Emile, your Ladyship. Welcome to Nirvana.'

38

8:00 pm
MEYRA

I had assumed my destination would be the Haven farmhouse, but I arrived at the palace next door.

An imposing party venue frequented - according to Emile after a judicious Nudge - by the very *best* people, high rollers who knew how to feed their appetites through the Dark Web at Haven at string-of-numbers/symbols/letters.hedonist. People with endless money and endless curiosity. We mixed here with people like the party girls whose paths conveniently crossed with what he rather chillingly described as "content" for the show.

My boundless curiosity charmed him. All of us were consumers in our own ways, side by side. According to each of Emile and Peter, woven into my little web, the connection with the Haven was *above their pay grade.* I was enchanted by the palace, ready to ignore its impossible economics - how it seemed to be there to support a homeless charity. I simply felt compelled to dance.

I forced myself to concentrate, tore myself away from the sound of music from the grand ballroom mere steps away.

In the car - carriage? - Peter had been confused as to how I fitted into his world. He knew where he was with the man in the grey beanie and the woman with the long ponytail at Brighton Station, even the two party girls. What was my story? Silly boy.

Emile suffered the same problems with me. I Nudged him to treat me as one of their

higher end prospects, introduced by one of
the seedier curators of the Dark Web via the
usual conduit. It was obvious of course that
this was the right thing for him to do for
someone like me, now that he had seen me
in the correct light. He obliged with alacrity,
giving me freedom to see how these places
were woven together; I trusted not into a
noose. Before I was allowed to dance - why
the delay - we repaired to a luxurious
lounge. Apparently some petty details were
needed from me.

There were impossibly colourful tropical
plants. My nose wrinkled with distaste. The
acrid smell of *Ma gic* corrupted the beauty of
the flowers, bringing me out of a reverie
filled with Bach and Handel. The *Ma gic*
warped the natural order so much that I was
surprised the woodland trees did not rise up
in rebellion. I kept my features composed
and did not protest, but each orchid's scent
felt like a blow to the chest for me. At home,
the gardener would have been fed to the
hounds. My discomfort was obvious to
Emile, he took it as my disapproval of the
delay. Emile hurried to explain that his tasks
would helpfully include guiding me through

the place and answering any questions that I had, such as *Where is the gym? What number is Room Service?* I suspected not, *What clandestine criminal conspiracy are you masterminding from here today?*

Emile sped through the paperwork with me, which naturally I lied and dissembled upon with gusto. The upfront charges were smoothly processed, expensive enough for even me to feel that I had been mugged by someone wearing sable gloves.

I have stayed in caravan trains of Bedouins, and in a Perspex tent under the Northern Lights, but they were commonplace in comparison to the final part of my check-in. I was asked to walk through what I was told was a full-length body scanner, *purely routine; to ensure my health for the time that I spent in Nirvana, and for the protection of other guests.* I had no wish for them to discern the anomalies - from their perspective - of my physical form, which would have made their analysis seem impossible, and my subsequent conversations with them overly awkward for me.

Before submitting to the scan, I took
advantage of the lavish bathroom facilities to
sink into the shadows and create a simple
Illusion of me returning and passing through
the scanner. It was what they were expecting
to see and as a result it is what they saw.
That done, I was taken to one of the
penthouse suites, better than five-star
quality; I have always been happy to settle
for the best. The quality of the room would
mean that during my future stays in Raffles
in Singapore I would find myself
questioning its champagne selection. There
was a tug at the edges of my consciousness, I
warned myself to remain alert.

The room was fitted with wall-sized one-
way picture windows of the surrounding
forest, best viewed from the super-kingsize
bed listening to music from the voice-
controlled Sonos playing elegant choral
music. There were two outbuildings, one
directly below the penthouse, the same
shape as the ones at the farmhouse but with
a larger footprint, tucked into the trees.
Maybe more living quarters. It had an odd

grille around the top, similar to ventilation stacks for buildings with heavy-duty air-conditioning systems, different from those at the farmhouse. The other was a windowless box, an absence of form and colour among the trees, a black square, mirroring its twin at the farmhouse. I wondered if Sam Franklin had been able to uncover the farmhouse secrets, and indeed where he was while I infiltrated this insane place.

There was no time for speculation.

It was important to feel the luxury. My attention wandered to the menu for eight different types of pillow to suit my every need; I refused the 24-hour male model butler as too distracting. A temperature-moderated cabinet dispensed brandy and cigars of the highest rank, and a range of other products helpfully marked with their strength and with the equivalent of tasting notes, such as *Notes of disorientation with a hint of paranoia.* The in-room amenities included a range of services from simple massage to *Mother would absolutely, unquestionably not approve.* I would not even begin to describe to her menu item B020

from Room Service, other than as highly
challenging and quite possibly life-
threatening; chain hotels until that moment
had meant something quite different to me.

Emile's voice was like honey flowing into
my thoughts, 'You are of course welcome to
participate in the festivities at any time, Lady
Kilbirnie ' – my preferred improvised false
name: it avoids complications and for these
purposes I never keep the same address;
Sam Franklin once said that in conversation I
speak like a Baroness. He hummed when he
said it and I never discerned why.

I framed my face as interestedly enigmatic
and explained that I would partake later in
the evening since I had things to do. He
bowed gracefully, artfully displaying rouged
cheeks and fluttered his gold filigree
handkerchief at me. When I looked at him
again, the handkerchief was no longer in his
hand, it had flickered and gone.

I reflected that it was espionage that
would be my first dance this evening, rather
than a minuet or a sarabande.

39

10:00pm
HATTIE PRYOR

Sergeant Hattie Pryor's sharp features softened as she thought about her coming summer holidays with Dave and the kids. She looked over at PC Hayden Chan. His back was to her. He was elbow-deep in the middle of the tall metal filing cabinet in the custody block.

He was cataloguing and storing physical evidence obtained from the back of the van that they had seized holding the three handcuffed muppets next door. He had a PDA to help on which he'd recorded a lot already.

'You'll be there 'til next Sunday,' she said, spinning and flipping a pencil through her fingers, idly looking down, conscious that it was nearly time for her to go home, just under another hour. What a *great* weekend it had been, work all day yesterday and work all day today. At least she had tomorrow off. Their family holiday was so close, she could almost touch it, almost taste the Aperols.

'Just got through processing the thumbscrews. Lovely people,' he said.

Hattie shuddered, 'I wish I hadn't said anything.' Not much of that sort of thing came across her desk. She tried to concentrate on her work.

She had no thought of an earthquake coming through the wall in Brighton's modern glass and steel main police station, into the basement Custody Block. But come through it did.

Bangs of Hattie's hair flopped over her face as she lay in an awkward position on the floor next to her upturned chair, her broken leg crushed under the heavy desk, the rest of her at an odd angle. Choking white dust swirled around the large office, the ceiling lights flickered in the clouds then

rallied. She did not know how she had
arrived in that position, but gravity does not
attend stakeholder courses on decision-
making, it simply does what it does.

She needed to pull herself together now,
get out from under the desk, get up on the
concertinaed floor, get over to help Hayden
Chan. Concertinaed? The floor was several
feet thick.

The state of the flooring was irrelevant for
the moment: she was unable to move. She
suppressed a squeal of pain when she tried,
and tried again. She coughed, a racking bark
of pain and frustration, and then slumped at
the shock of what was happening around
her.

At her level, through her shattered -
supposedly shatterproof - glass desk, aside
from the white clouds the only colour that
she could see was a stream of dark red. It
trickled from beneath the filing cabinet
which had been toppled onto Hayden Chan
with murderous ease by the force of the
explosion.

The CCTV had been taken out by
whatever it was. And no-one would believe
her about *any* of this. Even less when she

reported on whatever was beginning to emerge out of the clouds in front of her. A tall figure in a floor length silver robe, hood up. Hattie could not say which gender. It avoided stepping on Chan's outstretched hand and glided across the floor towards her.

Who the hell was this? She was terrified, the shattered and dust-filled room suddenly felt cold, like a mortuary in a blizzard.

Not an earthquake, then? A bomb? Charges fitted to the wall? But there had been no bang. There was no time for that now as the figure came closer, wearing a silver full length robe and deep hood, allowing it to blend eerily with the slowly settling dust.

A flash of memory came as Hattie recalled among her shredding thoughts their holiday in Tuscany, her broken ankle from those bloody tower steps, her trip in an ambulance to the local hospital, fainting with pain. She had woken up surrounded by men in black, rough cloth robes held around the waist by a cord, all of them peering at her wearing kindly, sombre expressions. She had thought that had been it; that those were her last moments on Earth. That incident at San

Gimignano's monastic hospital had merely been a foretaste of this moment.

An alarm was bleating, it may have been sounding for years. No-one had come yet. Too soon. It had been fifteen seconds since Hattie's world had changed.

The robed figure paused over Hattie, and moved on past her to the door to the Detention Cells. She knew there were only three inhabitants in this part of the station, the ones picked up from the van of horrors, the van that was like a serial killer's toybox.

The prisoners were barking mad, mostly sitting limply against the walls of their soundproofed cells, every now and again yelling and screaming about fangs and blood. Hattie's imagination heard them screaming now.

She lost consciousness again from the pain in her leg.

She didn't know how long she had been unconscious when she re-opened her eyes. The dust had mostly settled, and she heard receding footsteps. She caught a final glimpse of the robed figure. Of his or her back at any rate, leading the three prisoners in their cotton cell suits. They were shoeless, too much of a suicide risk in their rambling states of mind. They were chained to each other by the wrists and were half-pulled, half-dragged by the silent robed figure. They went through the tall, narrow hole in the wall.

She heard running feet from the direction of the main part of the station, shouts. Maybe they would be able to catch the four of them as they ran.

That became impossible, from this room at least, when she saw the wall close up into a regular smooth concrete wall, no seams, no cracks.

Just a fallen filing cabinet and a fallen colleague in front of where they had gone. And her. Her psych evaluation would be like a scene from Edgar Allen Poe if she wasn't careful. It would have particular focus on the fact that she was alive in a locked room with a dead officer and three unaccountably escaped batshit prisoners. On her watch.

Hattie heard boots outside, someone fumbling for a keycard. She took a picture on her phone of the three sets of scuffed footprints on the floor. They stopped at the wall.

There was the click of the door being released, then a low, silken voice, 'I shall take it from here, my darlings. I wouldn't want your youth corrupted.'

The boots retreated, the door clicked open again and Hattie saw a yellow-skinned squat form in the doorway wearing a sequined jacket and pink leather skirt.

'My, my, sugar, you do have *rough* parties down here. May I join in? I brought my fur handcuffs.'

40

10:05 pm
SAM

For such a lazy ball of fur, Pagoda had certainly moved fast.

She'd glided across town from the station, keeping to the rooftops. By the time I'd returned to the hotel from the Bird Cage, I found her maniacally scratching at my window, demanding to be let in, looking as agitated as I'd seen her in a long time.

I pulled open the window before she shredded the frame. I suppressed thoughts of the Bird Cage. Too distracting for her: her thoughts would veer towards *where's my bird?* And following close behind: *No, really. Where's my bird?*

For once, though, she was a cat on a mission, only momentarily delayed by the dried fish snack that I conjured up for her for sustenance, and then briefly delayed while she stretched out on my bed to compose herself. In the List Of Worthwhile Projects, trying to rush cats is just behind herding them, respectively at numbers 8,000,004 and 8,000,003.

We hunkered down for a Commune. As the Hex kicked in, an image of the interior of Brighton station came into my mind, seeing it through Pagoda's eyes.

Meyra was in earnest conversation with a blonde man. At that point I strongly regretted not having taken the free lip-reading classes offered at work. So much more useful at this time than the Ikebana classes at 5:30 on a Wednesday afternoon (although non-contact flower-arranging *had* helped me with my patience and tolerance). .

I wrestled with the view, on account of Pagoda's gaze having homed in fixedly on some battered hake that someone had discarded nearby, for a short while excluding everything else. *Pagoda, will you PLEASE GET ON WITH IT* - OK, I admit it: the Ikebana patience and tolerance thing still needs a bit of work.

Meyra and the man had sat and talked in a cafe for fifteen minutes. They appeared to come to an agreement and left the station with Pagoda dutifully padding behind them before Meyra and the man approached a parked Range Rover, glossy black, smoked windows. As she got into the passenger seat, I saw that Meyra dropped to one knee to tie up one of her boots. When she got up and sat in the car, there was a pale glow where she had knelt: *Sam Franklin, come to Haven, do not tarry. I am going in.*

How did Meyra end up in a Range Rover when she was investigating homeless people? There were evidently two ways into the Haven and she had as usual managed to find the first class ticket.

The car drove out of sight and a palpable feeling of confusion and nervousness came over the scene as Pagoda realised that her watching brief had suddenly changed to reacting as if the neighbour's Rottweiler had just dropped in for some cat treats (treats made out of a cat).

I closed the Commune and concentrated on resisting an almost overwhelming urge to shred a sofa, contenting myself for the moment with a soft prolonged hiss and a luxurious flex of my fingers.

Showtime.

41

10:30 pm
EMMA

The fire-breathing potion wouldn't be suitable. The wallpaper in the living room was not fireproof and it had only been up a fortnight. I blamed Sam. No, something else was needed. Something subtle which would break the minimum number of ornaments and not freak out the kids. They were currently asleep and prime candidates for hostages if I was not careful.

The kids had thought the two guys staying in our house were cool. At first. Both men - Tweedledum and Tweedledee; the Tweedles as their collective noun to keep it simple - managed to look delighted to be in our house, eating our food. At first. And, like the kids, they viewed clearing up as something that happened in another part of the space-time continuum, not their problem. Their job was to Protect Us To The Best Of Their Ability Against All Knowable and Unknowable Threats. They didn't say much, especially Bethany.

After a while, the kids looked at them as if they were alien life forms; annoyed as I was at their presence, which made no sense to me, they had my sympathy on that one. Welcome to our world.

One of them sat upstairs on the main landing, one sat in the sitting room, eyes notionally on a magazine, but not losing focus on his surroundings for one second. At night, they took it in turn to stay awake, no bed even though we had plenty. They were not pink valance or crisp sheets kind of people.

For all the disturbance, given the apparent potential threat to us, particularly the kids, I was glad they were on our side. As I'd said to Sam, no need to get Justin involved, these two had things well under control.

I changed my mind when I found the three body-bags in the cupboard under the stairs - the one which all of the family tried never to go in. All of us feared being attacked and drowned by the mountains of feral outerwear and kicked to death by the single shoes, the thirty year old hiking boots and the floral patterned Wellingtons that were too embarrassing to even *think* about wearing.

I had needed to brave the Coat Cupboard from Hell for some work shoes, and as I plunged my hands into the maelstrom, managing inevitably to grasp only one, the what looked like duvet bags surfaced for breath from the depths.

What was a little disconcerting was the fact that each one would fit the kids and me as if they had been measured up in Saville Row for us before a garrotting party. I decided not to mention the indelicacy of their bringing a host-murdering accessory into my house, and concentrated on getting Very Angry Indeed with them for their rudeness.

I put a Listen Hex to very good use when I heard the Terminator movie theme go off in the sitting room and saw a bulky shadow shift its weight and answer.

'The situation has changed. Bag them up,' I heard. A crackling voice at the other end, unrecognisable, but no matter. First things first.

'Moving or non-moving, sir?' asked Bethany, his voice low and soothing.

'Moving,' came the reply. 'To the usual place. We can switch to non-moving at a later stage.' The line went dead.

Andrews was upstairs. It would be unwelcome if the two of them were able to team up. Despite their monumental size, they were light on their feet, very helpful for performing a Charleston. Or a Double Roundhouse Kick. Both looked like they could chop wood without the inconvenience of going to find an axe.

I heard a long creaking sound as Bethany started to drag himself to his feet. I armed myself with a lemon squeezer and a spatula shaped like a flamingo: no need to overdo it.

I headed for the sitting room.

I was able to take comfort from the fact that the extra (padded, I noticed) body bag would come in handy when the kids next had any friends over to stay.

42

11:45 pm
WhatsApp: **River Smith** to **Sam Franklin**

Sorry to disturb you, sweetie. Things are racier here than one of my lingerie parties. One dead, one injured. Three birds flown coop. Signs of you-know-what used, culprit unknown. Still clearing up. Watch out, my cherub, they will be wanting to tie you up and beat you, and not in a nice way. Hastings *still* missing. Call me now, you bad boy.

43

11:45 pm
SAM

It was just before midnight.

Pagoda doesn't approve of nocturnal working, she likes to keep that time for playing, the cat concept meaning *hunting*.

She views her agreed working hours as around 2:00 pm to 2:45 pm at last count, She has a different view from most on the true meaning of a zero-hours contract, the clue for her being in the name. She'd been expecting several hours of well-earned

snooze after her cross-town adventure - part
of her seventeen-a-day – followed by a stroll
around Brighton looking for something
vulnerable to torture and kill, Charles
Manson in a fur onesie.

She fervently advanced the view, through
her hooded glower, that she hadn't signed
up for being cooped up in Jezebel festering
under the House Rule of 'Do Not Play With
The Steering Wheel'.

I swept up the campervan keys and my
phone, and the outraged Pagoda, and left the
hotel. I left my key at reception with Margit
who was on duty. She *always* seemed to be
on duty.

I crossed over to where Jezebel was
parked, and I dazzlingly charmed her into
starting, pleased that I had recently had her
swooned over by the Circle's head car
mechanic, Archie Prescott. So revered is he
at the Circle, that we all call him 'Preacher'
Prescott; he always does a great service.
There was a satisfying throaty shudder from
Jezebel, and I pulled out of the parking

space, knowing it would be there when I returned.

I saw the Pier brightly illuminated in the distance, outshining the more sedate lights of this part of town. I caught a glimpse of the Needle further along the beach standing out against the urban backlight like a 450 feet tall sentry.I turned left out of the square and followed Marine Parade out of Brighton. There was no traffic to speak of, not a surprise, and I sailed through Kemptown past the Brighton Marina. I saw the lights dotted on the rows of ship-shape buildings, barely visible from the road.

Then on past the angled and pointed buildings of the Roedean School for girls, set back starkly up the hill from the road, gazing timelessly over the Marina from its shadowy perch. A few dim orange lights glowed in the darkness, picking out parts of the elegant sprawl.

I turned on the retro-fitted sat-nav to update me on my progress and I was glad at that point that I'd switched back to the original voice – the primly named Emily -

from my dalliance with the Dirty Harry-voiced navigation, my Secret Santa gift from Dirty Harriet last year. Each time I'd fired it up, it had said in her Clint voice; 'Are you feeling lucky, punk?' More disconcerting was when she anticipated directions:

'Do you need the next right or the one after that? Well to tell you the truth, in all this excitement, I kind of lost track'.

Before Harry and Emily, DON'T EVEN GET ME STARTED ABOUT THAT BLOODY FUCKING BASTARD BASTARD BASTARD TOURETTES VERSION THAT I BRIEFLY TRIED OUT. Sorry, bad memories: taking a wrong turning with that one on had spelt trouble.

Overall, I'd probably stick with Emily for the moment. She informed me in her plummy BBC 1940s RP voice that I was around ten or so minutes away from Belvedere Farm, which nestled snugly in the hilly National Reserve. Would I be able to source any nylons for her from any nice Americans at my destination?

A little further along the main road, I passed through the coastal village of Rottingdean, yet more white houses overlooking the sea, radiating welcome in the darkness. More welcoming than where I was going.

And then I was turning up and away from the coast, past what looked like pretty pastel-coloured cottages picked out in the streetlamps. Emily asked in an urgent voice whether I would like to find the nearest air raid shelter. I'd forgotten that she was more assertive at night, especially about that sort of thing. When I left the village, I drove onto a narrow road with thinning houses and more trees along the route, the Downs gently undulating in different shades of black and grey into the distance.

The road went to a single car width just as the moon went behind a large cloud and I was completely reliant on my headlights. The road ran out of houses, no street lamps, no buildings, as I periodically snatched fleeting glances away from the smooth grey road surface playing out ahead of me.

The moon peeked out from behind the clouds, and Emily patiently explained that I was four minutes away at my current speed, and that loose lips sink ships. Very helpful.

The road – still tarmac, still well maintained even here in the back of beyond, with passing places neatly spaced out along it - continued up a long shallow incline, and I saw lights over to my right even at this time of night. A small farmhouse sat in the shadows, an abandoned beacon of civilization with a solitary porch light like a lighthouse.

I drove past it and carried on further into what was feeling more and more like undisturbed wilderness, soft and vast grassland, and woods. All of the features were transformed into threatening terrain, periodically patrolled by what appeared to be looming stone walls and towering barns that were elongated and warped in the night.

A large grey shape loomed in the lee of one of the rolling hills up ahead, a few white lights teaming up with patchy moonlight to pierce the sombre shapes: it was the

farmhouse and compound of Belvedere
Farm – the Haven.

'TURN THOSE BLOODY LIGHTS OUT!'
said Emily.

Obediently, I switched off Jezebel's
headlights for a discreet approach Through
our Bond, I borrowed Pagoda's Nightsight
so that I could still drive in the dark. I
reflected that it was a small price for her to
pay in exchange for feeding and litter
changing, or as she would term it my
catering and housekeeping duties.

Importantly here, though, I didn't also
acquire Pagoda's driving ability, which
might have made things a little tricky.
Otherwise I might well have taken off cross-
country after any mouse that skittered across
the road in Jezebel's path, or rendered
myself catatonic by watching the windscreen
wipers.

I found a place a short distance further up,
set back from the road, and parked Jezebel,
pointing her back down the hill. Just in case.
Prepared for a getaway, even if it would be a

rather slow and sedate getaway. If any bad
guys were chasing me in milk floats, then I
would be away from them in no time;
Jezebel's built for sass, not speed. I also set
up a Ward around the campervan to protect
her against intruders.

I peered at the Haven a short walk away
uphill and, in its brooding position on the
hill, it reminded me of the Bates Motel. It
made me want my Mother.

On foot, I cautiously approached the
outskirts of the Haven, Pagoda padding
along in the shadows near me, keeping a
look out, most likely for mislaid snacks.

PART FOUR

SUNDAY, AUGUST 8TH

44

2:00 am
SAM

There was no gate to the Haven property, just a rough driveway which would lead to the farmhouse. Security cameras were clustered around the entrance. I had an irritated cat, a large bag of boiled sweets in case things got *really* rough, and a fully charged mobile phone with no signal (no delivered messages since I'd left the Beachcomber). I was tooled up and ready to go.

It was a comfortable temperature, even in the early hours as I checked for any movement. There was none. Apart from Pagoda, who had already slunk off into the shadows. I hoped she was making a detailed survey of the surrounding area, but it was more likely she was on the lookout for insomniac squirrels.

The Haven didn't feel like a prison, no fortified gates, no guards, no dogs, just a few cameras to keep an eye on who was going in or out. From my vantage point near the gate, I quickly summoned and released a Sprite to check out the immediate area and report any activity, I received less lip than if I'd asked Pagoda.

No living creatures, other than Pagoda, over the size of a rat near the entrance. I allowed the Sprite to leave; they object to hanging around for too long unless there's treasure to be had. I flipped a small gold coin to her and she swept it away and was gone.

Emboldened, I Stealthed seamlessly into the shadows and eased past the cameras without disturbing them; Pagoda simply did what cats do.

I approached the farmhouse, slow and easy along the rough road. It would be embarrassing if I stomped around what turned out to be a generous, law-abiding community, looking for shadows that were simply not there. I was confident there were shadows, just not at the farmhouse.

The low square building from the Scrying was on the way, its windows tinted. I used a Focus to see inside, it became clear that it was a small medical centre for the residents, nothing sinister on the face of it. No patients at the moment.

I spotted a man from the blue files. I recognized his face as he passed through a patch of light, out for a late-night stroll, not supervised, not locked in. He moved slowly towards a large brazier that was burning a short distance away in the grounds in front of the farmhouse. It had been lit to take away any chill in a large seating area filled with deck chairs, hammocks hung on stands, and giant bean bags scattered on the floor. He settled down in one of the hammocks. An orange flare in the darkness announced a cigarette. No-one else was around.

The outbuildings were dark, aside from small dim lamps to illuminate their steps. The farmhouse was dark. A few soft lights were scattered around the grounds, giving illumination at night without disturbing sleeping residents. The place even had safety lighting, for crying out loud.

Pagoda flowed over to me, confirmed that Meyra was not in the farmhouse, and all she could see and hear were peacefully sleeping humans; she just about fought down the urge to comment on her wish to join them. No guards or other signs of duress.

My instincts told me that Meyra was elsewhere. Somewhere away from the farmhouse, in the shadows.

The gravel road turned and went away from the farmhouse, out towards woodland. Where it turned, there was the small area of gravel on which were parked four golf carts in a neat row.

I left the farmhouse complex behind and Stealthed, keeping in mind it would be blown if I were directly spotted. Invisibility is not yet in my Hexbook, but I live in hope. I looked for signs of movement, following an erratic route to take advantage of various welcoming pits of solid shadow.

There was clearly a place for this type of establishment that could provide comfort to the homeless in times of crisis, if run in the right way for the right reasons. I had seen nothing to suggest that it and the outbuildings amounted to anything other than an area for its previously homeless residents to be cared for and given the opportunity to take stock of their lives. Start again in a secure and supportive environment.

I walked parallel with the gravel road leading to the boundary fence.

Then two things happened, in quick succession.

First, I heard a door opening and closing from the direction of the farmhouse and looked back. Not loud, but loud enough in the early hours when it feels like you're wearing a red jersey in a Star Trek episode.

Three figures came out of the left-hand quarters, a man in another of those bizarre blazers was walking between two other men dressed in overalls, his arms draped across their shoulders. They went along a short path leading to the parked golf carts.

One of the men in overalls had a shock of blonde hair, clean cut and conventionally handsome; the other had curly brown hair and a mouth like a cheese slicer. They all seemed perfectly at ease, maybe even slightly intoxicated, the Blazer less so, gently guiding them along the path.

There was no evidence of coercion, just prompting. They had the general air of having had some drinks and being about to go out for a night on the town. None of them were rushing, all very relaxed and friendly, moving at an unhurried pace. Why run around at this time of night?

The blonde man giggled at something whispered by the Blazer. The scene was so convivial that I nearly felt like ordering a cocktail and joining them.

It was now 3 am: why were these men waltzing out of the men's quarters of a homelessness rehabilitation centre, to disappear into the night?

I retreated further into a patch of shadow under an oak tree and watched their progress. When they reached the nearest golf cart, the two residents climbed into the front and back passenger seats and Mr. Stripey settled down to drive, started the engine and quietly glided along the gravelled track. They were heading for the gap in the fence.

I kept to the shadows and let the golf cart pass. The three men were talking and Curly Hair's laughter burst out for a moment, then sank back into the darkness. The man on the hammock lazily waved to them as they drove past.

The golf cart reached and moved smoothly through the gap in the fence and drove out of sight.

The second thing happened as I edged closer to the fence, ready to slip through the gap.

I felt the unmistakable crackle of *Ma gic* under my skin as a Ward reached out to me and pushed me away.

45

3:10 am

SAM

Wards are the non-stick frying pans of *Ma gic*. At their most sophisticated, for example at the Beachcomber, they are designed to trick your mind that there's nothing there or that you should just *walk on by please, just move along, nothing to see here,* and slide away as you are distracted by something – anything – else.

Wards work well against all but a few non-practitioners; less effective against someone like me, someone with the Knack.

This one gripped me for a moment and then my training fought back. I burned something sticky onto this Ward's Teflon and kept my mind focused on getting past its slickness. The three men in the golf cart had not been stopped by the Ward so there was something more than go-faster stripes that had let them through.

I crept past the gap and stayed alongside the road.

I saw ahead of me that the trees parted and my section of track carried on to a tarmacked car park, with road to the left and gravelled tracks straight ahead and right radiating from the car park.

There was a hulking dark Range Rover parked at the end of the tarmac road, so I was confident that this was the right place. Also a Mercedes and a 7 series BMW. Somewhat incongruous. A golf cart was parked on the edge closest to the right-hand exit and was shortly joined by another from the right-hand track, driven by a man in a red and white jacket and gleaming teeth.

A pair of bright lights appeared from the road to the left and purred smoothly to a halt next to the golf cart. Another black Range Rover from another gate. Four people emerged, the driver remained in the car. One was a grey-haired man in his fifties dressed in a dinner suit. He was draped over by two stunning Philippinas in flaming crimson dresses wearing heels so high that they gave me altitude sickness. The fourth arrival was the man from the train station. He tapped his ear and said something, handing the guests over with a flourish to the Blazer who miraculously appeared moments later. He returned to the Range Rover. It turned around and sped off back down the road, lights steady on the smooth road.

The golf cart headed along the right-hand gravel track and vanished into the trees.

I followed it, hidden by the foliage, and reached the foot of steps cut into the wooded hill, saw above me into which had been built a large fountain carved out of a huge, ancient tree trunk. Through the water loomed a low, rambling wooden structure, with an unusually pleasing edge of dilapidation to its peeling paint and battered door. The outside of the structure was brown clapperboard, some hanging loosely, under a gently sloping roof. It would not have been visible from where we'd Scryed earlier.

There was a lean-to attached to the building, on which brightly coloured creeping plants gripped and wove. Two women, one with flowing green hair, were escorted by a Blazer through the entrance. Their forms blurred as they walked into the building, a trick of the light.

There would be another way in, one less public.

I edged around the building, avoiding a fallen gutter and dirty water from a leaking barrel. Pagoda gave the oily pool a wide berth. The door in the wall was not obvious, but its outline became clear when a man in red and white came out through it. There was a glow of blue light as he took a vape break under the stars.

It became a longer break when Pagoda hissed at him and he moved to kick her. Bad decision. She entwined herself around his ankles and he over-balanced like a demolished lighthouse. My boot to his head ended the evening for him. His jacket was a tight fit, but convincing enough. I scooped up his keycard and waved it at the door. It clicked open, Pagoda getting my drift that she should stay in the shadows outside while I was in the building.

Pagoda viewed that as an unambiguous green light to go hunting; she had already bagged one human tonight, so why not some other prey. As she broke away from me, she froze. I was fractionally behind her. She hissed a warning at the sound of heavy boots crunching on the ground towards us, coming around the side of the building.

There was a self-congratulatory purr from up a tree and the black-clad and helmeted figure walked past me, my ironic salute receiving no response, the jacket owner's slumped body tucked away behind the broken barrel.

I raised a Shield and opened the door. I found myself walking into a cavernous,

crowded, raucous New Orleans blues bar,
packed with revellers and the smell of
tobacco and spilt – in some cases dribbled -
whiskey. A quick glance around showed no
unwelcome interest in my arrival.

Music flooded over me from the large
stage at the far end, and my feet tapped
uncontrollably on the wooden floor to the
stripped down four-piece band: guitar,
drums, sax and a mean old guy with a
rumpled face on vocals. The balcony
wrapped around all four sides of the
rectangular room creating a performance
area in the round. Audience members hung
over the balcony to get low down and close
up.

The chilled band were easing through a
Chicago blues set; *Hoochie Coochie Man* had
seldom sounded so good. The audience was
standing, swaying, giving themselves to the
rhythm and I was entranced. My main
source of slight confusion was what the hell
was a blues club doing in the middle of the
South Downs next to a homeless commune?
Particularly with me dressed as Dan
Ackroyd, including an iconic black trilby

with its understated black satin band? Not a thread of red and white jacket on my clothes. Where had that gone?

Bartenders in red and white striped waistcoats were deep in conversation with customers at the bar as they poured shots of bourbon from thick, square bottles filled with tempting dark amber liquid. One of them looked across at me as I entered and stopped pouring. I kept my nerve, nodded back and he returned to his precious task. I relished the remainder of the song and its segue into a tasty rendition of Howlin' Wolf's *Smokestack Lightnin'*. The vocalist's throaty roared anguish when he asked his baby where she was last night was painful for all to hear. Majestic. I moved on, gently working my way through the audience, realising the need to tear myself away from the insistent music.

There was a heavy wooden door near the stage.

It opened before I reached it.

A figure came through and within seconds
my world turned upside down.

46

3:10 am
MEYRA

I had slept. Then I had bathed. Then I had put on the lavish make-up that the night demanded. Then I had fought my way into the exquisite layers of clothing that were all the rage, and finally I had organised my gorgeous hair. The full-length mirror was simply not long enough to take in all the splendour. I had vague memories of shadowy servants helping me at each stage of the long, long process.

But it had been worth it.

I must confess that when I looked through the ballroom doors even I was impressed by the marble floors, elaborate candelabra and sweeping curves of the staircases that led to a curved balcony reaching all around the room. It was painted and sculpted to within a dragon's compassion of every square millimetre on its walls and ceiling, with landscapes of nymphs and satyrs, gods and heroes, wine and absolute abandon, and hints of ghostly silver figures cavorting at the edges of my vision.

The distinctive notes of the harpsichord in the 36-piece Baroque orchestra were just to my taste, the stirring rendition of the Spring Concerto instilling in me a feeling of yearning, reminding me of home. A waiter deftly juggled a small silver tray of champagne towards me before I reached the threshold, his red and white velvet livery tracing streams of bright colour through the whirling ivory and white brocade of other waiting guests.

Sam Franklin had confessed to me once after too much ale that his picture of Elves enjoying themselves amounted to us frolicking gaily in the woods to the sound of soft flutes and pipes; I quickly corrected his bucolic Tolkien fetish - I prefer the full, round, dark tone of the bassoon. As a means of cultural acclimatisation, I had attended numerous parties when I had first arrived here, but although popular music occasionally found favour with me, based on the lack of dance cards, the excessive LSD and the mostly insufferable human beings, my interest had quickly waned. This place was the closest it had ever been to home down here, a revelation to me.

The enormous crystal chandeliers were exactly like ours at home. The male and female dancers elegantly mapped out their steps, finishing a flawless minuet. The ballroom was sumptuous. It was quite beyond what I had expected to see. I had anticipated crassness and overly forward behaviour.

The orchestra began playing the Prelude to Bach's Cello Suite Number 1 in G Major. Enchanting. The excitement of the Prelude took my breath away.

The men flaunted tight breeches and
ribboned, embroidered stockings, outdoing
each other with long tresses and facial hair,
the women floated in floor length,
shimmering in silk, with piled up hair styles
like tiered wedding cakes speckled with
emeralds and rubies, all vying for
supremacy over the colour spectrum,
ransacking shades of orange, as well as pinks
and peacock; never had I seen such
flamboyant perfection.

I could almost hear Sam Franklin saying in
his annoying way that everyone was
partying like it was 1699.

Glass in hand, I moved over to the
ballroom door and stepped in.

All seemed as it should. The dancers still
danced, the champagne still sparkled and
fizzed, the music still wove its spell. I
checked that the wiring was still sturdy
enough to support my anchored hair and
embellishments, my dress was sufficiently
splendid and devastatingly low-cut for me to
revel in its gorgeous shade of peach, what

could possibly make this occasion more
wonderful?

Then a figure flickered in front of me, a tall
man, dressed like a barbarian in a plain black
jacket, plain black trousers, and a white
blouse with a thin piece of black rectangular
cloth hanging around his neck. He was
wearing a hat, the beast, and worse it was
dull and black felt with an embarrassingly
narrow brim all round, pulled down at the
front. His eyes were covered with shiny
black circles attached to his ears by the same
material.

His mouth opened, it seemed to me with
surprise, and I noticed that bizarrely he had
no facial hair.

The air felt hot and static fizzed. My
sleeves had become rumpled and wrapped
in faded blue material, I wore long breeches
made of the same material, and goodness, I
felt it uncomprehendingly: my hair was
disgustingly short and naked.

In only a few seconds my world
descended into tumult.

A relaxed grin on his uncouth but familiar square face, Sam Franklin's words jolted me, 'Welcome to the party, Meyra. You just think you're at a different party.'

47

3:30 am
SAM

The men in the red and white blazers and waistcoats continuously calibrated and checked the room's settings: individual for each guest, every one of them swaying in time to a different rhythm and experience. Like attending a silent disco with your eyes shut, each guest when they arrived plugged into the room's *Ma gic*.

'I do not understand what is going on, Sam Franklin.'

'Not sure I do, but I think we were caught up in this building's Illusion. We saw what our subconscious wanted us to see. When our *Ma gic* fields collided, there was some sort of short circuit, or we could have been locked in here until we dropped.'

We needed to talk, and we needed to do that without being noticed. There was only one way.

I bowed to Meyra and she looked at her slim toes then me with – justified - trepidation.

We danced.

I saw flickers of her in her ridiculous gown shimmering under the lights, and I would never again be able to see her without thinking about her crazy sparkling beehive; she probably saw me as some sort of hobo from the Deep South. That wasn't much of a stretch for her; the main difference was that it was the Deep South of Croydon rather than the US.

The music for both of us staggered and sputtered and fragmented as if we were creating some maniacal Baroque Blues DJ set, the notes popping and stretching through our heads. But we hung in there, kept our respective form, held our nerve. What a sight we were, blending the two styles beyond breaking point.

'Nirvana', they call it, she said. 'They call this part the Clubhouse.'

'Nirvana? Perfect quiet and freedom,' I said. 'How appropriate.' Matched by the satin sheets of lazy blues guitar (not B.B. King's beloved Lucille, but close) playing *The Thrill is Gone*, the sweating vocalist's rasping voice a perfect counterpoint as he manhandled the lyrics.

'There are sixty-nine people in this place,' said Meyra. 'Including us. Some are from the blue files, two were picked up at the station yesterday', her eyes snapping to the two party girls lost in their private places.

'This still feels like a sideshow, but *Ma gic* is everywhere, as if people are waiting, or

being held, for a next stage. As if they're
being prepared.'

'For what?'

'That's what we're here to find out,
Cinderella,' I said, as there was another
flicker and flash of silk and jewels on and
around Meyra.

'We need to get out of here. Whatever's in
the air could get at us soon.'

'I concur,' said Meyra, leaning into me as I
bobbed from side to side in time to my music
and she twirled daintily around me, deftly
avoiding my heavy boots. Both of us just
about maintained our respective styles in our
nerve-wracking choreography.

Under cover of our routine, I stared at
some of the partygoers and felt flashes in my
head of where they had flown on their magic
carpets to La La Land: slave-draped Turkish
pavilions, howling festivals of death metal, a
tiny bar in Marrakesh, most disturbingly a
black, glistening dungeon filled with aged

leather and shiny PVC which I escaped from without more, all faces of the Clubhouse.

Without limit, enhanced by the Blazers and their weird machinery, fuelled by the unnatural chemicals swilling round this place. Thank the Gods for my Shield which had mostly protected me from the welcoming quagmire; Meyra had been on the brink, despite her different constitution.

We needed more information, more insight, just *more*.

'There is nothing else here, Sam Franklin. I have explored this place and it is merely a shell filled with vacuous people.'

'Or lost people.'

Whichever. It does not matter here.'

We agreed that I would check out the grilled building and Meyra would investigate the square box. 'It seems to be the same design as the one by the farmhouse, a medical facility, just bigger' I said. 'No windows.'

'I will find out.'

'We should meet by the wooden
fountains.'

'You mean the crystal pools with the
cherubs and dolphins.'

'Whatever. The one on the steps. Thirty
minutes.'

Now that I knew the trick to this building,
the sights and sounds of the fractured party
were almost overwhelming. I needed to get
away from this place; it was like a crypt
where the inhabitants moved, granted in
more colourful shrouds. Only copious
quantities of hard alcohol and drugs could
sustain someone through all of that for hours
on end. I think the same about golf.

A sense of Meyra's Mother - *always* a
capital "M" - came unannounced into my
mind. It really didn't matter that Meyra was
in human years not much younger than me.
Her Mother would be violently unimpressed
with me if Meyra had any big problems. Her

father traded derivatives accounts for the Triads, too, so no pressure. I'd rather be armed with a teaspoon and face off against a rabid pack of horned demons, whatever the colour of their horns, than clash with 'Mother' and 'Daddy'. It was disconcerting, unnerving: a reminder rather than a memory.

48

3:30 am
MEYRA

Sam Franklin drew me into the cacophony of his version of this world so that we could leave, a shame to replace my silk with his denim but that seemed to be a useful definition of our differences.

The music sounded like he had trodden on Pagoda's tail with spiked boots – fleetingly a pleasurable thought. It was darker there, easier to blend into the swathe of rancid audience members, easier to slip out into the night.

Pagoda was waiting for us outside, she was looking at her tail in a quizzical way, having picked up on my music critique from the various fractures of thought. She had scouted the area, no doubt looking for prey and useful intelligence for us in a descending order of priority.

Apparently, there were security cameras in a tight ring around both outbuildings. With that, Pagoda sloped off again out of sight. I wondered what fantasy world Pagoda might have experienced if she had come in here; it would probably have involved an orgy of grooming with giant tongues. Horrid beast.

I left Sam Franklin to the other outbuilding, and I Stealthed past the cameras circling the square windowless box. A black-clad guard tramped around from the side of the building and paused at what I took to be the main door. Sam Franklin had mentioned the existence of the guard, and he continued his patrol. This area was guarded by cameras and personnel, unlike the buildings by the farmhouse.

An unwelcome development. A second guard appeared, dressed in the same way, from around the corner of the mansion. Then a third from round the side of the Clubhouse. They briefly met at the door of the square building and dispersed on their orderly routes around the buildings. Ingress and egress were now complicated, but nothing that I could not navigate around.

I immediately felt *Ma gic* at the door and saw that a Ward had been placed on it in the form of a PRIVATE – KEEP OUT sign, with the Hex woven into it. Cameras, guards and *Ma gic*.

I Listened behind the door and heard nothing except for a quiet hum and some skittering sounds. I resisted the Ward and performed a KnockKnock on the keycard panel, which quickly succumbed. Time was of the essence before the next convergence of guards. The door obediently clicked open and I pushed it slowly.

Inside was an entrance lobby, stone floor, white concrete walls and a thick metal door straight ahead of me with a grilled window.

I peeked through to see what was inside and saw eighteen computer desktops with over-sized screens in three banks of six, all occupied by people in red and white jackets hunched over their screens, typing: the source of the skittering noises.

The screens were organised in an odd way, it took me a few moments to work out why they looked strange. They were all orientated in portrait rather than landscape, divided into quarters with an image in each quarter. A few screens held four images, completely filling the space.

Each section at the bottom had jagged graphs and was filled with changing numbers, none of which I could fathom. The striking images were above the graphs and figures, different sorts of figures. Sixty-three representations of a human body, different colours from a vivid palette, blues and greens with occasional flashes of black; a white circular dot with tiny numbers flashing in it, all in the same place in the neck of the painted figure. I moved forward to get a closer look.

49

3:40 am
SAM

Pagoda ostentatiously left me to deal with the lock on the grilled outbuilding. She takes the view with that kind of thing that we human beings are so pleased with ourselves as a species for having opposable thumbs that we should simply get on with it.

I dealt with the lock just as I heard approaching footsteps. One pair. The guard from earlier. I slid the door shut behind me with painstaking care and the guard passed by, Pagoda inveigled herself in with me,

warping the feasible dimensions in her
standard feline way.

I turned and saw hydroponics channelling
Day of the Triffids.

It was a large warehouse, like an aircraft
hangar, purpose-built, metal and plastic, lit
by dozens of lights with reflective shades
suspended from the ceiling, bathing the area
with soft violet light. And heat. The air was
dryer than the Sahara at midday. There was
a tangible fizz of *Ma gic* in the air, all around.
Musty fizz.

Ranks of sturdy spiky-leafed plants with
brown and purple buds stood in gravel.
They were at different growth stages; earthy
liquid fizzing with *Ma gic* sloshed around
the bases of the plants. It made gentle
burbling noises, contrasting with the
abrasive high tech of the porous tubes
wrapped around the plants, bleeding
nutrients into them. The wires and poles
rigidly encased and moulded them, holding
them up.

Dope on a rope.

I had seen cannabis before, it sometimes worked as a useful Hex component (very good for Levitation), but I had never seen so much in so cramped a space.

It was not just that. The flowers and buds of the mature plants were huge, the roots like cables, the stems bursting with life. Enhanced somehow. Green fingers used for the Devil's work, like a horror movie set waiting for some monsters.

The smell was cloying but not unpleasant, taking me directly back to days a long time ago, sitting on bean bags with a stack of Bob Marley albums playing cool tunes, with the inevitable accompanying – urgent – need for mountains of cheesy snacks.

Small black terminals with blinking blue and steady green lights stood at the end of each row, plugged into the system, monitoring. No wonder there's so much security, this was worth millions.

I broke off a leaf, crushed it and sniffed. Strong stuff. More bang for your bong; I should be in advertising.

Combining the effects of this stuff with the Illusions in the main building was literally mind-bending.

Through the exotic foliage, I saw a flash of reflection from some glass. I went over. Pagoda followed looking uncomfortable with the smell. Cat-nip was way better, in her opinion. Behind the tightly sealed glass door was a long room filled with benches holding large trays of organic material.

It looked like it was being stored for different stages of the refining process: cutting, drying and curing. And packaging. They were evidently maximising profits with some judicious distribution on the side, through the little white vans that were parked behind the building, visible through the back windows. Marked on their sides with: *Nature's Bounty – Premium Garden Products.* No shit.

I stared at the intricate production line around me. How did this fit into the so-called charity work at the farmhouse?

Pagoda stationed herself near the door and peered out. The heavy plants felt poisonous and unnatural, touched by *Ma gic*. Meyra would hate them. Pagoda gave me the claw up to leave the building and head off for my rendezvous with Meyra. The night air felt cold after the heat and dryness of the outbuildings. I took the long way round to the fountains to avoid misunderstandings with any perimeter guards.

I settled down in my red and white jacket, nonchalant, on a break. No-one bothered me, the action was inside the Clubhouse.

I shook my head to clear it from the heavy scent that still enveloped me from the warehouse. It felt like it had addled my brain without my having smoked anything.

A distant glimmer of early dawn touched the sky.

Meyra had not returned.

Lost in Plain Sight

50

4:40 am
SAM

No time to sleep until this was done.

As I'd instructed, Pagoda had gone to check out the square building to see if she could figure out what had happened to Meyra, why she hadn't shown up at our meeting place.

From her position at a sensible distance from the large square building (I knew that meant a comfortably long way away), Pagoda's report was concise and typically feline when she returned to me:

Too much going on, too many humans with short sticks around. Ate grass on the way back to you, made a splendid hair-ball.

'I'm so relieved. Nothing else?'

One of the men guarding the door asked whether the woman had been taken to the farmhouse, and the other one replied, 'Don't be stupid, she was sent for processing.' The first man said it was the end of his shift and he was going to get some food. No idea what food, sorry. The other said, you don't get it do you? Didn't you hear? All breaks are cancelled, we're on full alert.

'Processing?'

Processing.

It took us a long time to get to the car park. More security, more patrols, from the 'full alert'. Having worked our way past the cordon, there was a guard posted at the car park. To stop any other intruder escaping in the two Range Rovers that were there at the moment, and a golf cart.

I Stealthed up to the guard and hit him with my knuckleduster. I dragged him into the nearby trees and left him there. Pagoda bit his hand, she claimed to see whether he was properly unconscious, but I wasn't so sure that she wasn't playing with her food. We returned to the car park.

Where would they have taken Meyra? I made the call: not to the farmhouse - *Don't be stupid*. Why potentially create a scene among the residents? Nor back to the main road when all their infrastructure was inside this huge compound. I manoeuvred the golf cart out of the car park, onto the gravel track leading away from the farmhouse.

I got into the golf cart and Focused on its engine. I coaxed it and made it hum quietly into life. All those years with Jezebel hadn't been in vain. There was a rustling sound and something dark rushed over to me.

Pagoda had seen what I was doing and decided that there was no way she was going to go further on foot if a lift would be available. She scooted under the front seat and rolled herself into a ball like a plush R2-D2, her eyes roving over the area.

I followed the gravel track through trees for a while, using Pagoda's Nightsight to steer. I came to an abrupt halt when I heard a rhythmic whipping sound head, slightly muffled by a low hill. The top of the hill was level, regular, dipping down to the left; The track circled the left side of the hill then out of sight, bushes and trees obstructing the view beyond.

The sound was coming from over the edge of the hill.

I couldn't make out the whipping sound. I abandoned the golf cart by the side of the road, concealed from any casual observer; Pagoda had seen the writing on the wall about her ride and had already sloped off into the undergrowth, not appreciating the strange noises.

The hill was regular and covered with grass, with a few low bushes tufting out of it. I made my way up, crouching and crab-walking. At the top, it flattened out, then after 20 metres dropped away again. It looked out over a valley undulating into the distance, cut through with a stubborn river that sparkled in the new day.

I Stealthed forward slowly. I would not be seen unless I moved too quickly and attracted attention. Low-risk in my current position. A worthwhile risk. I spread myself out next to a short bush and peered over the edge.

There was a flat area below me that had been carved into the hillside before it fell away into the valley. Around 15 metres or so below was a large flat expanse of grey tarmac in a circular shape, clearly marked with a large 'H'. A helicopter approached from out of some fading mist in the valley, catching the first rays of sunshine on its spotless white fuselage.

It was front-on to me, the pilot was concentrating on not merely landing but landing as if in a feather bed. I kept my head down, but he was far too busy to notice me. The helicopter kissed the floor, a delicate peck on the cheek. It sank down with a sigh, the large side door pointing towards me at an angle, the rotation of the blades slowing, the whipping sound steadily decreasing.

When they had come to a halt, a man and a woman in green medical scrubs approached the helicopter, flanking another man. A golf cart was parked behind them at the edge of the helipad. The medics were walking, one on each side, at a respectful distance from the other man who was dressed in a long shapeless silver robe, hood up.

They all stopped, facing the door with their backs to me. The medics kept a discreet distance from the robed man. They looked around constantly, on edge.

The door of the helicopter slowly swung open, and I saw figures moving in the aircraft.

Two men in dark suits and mirror shades, not a hair on either man's head, jumped down to each side of the door. They gestured curtly to the two medics to stand well back, and they didn't argue. The bodyguards were

way over six feet tall, carved out of rock-
hard muscle with extra bulges under their
armpits which, sensitive as these guys may
be, were unlikely to be spare bottles of body
lotion.

They checked their surroundings and
waved into the back of the helicopter. A
woman's face appeared in the doorway,
straining. The two medics rushed forward
and there was a glint of early sunlight on
metal as between them they eased a wheeled
gurney down to the floor of the helipad.

The body of a woman was lying supine
under a thick white blanket, strapped onto
the trolley. The robed figure leaned over and
placed the palm of his hand on her chest for
several seconds, then secured a bracelet on
her wrist. He handed one to each bodyguard
who took them without comment; they
barely went around their wrists.

The attendants fussed over connecting a
drip to the patient, retrieved and placed ice
packs around her body and wheeled the
gurney across the smooth surface of the
helipad.

They moved at a funereal pace, the robed figure pacing behind them and disappeared from my line of sight behind the mound. As the party passed below me, I had a long look at the patient. I recognised her from her pictures in the press, all over the press.

Natasha Shevchenko.

She'd been all over the business pages, and the tabloids scenting a story with a blissful mixture of sex and crime. A young female owner – still remarkable in itself - of one of the monolithic energy companies that had carved up the market in Russia. A hint – more than a hint – of her jewel-encrusted fingers in organized crime pies in Russia and across Eastern Europe.

Lurid stories of remorseless excess had surfaced. From her drawn and pallid face and her unmoving form, her lifestyle choices had bitten back. Her arrival was at odds with the publicity shots of her in the Bahamas at the moment. Not Brighton.

Discovery of her presence here rather than on a golden beach surrounded by her entourage would be high profile; *big* news. If she were seriously ill - the pallor in her face and all of these measures suggested exactly that - it would have serious implications for her conglomerate. More than that, a sweeping knock-on effect on the global energy markets. Big money was at stake, and the markets needed to be fooled into thinking that all was well. Her Russian Rope Trick was maintaining the illusion.

The engines started up and the helicopter rose gracefully into the air, turned around and headed in the direction of the coast. I half-crept and half-scrambled as quickly as I could over to the far end of the slope. I wanted to look down and see the road to find out where the gurney was heading from the helipad. It couldn't be far. I wondered if they might get into some sort of ambulance, although I hadn't heard anything arrive. When I reached a good spot, I looked down and around, stumped.

The golf cart was where they had left it at the edge of the helipad; there was no other vehicle in sight and no sign that there had ever been one.

Where had the granite bodyguards and the robed figure gone with the 'patient'? In that short space of time, they had vanished with the gurney.

Not even a puff of smoke.

Abracadabra.

51

6:00 am

SAM

I retraced in my mind the path taken by the gurney: straight across the large helipad, out of sight from me for two or three minutes while I'd waited for the helicopter to head off. They had vanished by the time I'd followed them.

I didn't understand where they had gone so fast. Someone in Natasha Shevchenko's condition wouldn't have been able to go very far. And there had been no ambulance.

There was another layer that I hadn't picked up on that would explain the Shevchenko-lessness.

Forget the Haven with its homeless people and charity teas; forget the on-tap booze and drugs of the Clubhouse. This felt like the core of it all. The Haven was for people lost in plain sight in the system, the Clubhouse for cash-rich wasters and people lured or taken out of the commune, but now this? Natasha Shevchenko was big league, glossy magazine and financial section fodder.

There was no-one in my field of view at all, so I scooted down the hill back to the road and cautiously followed it round. There was still nothing and no-one to see. I reached where the hill dipped down to meet the road as it swept round to the helipad. Now on my right, the hill came down to a rounded end. It was obvious from this angle that the hill had been man-made, the grass covering it having accumulated over a long, long time.

There was a set of four blocks at the narrowest part, two vertical blocks of stone with one supported by both to make effectively a crude lintel. There was a large plug of stone sealing what otherwise would have been a doorway, which had the practical effect of a very large baby's dummy. There was no way the gurney would have fitted through the gap, even without the presence of the plug.

Nothing in the nearby bushes or trees.

Pagoda emerged from the nearby undergrowth, her tail furred up to twice its normal volume, eyes narrowed, not looking at me.

She stopped in her tracks. She was staring pointedly at the mound. I Focused on it and, when my gaze turned to the stone blocks, I froze. A large glass door shimmered where the plug had been. A path behind it led downwards into the hill, all previously Hidden from view.

I used the Bond. Pagoda's fine-tuned senses had been spooked by the *Ma gic* discharge when the party had passed through the entrance and disrupted the field. That would have ruffled her fur no end. The

Illusion of the central stone plug had been enough to head me off; Pagoda strutted up to me in triumph.

We retreated into the bushes to wait, we wouldn't be seen from the glass door if anyone appeared. Like for a cat, high points were des-res for the mound when it was built thousands of years ago, Anglo-Saxon, maybe Bronze Age.

I concentrated on the door. There was a keypad next to it built into the wall. I hoped that someone would be along soon to oblige with the code, seeing as how I'd stretched, and indeed over-stretched, my dead-people-in-dark-places knowledge. I recognized, with a tinge of sadness, that I wouldn't be likely to shine on this if megaliths ever came up as a round in a pub quiz. It reminded me a bit too much of a giant burrow - Watership Down and the doomed bunnies.

As I concentrated on how to get into the mound, I endeavoured not to look like a doomed bunny, although Pagoda caught a little of that drift through our Bond and started to look interested. I made myself more comfortable in my makeshift hide and watched the entrance.

This place must be connected somehow to the drug den Clubhouse unless the respective personnel had a shared tailor; Natasha Shevchenko had been brought in by a low-flying helicopter to land next to an entrance to the underworld concealed by heavy-duty *Ma gic*. She had been taken down the secret rabbit hole for urgent treatment and care, in the hope the burial mound wouldn't be needed as part of a one-stop shopping experience.

I heard a soft warning hiss from Pagoda, followed shortly afterwards by a low whirring sound. A golf cart was trundling along the road towards us, then past and round to the edge of the helipad, opposite the glass door. It was a six-seater and there were two blazers, one driving, one at the back. There were three other men in the passenger seats.

I did a double-take when I saw them.

The passengers were my three assailants from Friday evening, the ones supposed to be in police custody rather than about to descend into a burial mound.

52

6:15 am

SAM

The three men were quiet, deflated. They looked guilty and defiant at the same time, and nervous but trying not to show it. I saw traces of Justin's effect on them as they started at every shadow.

But how were they here? River would not have released them. They were too important a link to what was going on. So that suggested the Haven's reach was further than we'd previously thought.

The one I'd called All-Black, but who was like the other two dressed in the blue Haven uniform, fiddled with his bracelet. He said, petulantly 'I keep telling you: it wasn't our fault. A wild animal attacked us. Some sort of - werewolf.' At that thought, his voice tailed off. There was a snort of derision from one of the blazers. The other two thugs cowered in the golf cart at his use of the word as if it would conjure up the monster. The blazers were stony-faced, contemptuous.

'I jus' can't remember,' said Karnage. 'All I see are the nightmares. That face, hairy, drooling, teeth like a shark.' Thanks a million, Justin, I thought, I wouldn't have been able to put those Apparitions together without you.

The other blazer said: '*Really*? You clowns might have screwed up this whole deal if you said anything to the pigs. We need to know. Did you really think it would just go away and everyone would be fine about it?'

'I told you. I had really bad dreams,' repeated the leader, whining, afraid.

There was another loud snort from one of the blazers. 'Bad dreams? Poor baby. It's more a case of what shit you were using when you got caught'.

'Well, you'll have a different job now. No more mixing work and playtime,' said the other one. 'Think of it as a permanent position.'

The hairs on my neck came up when I heard that. The three men didn't seem to notice, feeling sorry for themselves and trying as hard as they could to keep their heads down, hoping that the crap would fly over them somewhere else. Good luck with that.

I saw they were not tied up, but I could certainly feel that they were in serious trouble. It felt to me like they were at risk of more than being merely fired.

Karnage asked what the new job was. 'You'll find out soon enough,' said the blazer at the back of the cart. 'Put these on or you'll come across something that makes your werewolf look like a pussycat.' Pagoda nudged me twice, narrow-eyed, making it clear that using cats as the harmless part of the comparison was a *big* mistake. The blazer handed over three bracelets to the thugs who meekly put them on.

The blazers and the men got out of the cart and headed towards the glass door, as if it were plain for all to see.

The blazers' name tags fizzed and allowed the five men to see the door.

One of the blazers punched a sequence of six buttons on the keypad. With my Focus stretched as far as I could, I saw the buttons and their place in the sequence, and then watched the glass door slide smoothly open. The five men entered the tunnel through the open door, which slid shut behind them.

I waited for a short while and then, not having detected any further sounds or movement, I went to the door. There was a dark blur in my peripheral vision.

Pagoda ran up onto my shoulder and gripped onto me like a limpet. I approached

354

the entrance from the side, the opening must have looked like an oversized mouse hole. I repeated the code sequence on the keypad and the door slid open with a slight hiss. I moved into the tunnel, cat still attached.

The wide tunnel angled smoothly downwards, with soft floor lighting providing pools of illumination as we went. I used Pagoda's Nightsight to enhance my senses as we crept along, still Stealthing.

There was something badly wrong here. The rest of the Haven complex was a twisted combination of Mother Theresa and your local crack dealer, but this felt like something else, something darker. The charity stuff by itself was fine, possibly even great; the sorcerous Disneyland not so much: *have a Ma gical day.*

But this? I had no idea where it stood on the Evil-ometer, but I suspected that ultimately it would go all the way up to 11.

The tunnel opened out into a chamber and I took in the surroundings.

It was over 20 or so metres wide, directly under the mound that I had walked over.

The smooth floor contrasted starkly with the rough-hewn stone blocks supporting the roof, which had been interwoven with modern concrete for extra stability. That was slightly comforting. Chalk, one of the mainstays of the South Downs, has never been prime building material.

Starting at just above head height, I could see that the walkway went straight ahead without deviating, while the height of the ceiling rose to around three or four metres. I could see entrances into what looked like small chambers at regular intervals on both sides. Chambers for important buried occupants: en suite sacrifices, complimentary shroud changes every few centuries. They would stay like that for several more centuries. I concentrated n the walkway, kept my Stealth going.

The chambers started at floor level. Eventually, the floor angled downwards so that the straight line of chambers seemed to float upwards away from the ground. That was an optical illusion: the floor had been excavated, going deeper.

I followed the walkway, Pagoda still clamped to me. It blended into the gloom ahead and disappeared. Off to the sides, there were small pedestals of stone that had been deliberately left out of the re-shaping. On one, I saw some cracked pottery and what seemed to be beads that had been carefully preserved. On another there was a glint of gold, perhaps a necklace, which had been left untouched?

Further along was a circular furrow cut into the floor, a couple of metres in diameter. In it was a well-preserved skeleton. Maybe a participant - willing or not - in the original burial ceremony, left to rest in peace while the rest of the burial mound had been re-shaped around him.

The silence was broken only by my careful tiptoeing. Soft blue lighting chilled the atmosphere of the chamber, which hadn't started out particularly festive. No honky tonk piano or dancing girls down here; death metal seemed more on the playlist.

357

The place was tomb or a museum, not a hospital. The only things missing were some glass display cases and some turgid descriptions of shards. No interactive buttons either, come to think of it, although that may have been a good thing in the case of the skeleton.

I had nearly reached the centre of the lozenge-shaped burial mound with the pale path through it. Ahead, at the exact centre, it dramatically widened into a large stone circle. Beyond it, the walkway carried on as before. The circle must have been around five metres in diameter, and it had an inset silvery metal circle in the middle at least a metre across, seamless with the stone.

Why? There were real issues if they wanted to use it to land a helicopter in here; and it would clearly have been an ill-judged place to build a patio.

Various signs and sigils had been deeply carved – recently - into the stone around the edge; the centre circle was completely smooth. The carvings had been executed with great precision, possibly with lasers by the look of it given the sharp relief of the shapes.

I didn't recognise many of the symbols, although there were some that were familiar to me. Depressingly, those tended to be the ones that related to sacrificial murder, entombment and grisly death. They were among the fun activities avidly pursued in places like this. These were not the sorts of shaped stones that you would normally find at your local garden centre.

I really hoped for Natasha Shevchenko's sake that the circle wasn't the operating theatre for her; a bit too Grand Guignol for my taste. With no encores. Careful not to bring the house down.

It seemed highly unlikely that the people behind this place were going to sacrifice her, but I did wonder whether there might be an unwilling understudy. I padded on and then stopped suddenly. Pagoda's claws dug into my shoulder and she let out a short rumbling growl.

Voices were coming from behind me from the direction of the entrance.

And sounds ahead of me, slightly muffled, coming from wherever the path led.

Awkward.

Pagoda and I were about to become as welcome as veal tartare in a Vegan sandwich.

Well, I was anyway. Pagoda decided that she would find a more suitable perch than one which was about to find itself between two sets of converging individuals who might inexplicably not like cats. And she wanted to start batting that necklace around to see it glint in the lights.

Both sets of sounds started to get louder. And closer.

53

6:30 am
SAM

While I had been dismissive of my splendid feline companion a moment ago, in the event I really felt that I owed her an apology. And a cat treat or two.

I looked down on the walkway from one of the burial chambers set into the sides of the burial mound. I knew for certain it was a burial mound because I had landed with a crunch on a mummified body in my haste. I was smeared with chalk dust, although this wasn't the time to shake it off. I brushed a

few crushed bone fragments off my
shoulder, though. It's important to try to
keep up appearances.

I had a box seat for what came next when
the two sets of sounds resolved themselves
into people arriving at the stone circle. I was
relieved not to have been standing there
waiting to show them to their seats.

Bless her, even though Pagoda had had it
away on her claws at the first sign of
possible trouble, she had made sure that she
was close enough to me for me to Borrow
some of her cat–ness to help me out. I had
hastily tippy-toed, cat-like, away from the
walkway (rather than relying on my natural
stealth: that would have resulted in my
breaking pedestals, scattering artefacts and
ultimately landing on top of the skeleton in a
compromising position).

When I'd managed to get to the wall, I had
seen that the closest entrance above me was
around three or four metres up. Rough-hewn
the walls may have been, but they didn't
have comfortable footholds or handholds,
which had from my perspective was a

design flaw. I'd been able to impress upon Pagoda the urgency of the situation and she enabled me to Spring up to the entrance of the chamber and scramble in for my tryst with the Mummy.

Although my Stealth had wobbled at that point, my acquisition of Pagoda's vertical-take-off-and–landing skill had done the trick.

At this point, I was principally concerned with keeping still and quiet. That was at odds with my post-feline urge that had triggered in me a strong need to self-groom in that acrobatic and frankly unsavoury way that cats have. At this sort of sensitive time, and for that sort of complicated self-grooming, additional high-level yoga training would have been too embarrassingly essential.

I could now see who had met in the circle.

From further into the mound had come two men in blazers. Odd outfits for working in a graveyard. For fashion inspiration, I would have looked no further than Goth. How many of these mercenary vaudeville

artists there were? One of them was
Endymion Walker.

In person. In a candy-striped blazer.

Of the three coming from the entrance,
two were men, neither of whom had I
previously seen, one had a buzz-cut, the
other darker short hair and trendy stubble.
Easy to tell apart. The third person was a
woman, walking docilely in front of them, a
woven bag over her head; they had been
prodding her in the back periodically, and
not gently.

I recognised her immediately from how
she carried herself even in her captive state.
Unconscious elegance.

Meyra.

How had she ended up behind me? By the
time Pagoda had reached the square
building to investigate Meyra's no-show,
according to Pagoda Meyra had already
been removed from the scene. Realistically,
there was nowhere for her to have been
taken other than the farmhouse or the

Clubhouse. So where had she been until now?

I examined my precarious position:

- I was in a hole in the wall with my cat, lying prone on a withered corpse.
- Meyra had been attacked and captured.
- Endymion Walker (or someone in Endymion Walker's body) was standing below me.

We had what was indeed the class reunion from Hell.

'Who's she?' asked the blazer alongside Walker, dispensing rough justice to some offending chewing gum.

One of the men who had been herding Meyra lazily scratched at his rough stubble and pulled off the bag. Meyra's face was puffed up and heavily bruised. He said in a bored voice: 'Here you go, knock yourself out. We caught her earlier trying to poke around in the data centre. Stupid bitch must have thought we were all high and she could look around and do as she pleased.'

'We showed her different,' said Buzz-cut, with an unappealing grin.

'We checked her out, and she came out with some funny readings,' said Stubble. 'The boss'll be interested.'

'Hold your horses. Chill out,' said Not-Walker. 'Let's not get ahead of ourselves. I'm not bothering him with some nobody with itchy fingers. We'll ask her nicely who she is and what she was after. Dot our I's and cross our t's - you know what he's like. *Nothing* de-rails the Shevchenko thing, OK? If we let that happen, it'll make life miserable – and short - for all of us.' He rubbed his face. 'Anyway, I've got my own fish to fry on that front,' he said, pointing at himself and grimacing. 'I want this fixed before it becomes permanent. This guy must have been eighty or more.'

'Your nightclub days are over then, mate,' said his companion, making a smacking noise with the gum.

'*You* volunteer next time,' Not-Walker spat back.

I tried to home in on what was odd about this Walker. Aside from Walker being dead, of course. It was the voice that did it for me. He was clearly not happy about his appearance. It would be why he hadn't spoken at the hotel.

Stubble said, in a hard voice, 'OK, Reynolds, no more sob stories. You were picked out for that job, so deal with it. It'll get fixed when the woman's been sorted out.' His mouth twisted. 'You're not exactly top of the list, y'know. I realize you want your gorgeous golden locks back as soon as you can get your face on them, but that sort of stuff's why we all get paid so much here.'

Walker – Reynolds – growled and rubbed the back of his neck, irritably, as if it didn't quite fit perfectly.

It was easy to see how he'd managed to pass himself off as Walker; and how the Beachcomber staff, and Meyra and I, had been fooled. He was of a similar build and the general shape of his face was comparable to Walker's. That would have been why he'd been the lucky one chosen to have his face and body grabbed, he would have felt more comfortable in his makeshift body.

He was always going to have a reasonably good shot at a place in the Endymion Walker Tribute Band as its lead singer, but this had given him an unfair advantage. That made me think of one of my favourite stories about Charlie Chaplin, that around 1920 or so he'd entered a competition at a fair in the US to determine who could best imitate the Charlie Chaplin walk.

He'd come in twentieth. Who knew?

Now I knew for sure where Reynolds had been at around 7 am last Thursday: in the Beachcomber, opening the door to Walker's room, having performed a passable Walker impression in the lobby. Even his walk had been convincing enough.

Walker had probably succeeded in tracking Olivia here, to the burial mound, and been killed, maybe trying to sneak in? Given where I was right now, I really didn't want a repeat performance. And I still didn't know what had happened to his daughter.

What I did know was that Meyra hadn't reacted to 'Walker's' appearance. From her expression, she'd been drugged to make her compliant, which was probably the only way to get her cooperation in this type of situation.

To get her into a drugged state around here all they'd needed to do was to ring for Room Service.

54

6:45 am

SAM

Meyra was pushed over to Reynolds and the other blazer, and without more they turned around and started to walk across the circle and back onto the walkway. Further into the mound. Away from the entrance. Downwards.

The other two hung around and watched them go.

'Back to work, then,' said Buzz-cut. 'No peace for the wicked, right? They've stepped up security round here even more than before, after we heard about the Russian rich bitch coming in for her op and taking that girl – Lydia? Olivia? Whatever.' My ears pricked up so much at his words that I thought I was probably starting to look like a bunny. Not an advisable look when there's a vindictive feline to hand; Pagoda's eyes briefly narrowed.

Buzz-cut's companion looked thoughtful and rubbed his stubble, making a rasping noise. 'You're right. Now this one. It's made it too risky. I've had it up to here with all this – that guy's weird cosmetic thing was about the last straw.' He squinted across the circle into the shadows that had now swallowed up Reynolds with his sidekick and Meyra. 'I don't want to be next for plastic surgery.'

Stubble swallowed, looked around, carried on: 'Someone'll find out about this place soon for sure, and bring it down. I don't want to be here when that happens. I'm thinking when I've caught up with my money for all this shit I'll call it a day here before everything blows up. The stuff with Bill freaks me out as well.'

Bill?

'Yeah, freak. He does scare the crap out of me, not gonna lie. I wish we didn't have to go back that way.'

'Devil and the deep blue, mate. Down in the caves might be worse though.' He paused for breath, eyes flicking from side to side in reflex, making sure he hadn't been overheard. 'Yeah, the money's good, but some of this shit's too full-on for me.'

'Difficult to give up the cash, though, right?' Buzz-cut glanced in the direction of the entrance and pulled back his shoulders, set with sudden purpose. This next job was definitely not on his want-to-do list.

'We'd better go let Bill out. He's been resting, alright for some,' he said, trying to sound cheerful, not getting beyond anxious. Overall, he looked like he'd had similar thoughts to his colleague, but the cash had won him over. Stubble looked nervously back over his shoulder when Bill's name was mentioned. He unconsciously fiddled with his bracelet and turned around to keep the entrance in sight.

Buzz-cut shrugged and then chuckled. 'Anyway, I don't know who came up with that name. It's so perfect, right? Genius... Raaaargh!' he roared, and put both arms in the air, waving them violently at his colleague.

The man visibly jumped, much to Buzz-cut's great amusement, until there was an answering throaty roar a few moments later from near the entrance to the burial mound. At that point, both men went very quiet indeed. Pagoda and I kept even more quiet.

In the next few moments, while he tried to pull himself together, Buzz-cut whispered conspiratorially: 'Bill's drugs must be off the charts. Completely barking. Look what he did to that old guy last week.'

'Weird shit,' said Stubble, heading off with his partner back down the walkway towards the entrance. 'Let's get this over with and get the hell out of here.'

'Just make sure you check that gizmo is working – No idea how it works, but let's not find out the hard way that it doesn't.' Stubble grunted his agreement and I could see him fiddling with his bracelet to tighten it. He seemed too nervous even to let go of it.

'Here, Billy, Billy. Feeding time,' called out Buzz-cut, having recovered more of his composure. He said it in a mock-wheedling voice. The answering rumble made it less mock.

They switched on electric torches and I saw that their beams criss-crossed in the dusty air, as they went off the walkway and towards one of the burial chambers on the opposite side. It was nearer the chamber entrance, at the level of the walkway. I was suddenly pleased we hadn't explored the side chambers.

Easy access for the two blazers for whatever came next. It was at the outer edges of my Focus, but I stuck with it. My elevation helped. From what I'd heard from these guys, staying up here would be good.

Pagoda's agreement was total, I could tell by the warning grip of her claws.

The two men overlapped their torch beams on the entrance and one of them made a complicated series of hand movements. I saw that it was the reverse of a Ward – a strong one from what I could see. Clumsy, but effective.

I could tell that the blazer didn't know that he was using *Ma gic* – rote learning, too mechanical. The effect was something like one of those video game motion detectors where you play the game by moving your hands in front of a camera. Getting those gestures wrong here would have resulted in a bad case of Game Over.

There was a crackling sound audible even this far away in our lofty perch. Then a flash of blue light as the Ward went down, and I saw that a figure had appeared at the entrance to the chamber. The man's face, still partially in shadow, glowed slightly, possibly in the lights of the burial mound and the men's torches. He came further out of the chamber in which I presumed he had previously been sleeping, awoken by Buzz-cut's stupid prank.

A chill worked its way up my spine. Pagoda hissed quietly with sudden and deep fright by my side.

On his head were six or so short conical shapes attached to his temples and ringed around the top of his head.

Horns.

Some stunted and warped, some curved and gleaming, but all horns.

The glow around the figure was blue. It seeped out of the figure's body, creating a corona around him.

A blue *and* horned demon (rather than a demon with blue horns), man-shaped, wearing Hastings's clothes and Hastings's body. His black clothes were torn in various places by sharp appendages violating this caricature of a human being, his dress code set at casual feral.

He – probably more accurate to say 'it', but on reflection 'he' sounded more manageable psychologically - sniffed at the two men, particularly their bracelets, and snarled at them. He looked like he'd want nothing more than one of them to take off his bracelet. He had the air of inspecting his food in the market before it was slaughtered and served for dinner.

After he'd finished examining them, he made a disappointed snarl and stepped back, making no aggressive moves. Those trendy New Age bracelet charms - probably 3 for the price of 2 from *Mirror of Galadriel* - sold as fiendship bracelets – evidently worked.

Naturally, I was delighted for the two men. Made up that they were protected from the attentions of the slavering demon. The position was more sub-optimal for Pagoda and me. Pagoda let out another hiss her tail now big enough to be used as a Beefeater's helmet.

There was a lighter blob of colour on the figure's chest.

With a start, I recognized it as a picture of a burning airship on a T-shirt.

The creature was what remained of the missing policeman.

Kieran Hastings.

AKA the 'Bill'.

Literally one of our Boys in Blue.

55

7:00 am
SAM

Hastings had been manipulated and possessed, his being inhabited by a beast from Beyond. His original form had been ripped apart to become a channel for hatred and mayhem. I *really* didn't want to dial 666 and have my collar felt – more likely chewed off along with the rest of my head - by Bill. Demons don't just turn up, they are invited in and provided with a vessel: Hastings.

I was overcome by a mixture of primal fear of the demon and nothing short of hatred of the people who had done this to him, corrupting his life force. He'd been turned into an assassin. Eventually a further price would have to be paid. It remained to be seen by whom.

I shrank back into our temporary lair. I genuinely hoped that Bill had had a cosy and relaxing sleep, and was well rested and happy. I'd even be pleased to offer him toast and marmalade, and a copy of his newspaper of choice, to make his waking up more comfortable. Maybe his favourite slippers, too. No coffee, though, he didn't need caffeine.

The snarling just now had not been Bill politely asking for a couple of soft-boiled eggs with soldiers, unless I suspect they were real soldiers, kit bags and all. Instead, I was concerned that some other serving of a late breakfast would shortly be on what was left of his mind:

Me, with a side order of cat.

I saw that the two men had left Bill to it, and had rapidly retreated towards the entrance of the mound, in silence so that they didn't provoke him. Bill was the guard for the burial mound to stop intruders, no doubt with his heart-juggling trick. Hastings had been consumed by the demon, it looked as if the process had gone too far to be reversible. It would be a matter of trying to get round or through him.

If that couldn't be done, I'd be forced to take up adverse possession of this bijou burial chamber. It was a little draughty, with no cable TV and it did have a desiccated corpse in it, so I thought I'd prefer to give it a miss. That said, it was still quite a lot nicer than some of my early student digs.

His two handlers had evidently decided, for the sake of their sanity, to convince themselves that Bill was a pumped-up drug addict with a really big skin problem and profound anger management issues. That would have worked a lot better for them than any other explanation that they might have nightmared up.

With them gone, there was no way from here that I would be able to get my hands on a protective bracelet. Reasoning with Bill? That would be a no. I needed to come up with something cunning and devious. Shame that my *Ma gic* repertoire didn't run to fireballs and thunderbolts; something more indirect was in order.

A game of pinball.

Bill as the ball, Pagoda and me as the flippers.

Bill was stretching and pacing outside his lair, then he then lurched on the spot from side to side, undecided where to go first with his new-found – partial – freedom, a lethal hound on a very short lead.

An uncomfortable realisation: he was looking around for something interesting to divert him, I could see that he elongated his forearms and hands into long razor-sharp clawed appendages, pretty much flexing them. It made me want to play with him even less.

I intensified my Stealth to stay out of Bill's way and then set to work. There was no time to lose, at any moment he might come calling and scones were off the menu, I didn't want him to be inconvenienced by having to remove bits of Pagoda and me from his nice sharp teeth.

I used Pagoda's Nightsight and assessed the cramped small chamber. There was a cracked brooch and a broken bowl, things to ground the Ward. I pictured its form: the reverse of the spell that the Bill-handlers had used to release him. I knew that that Ward worked on him and trying a different form would be courageous, bordering on suicidal. Tried and trusted here, no room for mistakes.

And then I drew it out twice on the items and activated each of them. I placed the brooch in the side of the opening opposite me and I held the cracked bowl, its inside facing the entrance. I explained my plan to Pagoda. I can't say that she looked thrilled about it, but she could see there weren't many choices in our position. *Needs must when the Demon drives.*

Skulking was not a long or even medium-term option.

We would be lucky if it stretched to short.

I reproduced on the floor in the entrance to the chamber another Ward, ready to be activated when needed. I left it primed for me to trigger when we ended up on his brunch menu. We had to control as far as we could how this played out, unless some unlucky blazers were going to wander into the burial mound and hand their bracelets to Pagoda and me. No, I thought not.

We needed to hunt Bill before he hunted us.

I Sprang down with Pagoda, fixing the position of the side chamber in my mind. I realised that a sense of direction failure here would be costly – I could almost hear Clint the Sat-nav saying 'Turn around when possible, punk. Put your hands on your head. If they're all still attached to your body'.

Then, heart in mouth – hopefully not my heart in Bill's mouth - I created a fiercely orange fluorescent Lantern which I held in front of me like I had a flare at a South American football match. Pagoda gave out a frightened yelp as she realised what I had done.

There was a roar in the distance as Bill detected the change in the light levels and fastened onto the Lantern.

And onto me.

He looked a combination of confused and intrigued for a very, very brief moment.

Why had anyone dared to announce their presence in *his* territory?

But the most important thought that came into his head – rather frighteningly, like my kids at about midnight – was:

Food!

He slithered towards me. I must say it's difficult to slither when you're on two legs,

but he managed it. He was unnervingly
quick over the ground, low down, nearly on
all fours, an expectant growl coming from
his throat. I could see each of his forearms
and hands changing shape again to house
those elongated claws. Freddy Krueger with
extensions.

Pagoda would have been green with envy
about those claws if she hadn't already been
concentrating on ensuring that her tail went
to Def-Con Squirrel. She was forced to make
a call in the game of Fight or Flight.

Well, between *Flight Now* or *Flight Sooner*; I
picked up through our Bond the feline for:
Fight? Are you kidding me?

Flight Sooner won. Claws down.

Bill's fully-formed claws now helped him
to eat up the ground towards me, as I saw,
out of the corner of my eye, Pagoda hurtle
up the wall to the high ground of our burial
chamber.

I wasn't far behind. I Sprang back up to
our chamber and steadied myself on the left

of the entrance, opposite the carefully positioned brooch.

It didn't take long for Bill to arrive.

He hurled himself up into the air, in a long urgent arc, perfectly homing in on me, ready to impale me on those long, tapering, razor sharp claws. Ready to disemheart me, just like he'd done with Walker.

While he was in the air, I felt my heart thumping in my chest as I saw him rushing towards me, and I really wanted it to stay on that side of my skin. And still thumping.

Just as Bill reached rending distance from me, I held my Ward straight out and he faltered in front of it. I twisted my grip and he lurched into the centre of the opening away from me, you could say I had bowled him. He was ripe for Pagoda's move. I'd explained it to her as if she were playing with a dead mouse, and she got it perfectly, flicking the brooch with practised ease at Bill who was pushed back, into the chamber. I activated the floor Ward and he snarled with anger as it crackled into life across the whole of the entrance.

Ker-ching. Flashing lights! High score!

It's unusual to use a Ward to move something rather than act as an obstacle, but it worked here, the old one-two.

I. Am. Very. Pleased. To. Say.

It was nice for Bill to have a change of accommodation, notwithstanding the long-dead body and the cramped un-living space; our chamber probably had a much better view over the stone piazza below. Location, location, location, right?

I could serenade him from below with a thankfully live version of *Sympathy for the Devil* if that might make him feel better. No need for that sort of cruel and unusual punishment: he'd suffered enough. I'm not so sure that he agreed with my estate agency or showmanship. Instead, he hurled himself against the invisible – happily, solid - barrier. He let out a high-pitched scream of pain and anger from the impact. And then he tried again.

He was repelled again.

It hurt him again, but he didn't get through.

As I watched him, I placed my hand on the left side of my chest.

Still thumping.

Still there.

Visitors to the chamber were going to be few and far between with Bill apparently roaming the area looking for an All-the-people-you-can-eat buffet; his growls would be put down to his usual jolly self; and hunger. I scooped up Pagoda and Sprang down.

In celebratory mood, I pulled out a few tasty dried liver treats for Pagoda, the least I could do: what a guy. Given all that Springing, I must confess to having snaffled a few for myself.

I looked up. There was a blue glow
coming from Bill's new digs, which I thought
was a nice touch. I loved what he'd done
with the place. Especially how he had
quickly trashed the remaining contents even
further, for a casual look.

His complaints were still audible, but as
his loreyer I was only required to respond to
complaints within 28 days of receiving them,
after I'd properly considered them and
addressed his concerns as far as I reasonably
could. I promised to get back to him.

He did present a longer-term problem
over and above his tenancy rights in the
chamber; what about his tenancy rights over
Hastings's body and spirit, soul, whatever
you want to call it? We would at least need
to try to rescue Hastings from where his
being had been imprisoned and ravaged,
subverted. It seemed a hopeless task; one to
add to the list.

But Meyra was still a prisoner, and I
needed to make sure they didn't do the same

things to her as they had done to Bill, or worse.

It was time to go further underground.

Into the caves.

56

7:30 am
SAM

I'd worked my way further along into the
burial mound, Bill's muffled growls faded
behind me. Pagoda had followed, sticking
with me rather than chancing what else she
might find down here. I'd found a recently
constructed large arch with a modern tunnel
behind, descending below the surface of the
burial mound. There had been no sign of life
ahead and I'd quietly followed the tunnel,
finding myself in darkness. Motion sensors
had kicked in to keep pace with my walking
speed, lighting up the way ahead.

The main thing that always came to mind
for me when thinking about chalk caves –
which to be fair wasn't very often - was the
uncomfortable thought that they are
inherently crumbly and unstable. In fact, in
this area they're not normally 'caves' at all,
but typically man-made, six or seven feet
square in cross-section, arched for strength
with brickwork judiciously inserted in
relevant places at intervals to shore up the
walls and roof.

I knew stories of Vikings digging holes for
hiding away, keeping their hands in while
waiting for the next bout of raping and
pillaging, druid gatherings underground,
even the Romans getting in on the act. For
the most part it seemed to be a bunch of
inflated legends and other rubbish, much of
it for the tourist crowd.

I knew for a fact that a network of druids
had operated in Southeast England off and
on over the centuries, taking advantage of
places of power, like the brooding presence
of the burial mound above. All of that would
add richness and strength to *Ma gic* castings

in the area, so maybe the druids had been re-inventing themselves here.

The main reason for many 'caves' like this had nothing to do with *Ma gic*, it was a much more prosaic: mining for chalk and flint, fighting with the walls to dig it out metre by metre in semi-darkness, to be dragged to the surface in carts, later horses, even maybe a small train as the technology evolved. The tunnel in which I found myself burrowed into the hillside and quickly turned from new to worn, looking like a connection had been dug between these caves and the burial mound; a strange bridge built across centuries and civilisations.

The walls were rough-hewn, the surface giving the illusion of it having gently oozed out of the walls and ceiling and then crystallised. The floor had been smoothed out as far as possible, allowing easy passage. There would be miles of caves, chipped out of the rock in a bewilderingly tight pattern of opportunistic digging. Small chambers and large chambers, all connected by a labyrinth of passages. There were chalk workings all

over this part of the country, dating back
hundreds, sometimes thousands, of years.

I remembered stories about chalk and flint
mines like this, which had had indoor
gardens built into them by eccentric owners,
and train tracks to move the mined materials
to the surface. The networks of caves had
vertical shafts connected into them and
corkscrew shaped pits. One of the mine
systems nearby had been used as an air raid
shelter, and as a place to store explosives
during the Second World War. Not at the
same time.

The walkway ahead sloped down. I
noticed some rubber matting on the floor to
help with grip. I could see scuffed tracks of
gurney wheels on some of the matting. I
reached a crossroads, now bathed in soft
continuous lighting and revealing three
tunnels snaking further into the hill.

There were gurney tracks in the chalk dust
turning to the right. The ground continued
to slope down. This part of the shaft had
been here for a *long* time.

The shaft to the left, led in the direction of the hillside, ending quickly in untidy - and a frankly rather worrying - pile of chalk and stone. There had been a recent roof collapse, perhaps caused by the mining work.

The right-hand tunnel had been heavily worked on for stability. I ventured with Pagoda further down and the passageway turned right again. With no map and the eerie dimness, punctuated by more motion sensor lights, it was hard to keep track of where I was. I saw that several holes in the walls – other tunnels – had been filled in and the surface of the rock and the floor had been made good to allow easy passage through the tunnel.

The corridor continued to slope downwards.

There was a bright smear of harsh white light ahead, and I could see a junction of tunnels, one carrying on ahead and to the right. The right-hand fork would come out directly under the burial mound; I had no idea where the other tunnel went. I was starting to feel like I was in the middle of a game of Mornington Crescent, but with fewer rules.

I heard noises ahead, and she was so jumpy that I *heard* Pagoda's hackles rise.

I crouched down and Listened, trying to soak in as much sound in as much detail as possible from my immediate area in the complex. The Hex didn't carry very far, but I caught the sound of three heartbeats beyond the junction, straight ahead. One of them was slow and regular, the others strong and fast, stressed. All stationary, close to each other.

There was distant murmuring from the right-hand tunnel, too far away to identify, like the rumble of waves at the beach; no sounds from behind me.

I concentrated on voices that matched the heartbeats – two voices that mapped onto the rapid pulses. I quickly recognized the man I had come to know as Reynolds; and his companion in the burial mound. That gave me hope about the third heartbeat.

Meyra.

'What is wrong with her?' said Reynolds. 'We can't finish her sphere until we've found out what she knows. And he'll go ballistic with us. I'm worried. Maybe we ought to have said something to him sooner.'

Sphere?

'You've always been a glory hound,' the other man replied. 'We've bitten off more than we can chew here. I reckon we need help from the tech bods,' he said, sounding annoyed. 'She should have come off the juice by now and be ready to talk. No-one's ever resisted before as long as this.'

The interrogation didn't sound like it had been going too well. As I'd suspected, they had drugged her, but she seemed to have found a way to combat its effects, probably her better resilience. I crept past the junction with the corridor in which I'd heard the murmuring – that would have to wait. I homed in on the voices ahead.

Homed in on Meyra.

I reached a small chamber. Empty. The voices had been coming from the left. Pagoda scurried and showed me a sparsely furnished side chamber cut out of the left wall of the tunnel, three people, not much else. The people had my attention.

Reynolds, in his Walker body; the other guy from the burial chamber, both in silver robes with the cowls pulled back, still reassuringly creepy. And Meyra, tied to a chair, her closed eyes racing to escape from the confines of her eye sockets, in her own little world, oblivious to the men who stood over her trying to figure out their Plan K for her, Plan A was a distant memory.

I decided on a direct approach.

I reached into my pockets for a boiled sweet, and for my knuckleduster which I slipped onto my hand which was proving to be very handy indeed.

I wasn't going to use my knuckleduster as a door-knocker. And the sweet wasn't to calm my nerves. It fell under my direct approach.

57

7:45 am
SAM

I took a long and steady breath, let it out slowly and strode into the chamber. I nodded curtly to the two men as they heard my footsteps and turned their heads towards me. I had gone for a managerial, officer-on-the-deck look, startling them and making them feel guilty at the same time; it could only have worked better if I'd been carrying a clipboard.

Reynolds' eyes flickered with uncertainty; the other man reacted more quickly.

Him first, then.

I flipped my sweet into the air - I like to think of this as my hard-boiled investigator style.

I aimed it at him and made a low but intense roaring sound as I threw my hand out violently and fired the boiled sweet at him. I'd discovered over the years that this particular brand of boiled sweets - apart from having a syrupy and slightly nutty caramel flavour - worked very well as the equivalent of a baton round.

A real gobstopper, .45 calibre.

The sweet smashed into his chest - Hydrostatic choc! – and it explosively released its stored energy into him, inelegantly lifting him off his feet and dumping him on the floor, motionless, his eyes rolled up in his head.

I noted this as further proof that too much sugar has always been bad for your health.

I Sprang forward, cat-like and crashed a heavy blow to the side of Reynolds's head with the knuckleduster before he could react; he went down, pole-axed. It felt odd hitting someone who looked like one of my colleagues, but then again we all feel like doing that at work sometimes, right?

I purred with satisfaction and licked my fist. I started to bat at the two prone forms on the floor, getting ready to edge them round the floor with my feet, sidle off a little and then rush back and pounce on them again.

Then I pulled myself together. Embarrassed, even though no-one apart from Pagoda had been watching (which was plenty), I bound them with plastic cable tags from the table next to Meyra's inert form. Her eyes hurtled around beneath her eyelids in her swollen face, her random eye movements showing no signs of slowing down.

I cut the tags that had been used to restrain her, and I arranged her as best I could on the seat, checking out her aura as I did so, which showed that she had retreated into her Mind Fortress to protect herself.

I secured the room. I noted that there was a table scattered with bottles and syringes, and a smashed bottle in the corner, perhaps from a struggle but more likely hurled there in a display of frustrated anger from one of them, thwarted by Meyra. They hadn't needed to feel bad about that: I'd been annoyed and confused by Meyra ever since I'd met her.

I was disappointed that there were no CCTV screens, but I could only begin to imagine the IT difficulties in tunnels and caves like this. The Circle's IT department had spasms when any of us tried to set up a conference call with three or more people. On the positive side, it would have been difficult to pick up 'funny' cat videos down here.

Pagoda caught a whiff of my thought through the Bond and looked haughty, disapproving on principle. She's made it abundantly clear about her position on cat-related amusements, such as an absolute ban on novelty antlers being bought for her at Christmas. She graciously indicated her flexibility on the antlers issue when it came to other cats. With all those positive thoughts banked, I persuaded Pagoda to guard the entrance while I attended to Meyra's release from her Mind Fortress.

The rooms in a Mind Fortress are a complex representation of someone's memories, dreams and thoughts, built up into a complicated artificial world in which the creator could maintain and recall memories, but also do a whole lot more. It provides a fascinating evolving snapshot of the individual's self–image, core values and drives, albeit depicted for outsiders looking in, or visitors, in the subject's typically highly personal and stylised way. The technique had allowed Meyra to create special safe areas in the fabric of her Mind Fortress to protect herself, in case her defences were breached.

Effectively, Meyra had mentally boarded herself up in her Mind Fortress and hidden the contents of her mind from outside persecution and danger: Reynolds and his sidekick. Torturing her or threatening her while she was there would have meant nothing to her; it would not even have registered with her as happening.

She had removed herself from the normal world while she was in danger of providing her enemies with crucial information. That had been in the knowledge of the obvious drawback of a Mind Fortress, that the caster is effectively dormant, helpless, unable to defend themselves in the physical world. Normally, it would only be used in a place of comfort and security for meditation and contemplation, here she had used it as a fortress.

It looked like she had taken it too far. The Mind Fortress was still active even though the danger was for the moment gone. I hoped she didn't regard me a a danger. That would have made retrieving her much harder.

I carefully checked the bonds holding Reynolds and his side-kick, and then I settled myself as comfortably as I could in the small chamber and fell into a self-

induced trance. Then I did the *Ma gic*
equivalent of knocking on the Mind Fortress
door leading into Meyra's mind. Given that
this was Meyra, I needed to use the
tradesmen's entrance, but at least there was
an entrance.

I found myself in a cobbled street with
quaint, delightful boutique shops, squat
Victorian establishments lined with
unknowable treasures. The shadows were
starting to creep up the buildings, oddly on
both sides, and the sky was heavy with deep
purple clouds and flashes of livid lightning.
There was a continuous rumble of angry
thunder. The climate perfectly matched
Meyra's situation, and most likely her mood.

I turned down an alleyway, past a
bookshop filled with books covered in
rainbow hues. I saw shoals of dis-embodied
eyes looking through some of the windows,
watching me impassively. Periodically, I
caught a glimpse of a shadowy form to
which the eyes belonged, sometimes more
than one pair.

My journey took me through castle gates, across a moat teeming with scarlet crocodiles. Then I arrived at a junction with thirteen roads. I knew from experience that all but one of them would to an eventual dead-end after a long and difficult, and hazardous, journey.

I instinctively knew which road to take.

It led to the entrance to a clearing in a thick forest, towering oak trees looming over me as I approached, their branches intertwining in my path, whispering at me asking why I was here, combining Wards to push me away. I fought my way through the branches, found myself in the clearing. At its centre, her safest place in her Mind Fortress, the place that I knew of but had never discussed with her. Ever.

Her *My Little Unicorn* spot, with attendant sparkles of bejewelled heaps. The site, if needed, of her last stand.

I moved further in. Meyra was surrounded by white, pink, lilac and purple unicorns of various sizes.

I had hitherto been rather dismissive of unicorns, particularly cake icing-coloured ones. However, my mind was appropriately changed by these unicorns all being armed with extremely pointy horns. The horns reminded me too much for comfort of elongated drill-bits. So, yes they were pretty colours, but they were also easily able to punch through walls. I decided that in due course, when this was over, I would revisit the dragons that I'd created for my Mind Fortress to see whether they were quite as hard-looking as these. I might need to re-do them in rosy pink.

Meyra was sitting on a sumptuous padded pink and white throne, legs curled up beneath her, wearing a soft pink onesie and a dazzling diamond tiara in her dark hair.

Dressed to kill.

Well, dressed to kill intruders.

She looked at me carefully and sent one of her unicorns over to sniff at me. It was a fetching candy pink creature, with eyes that

were pools of solid black. The unicorn
breathed in heavily over me, whinnied and
then tossed its head back dismissively.

'Hello Sam Franklin,' she said. 'I am
pleased it is you. If it had been anyone else, I
find that disembowelment spoils the
ambience in this place.'

'I see you've had the decorators in since I
was last here. I love what you've done with
the place. I looked around me. 'It worked!
They were so confused why they hadn't
broken you down that they were just about
to send for some people to come in and
winkle you out.'

'If they had done so, Spiker and Sabre
would have been ready,' said Meyra,
stroking the mane of one of the fearsome
beasts. Little sparkling stars came off its back
in rhythm with the stroking. Sweet. Those
stars looked like they could shred milled
steel.

She smiled at the sparkly unicorn and its
neighbour. Spiker. Sabre. Fair enough, I
conceded that names like Puffle and Binky

really wouldn't have suited them. They pawed at the ground modestly; their horns pointed in unison at the direct centre of my head.

'Twinkle Bunny, too', she said, glancing across at the candy pink unicorn.

Twinkle Bunny was foaming at the mouth with annoyance, and no small amount of frustration. Its name did not quite live up to its homicidal air. Maybe Stiletto? Sabrehorn? Stabbie McStab-Face?

Whatever its name, Twinkle Bunny *really* wanted to make a Sam shish-kebab.

I put to one side for the time being the knowledge that this candy pink stabbing machine was a part of – hopefully, as far as I was concerned, a small part of - Meyra's psyche. Maybe another team building weekend would be needed soon?

I said to her, eyeing the unicorns cautiously in case they wanted to turn me into a unicorn's equivalent of a glove puppet: 'The Palace has done more than enough. We need to get out of here, Your Majesty.' Meyra looked pleased at the use of the honorific in her Kingdom. 'We have work to do, I'm afraid.'

She nodded. 'You first, I think, Sam Franklin' she said. 'I need to lock up and set the guards free.' She blew fond kisses to the unicorns.

With a short wave – my ruby slippers were in for repairs – I returned to myself.

58

9:00 am
SAM

I was disorientated. A normal and predictable reaction to visiting someone else's head. Especially when it'd been infested with homicidal unicorns. Granted, the use of the word *normal* was a stretch. I gently shook my head to clear it, making quite sure that there were no residual pointy unicorn horns inside to pierce it.

Meyra was starting to emerge from her self. It would take several minutes for her to sort herself out and I tactfully left her to it. Pagoda intently watched me to make sure that I'd come back and not brought anything nightmarish with me.

Meyra's eyes, particularly her pupils, had returned to normal, and she was coming out of her trance. She looked rough, but if I put it that way she would have turned Twinkle Bunny on me in my sleep.

Instead: 'Do you want to stay here and guard these guys while Pagoda and I look around?' Pagoda's face swivelled towards me indicating that she would be more than happy to stay behind and guard Meyra.

'I believe you must be jesting with me.' Meyra said in a quiet voice. I took that as a no; Pagoda looked disappointed.

I turned to the two men tied up on the floor. The one with the sugar overdose in his chest should be out for hours yet. I eyed up both. Luckily, their clothes sizes were not far off those for Meyra and me. I thought that, with my height, I might well carry off a robe rather dashingly.

As a starting point, Meyra and I quickly changed our clothes with the two men so that we could blend in. They were still wearing their bracelets, which I took, in case Bill got loose or he had a few like-minded friends. I checked; they were working. We each found in a pocket a neck chain of beads in a pouch which we slipped on.

I looked over the various bottles on the table and saw they were more designed to keep a subject conscious and in pain rather than anything else; truth serums belong in spy novels.

We took our time and finished up with the unconscious men, the final touches taking a bit longer than just trading clothes. Pagoda looked on impassively, she knew we were our usual lovable selves in spite of what her eyes told her. Cats *know* the guiding mind behind feeding them.

The three of us left the chamber and went slowly to the entrance of the other section of tunnel. No more sounds at that moment. We edged along it cautiously.

We had Snakeskinned into the bodies of
Reynolds (in Walker's body) and his
colleague, me taking over Walker's body
from Reynolds, Meyra kitted out with the
bodyshell of the other one, the one who'd
tortured her. Her disgust was evident: he
was way bulkier than her, and taller; more
tattoos. I imagined he wouldn't get it back in
perfect nick when we reversed the
Snakeskin; knowing Meyra, she'd decorate it
with a few dings as payback. In the
meantime, she wore it with her very own air
of disdainful elegance, not a look the owner
would've been known for. She'd need to
tone that down when we mingled with
anyone else down here. I'd bet a lot of
money that they'd be confused if he started
delicately sipping some Chardonnay.

Our hostile takeovers had been made easy,
they'd both been unconscious, unresisting,
but it had been far too weird for comfort my
getting into Walker's bodyshell and kicking
Reynolds out, like invading a tomb; nobody
home. The echoes of Walker's dead form
must have been playing hell with Reynolds's
sanity - I needed not to dwell there any

longer than could be helped, to avoid lasting damage from the echoes.

Now I was getting acquainted with my new Reynolds/Walker bodyshell, like wearing in new trainers (or, in Meyra's case, Jimmy Choo pumps). Granted, my face itched, and my left elbow felt a bit stiff, but overall my compliments to Walker for having kept himself in good condition for his age, putting to one side of course his having died with his chest ripped open (that must have really freaked out Reynolds). I glossed over that bit, the warts-and-all bit of a Snakeskin is a bit of a nightmare, infinitely magnified by the Snakeskin target's body being a corpse. Until I came along, Reynolds had been inhabiting Walker's bodyshell. I couldn't help thinking that I was wearing Walker's bodyshell better than either of them; comfortable in my newly adopted skin.

The downward slope ran out after one hundred and fifty metres and the wall ahead fell away into a huge regular cuboid pit which had been sculpted by *Ma gic* out of the rock in one smooth Dig Hex, not clawed and wrestled out by anything as uncouth as a tool. We were eight or nine metres below the roof, twenty metres above the floor, standing on a gallery section that wrapped around the whole of the pit. A thin metal chain acted as a barrier, held up by thin rock pillars dragged upwards and twisted out of the floor.

We were at the mid-point on one of the long sides as I looked down at the huge volume of disembowelled interior, heightening my sense of the sheer weight of rock poised above it. And above us.

Meyra's eyes were wide. She didn't suffer from claustrophobia, but she did have her people's deep yearning for leafy glades and burbling streams rather than cavernous underground holes stashed away in the middle of a hillside. That sort of thing should be left to dwarves and nomes. They were more designed for that sort of thing, the roof taking longer to reach them when it fell in on their heads. Pagoda's response was simply to keep her tail at times-two for the moment, pending further developments, still hoping to find the extremely big mouse that lived down these tunnels.

The area was so busy that I was confused where to look first. My eye was drawn to the imposing central silver column, but first I looked around the gallery to identify immediate threats, on the basis that there were plenty of imminent and longer term threats to hand below.

To our left was a brightly lit alcove cut into the side wall of the gallery. Cold lights glared on metal and reflective white plastic equipment of some kind. And the light also reflected from part of its floor. Strange. The alcove marked the start of a gentle spiral walkway down from the gallery to the floor of the pit. Opposite us were living quarters for around twenty people, crude but serviceable, built into the wall, presently empty.

Two threats walked out of the alcove: the two bodyguards from earlier. Alert, instinctively hunting for danger, escorting the two green-clad medics with their unconscious burden. We were hidden from them and intended to stay that way until we could see what they were up to.

They all reached floor level at a controlled, sedate pace, passing a cluster of three-metre diameter spheres which to my horror seemed to contain floating human beings which were tethered to the ground. They skirted the two-metre diameter central silver column in the centre that dominated the huge cavern below our galleried perch, surrounded by milling sinister figures in hooded silver robes, all watching the procession from under their raised cowls.

The group reached what looked like an occult play set complete with twin marble slabs set a few metres apart surrounded by a sea of lit creamy candles, and a Deranged Hooded Action Figure ™ . The guy from the helicopter: although dressed the same as the others, he was instantly recognisable as the one in charge. Something nagging me about him.

One of the medics applied the brake. The gurney stopped by the right-hand slab; both had human shaped indentations. The medics leaned forward. End of the line.

I said to Meyra in a low voice: 'Passenger announcement: This is Goth Central. This service terminates here.'

'If we are not careful here, Sam Franklin, so will we'.

59

9:30 am
SAM

The leader placed his hand on
Shevchenko's chest as he had at the helipad,
nodded and gestured to the medics to move
her onto the slab. They struggled with the
body but eventually managed to manoeuvre
it into the depression; the bodyguards didn't
help, they were too busy looking around for
trouble. The leader gestured to them in a
way that seemed to convey that all was well.
They looked around them, glanced at their
boss's body and withdrew across the floor of
the pit, to leave these weird doctor-types to

work on her. A successful outcome was not negotiable.

They took up station at the bottom of the spiral walkway, maintaining admirable spring-loaded attention.

My eyes were inexorably drawn away from them, back to the cool beauty of the column. At the foot and at the top, the smoothness of the column gave way to tendrils of metal that burrowed into the floor like ancient roots and grasped upwards to the burial mound like a glittering corpse breaking free of hallowed ground. Was this the *Tree of Life* from the scrap of paper in Walker's room? And was it giving or taking?

From its position, the column would come from below to meet the circular centre of the sacrificial stone circle in the burial mound above all of us. That wasn't terribly comforting in the light of the sacrifice thing. It could meet something more terrifying below. The connection between this chamber and the ancient burial mound hinted not very subtly at an enormous reserve of *Ma gic* potential having pooled in this place.

Dizzying. I tore my gaze away, saw that Meyra had done the same; I nudged Pagoda, who had also been captivated until I broke the spell, 'What are you, a cat or a magpie?'

The column was the main support for the pit, in a very practical sense its centre of gravity. It glistened in the industrial floodlights that studded the cathedral-like ceiling, so much more than just an RSJ with ideas above its station. There was something dormant and patient about it. Alive. Fluid.

Unnatural.

Overall, the pit made me think of what you would end up with if you went to your local homeware superstore and bought a deluxe flat-packed Abomination Castle (with Monster) kit. It would need a catchy Scandi name, maybe *Mönst,* packaged in red and black not blue and yellow. It would combine easy-clean paint (splatter-proof, to help clear up the blood); easy self-assembly by a minimum of two henchmen (for safety reasons); fire resistant against all but the hottest torches carried by vengeful villagers.

Absolutely essential to buy and build on a rainy public holiday in Transylvania. As for the Monster, at the end of the exercise you would *know*, with a sense of ineffable dread, that you'd find an unexpected extra hand or spleen, just when you thought you'd finished putting it together and were looking forward to a celebratory cold beer.

I looked up at the floods and back down at Meyra, 'I think there's a light over at the Frankenstein place,' I said. 'Don't get me wrong, I love *Rocky Horror*, I just don't want to be a cast member.'

60

9:45 am
SAM

No-one was on the gallery level after Shevchenko's descent. Everyone seemed to be downstairs for a cheeky Satanic ritual.

The robed figures started to arrange themselves in a circle, congregating in a tight and precise formation around the base of the silvery column. There were obvious sphere-sized gaps at each of the Cardinal points of the compass and two spaces between each of those points for a congregant. There were six of them, wearing silver robes, the same as ours, with beads around their collars. Two missing…I looked pointedly at Meyra; this could get awkward.

The bodyguards had settled themselves into a comfortable pose for a long vigil, potentially punctuated by excessive violence: a difficult balance to strike. They looked more at home with the violent part. They displayed no interest in the floating bodies in the spheres; they usually used a river for their waste disposal.

I examined the spheres. There were seven of them, held in thin netting and tethered to the ground by short thin cords. The arrangement made me think of a baby Hydra having been given its first pack of bubble-gum. Charming.

The spheres bounced gently against each other and the orientation of the figures changed as they moved, arms and legs gently resting at their sides one moment and then, in slow motion, flailing out at random the next, and then back. Pagoda followed my gaze and sat fascinated. She hissed when she saw one of the occupants: Karnage, in his blue uniform. Now that I had the opportunity to take notice of the occupants, with one exception they amounted to a collection of human jigsaw pieces from my time down in Brighton. Apart from Karnage, there were his two companions, and this was the tantalising new internal posting to change the direction of their careers with Haven. It seemed unlikely to have much in the way of long-term prospects.

Although I had never met him, I recognised Asim Hussain from the file of pictures in the shop. No signs of damage. Yet.

And Olivia Walker: not how I had envisaged meeting her or wanting to meet her. Her arms were outstretched, gently drifting, as if she were relaxing at the spa. She looked peaceful and calm, vacant.

There was another woman, currently upside down, clearly young. She had long mousey-coloured hair that was not tied up and swirled lazily with her movements. I remembered her face from the files, one of the yellows: Becky Carpenter. *FAST TRACK* to what?

Finally - in all senses - there was a black sphere set slightly apart from the rest, forbidding and desolate. Despite the darkness, I was able to see into the interior: a man. I didn't recognise his face, but I could see his flurry of golden hair. *I realize you want your gorgeous golden locks back as soon as you can get your face on them, but that sort of stuff's why we all get paid so much here.*

It was Reynolds's bodyshell. Walker's body holding Reynolds' bodyshell, Walker's bottomless dead eyes staring blankly out, merely being used as a place to store Reynolds' bodyshell until the hooded figure got round to transferring it back. Walker's form was playing the role of a mannequin as a final insult.

I had heard the yearning in Reynolds' voice to have his own face and body back. *It'll get fixed when the woman's been sorted out.*

Reynolds would need to keep up, I thought, with a tight smile, like in a game of Find the Lady.

The auras of the people in the spheres, apart from Walker/Reynolds, were stable, peaceful even. The reason for the blackened sphere around Walker was straightforward: Walker was dead; there was no aura to display. Just unbroken emptiness. As peaceful as it gets.

Each of the two slabs had been set at a level high enough for an average-to-tall person to lean over it comfortably. In the circumstances, I was relieved to see they were not set at a comfortable height for a buffet.

A metal table stood between the two slabs, holding what appeared to be a collection of shiny instruments and tools, as well as candles – no doubt scented with *eau d'emonic*. Next to the table, at the head of each slab, was a tall lectern on which a skinny book was propped. When I say it was skinny, I don't mean that it was thin. In fact, it had a lot of pages.

The cover was made out of skin, probably Caucasian. Skinny. It was open, preferably not at dish of the day. A bank of three enormous flat screens, currently nearly as black as Walker's eyes, loomed over the slab, one each and a central screen behind the lectern, maybe for Boris Karloff movie nights on pay-per-view.

Natasha Shevchenko was clearly the headline participant, with space for another human being on the other slab. Pagoda indicated with a swish of her tail that she was absolutely fine with that, comforting herself with the thought that neither of the slabs was cat-shaped.

If not some sort of operating theatre, then a spa retreat for the Addams Family.

61

10:00 am
SAM

The three men and the painfully young woman drifted in the centre of their spheres, their heads, arms and legs roaming in random directions like drunkards in a space station, their faces empty of expression, not waiting but passively accepting time passing until whatever happened.

Below us, near the foot of the spiral slope, the two dark-suited bodyguards kept their positions, watching. Their attention was fixed on the dying Russian woman at the far end.

Their peripheral vision took in the other
two occupied spheres bobbing near them,
the activity around the central column, and
the motionless Olivia Walker on the other
slab. No sign of tension in their shoulders,
everything appeared under control; no need
to do anything for now. Just waiting.

Patient, but ready.

The leader stood at a control panel
between the two slabs. He stabbed a button.
Even in that simple action, he exuded a sense
that the world needed to be slashed through
not lived in. The lights dimmed at his touch.

Three large flatscreens behind him
snapped into life, one moment lifeless black
monoliths, the next a triptych of Modern Art:
digital doppelgangers of the inert women
that seemed to hover in the low light, their
bodies picked out on the screens in intricate,
shifting 3-D blue tracery. The right-hand one
was disfigured by ugly blotches of crimson
and thick smears of inky black. Natasha
Shevchenko.

The images flanked the central flatscreen, displaying a good old-fashioned blue neon Portent of Doom: a timer, counting down, imprinted on flashing subliminal images of an old man trailing a broom, a hunter, a sly individual wearing a plumed hat, a warrior figure wielding twin sickles, an angel in white robes, a mighty figure wielding lightning a woman draped in jewels and beads, and a stunningly, impossibly beautiful female, all interlocking and breaking apart and implanting their power. Pagoda's huge eyes were like full solar eclipses; they reflected the changing numbers as they steadily decreased to zero at Noon; at least not Midnight, a refreshing challenge to convention. Noon came quicker: time is money; no need to pay any overtime.

The leader raised his hands and the sound of African drums boomed around the caver, circling and enmeshing the chanting, making a single throbbing sound.

The leader intoned in a voice that melted into the drums and the chant as the chorus writhed in anticipation, all in time with the ancient rhythms:

'Babalu-Aye, Oh Lord of Healing, Lord
Ọbalúayé, Wise and conquering One, Your
Worshipfulness Erinle, Your medical
wisdom we need and implore, Lord Esu,
Your Tricks and Wit are our Guide, Lord
Kokou teach us your Warrior ways, Obatala,
help us to create human bodies in your
divine image, Lord Shango put your trust
and lightning in us, Lady Aje share your
bounteous wisdom and wealth, and Mistress
Oya, let us know the secrets of your *Ma gic*,
we beseech you.'

The leader motioned to his entranced
entourage, like a king cobra conducting at
the Royal Albert Hall. They responded
immediately. I am horrified to say that we
responded immediately, just far enough
away to escape the strangling power of the
combination of beat and words and song.
The circle of acolytes and spheres tightened;
the intensity and volume increased. I could
smell its dark ululations, feel the texture of
its cloying taste, hear the jangling of harsh
colours, even from where we were. The
images behind the countdown flickered and
became one.

The "Casa" of Life on the list, merging with the "Tree of Life" - the silver column - now made sense, this was a Santeria house temple built in the cult's image, the chaotic and unstructured religion of Cuban Santeria: the power of Orishas - African Saints - weaving *Ma gic* below the rolling South Downs.

02:12:00 to go.

The leader moved out from behind the console, headed for the closest of the four spheres. His silver robe swirled around his ankles as he walked. When he reached the sphere, he stopped, stiffened, like Arctic water forming a spiked shard over an ice cliff. Ready to impale. He placed his palm on the sphere – I was surprised it didn't burst - and closed his eyes. An image of his handprint appeared on the other three.

Sympathetic *Ma gic;* no trace of sympathy.

It was a signal, a call for even louder and more intense chanting. Faster, booming. Echoing. Deeper drumming. An intense

436

crackling of *Ma gic*, stronger than any I'd ever felt. The walls pulsed, almost breathing. With elaborate hand movements, the leader shredded the air in front of him. The four tethered spheres began to glow, matching the central column.

He glowed; the acolytes glowed. Our beads were now glowing, reached by the power of the Incantation so that the three of us glowed.

The hairs all over my borrowed body stood to crisp attention; all the fur on Pagoda's body was upright as if she'd been rubbed vigorously with a large balloon; even Meyra looked uncomfortable in the thug's bodyshell, as if she'd found a typo in one of his tattoos. Excitement and longing licked over me. Stronger than before, inviting me to scream for inclusion in the circle.

Pagoda made low mewling noises in time with the chanting; disconcertingly, so did I. Briefly. Until I reined myself in: our Bond has a lot to answer for sometimes. Meyra's cheeks flirted with a hint of colour, battling her iron control.

Below us, there was a pause, stillness, unseen figures saying grace before a feast.

The leader swept a hand up, then straight down.

Energy burst out of the four occupants of the spheres in searing lines of intense white light. They tore into the column, weaved patterns on my retinas. The leader fought to control the flow, sweat popping out on his face, his hair bristling like a hedgehog in the dew.

I did not want him to succeed in controlling the surge.

I wanted it to bathe us, *feed* us: without delay; without limit.

Pagoda's body shook, going through the same struggle: I felt her strain as she resisted. And she felt mine. Meyra was also under pressure, although to anyone else she could have been ordering afternoon tea at Claridge's.

The four diminishing victims leaked in agonising torrents, their expressions no longer peaceful, their faces grey and distorted. The three heavies had chosen their paths, Vanessa Grant had simply asked for help; none of them deserved this. The acolytes' chanting became feverish, delirious. One whirled and danced, overcome; her eyes like upturned bone china saucers, white and fragile. She swayed and stumbled, arms outstretched. The light skewered her body, held it as if she had been nailed to a church door. Her essence joined the stream flowing into the column. The other acolytes were oblivious of her fate, nestled in their luminous introspection.

The beams. Blinked. And were gone. The four spheres were like black holes wolfing colour from their surroundings; they started to implode; the five bodies slithered in stages to the floor, extinguished. No more chanting.

Silence.

The column shone and glistened, turbulent.

The leader strode back to the control panel. The surviving acolytes turned as one towards him. They stood transfixed.

He reached up and folded back his hood. The piercing glare; that spiky beard. Sparkling eyes under circles of white face paint around each eye, drawn down over the centre of his nose and connected around his mouth, seeping into his beard, the rest of his face smooth and tanned. No doubt who it was.

Gideon Winterbourne.

It made me momentarily nostalgic. It was like a Scooby Doo villain reveal: *It's Mr Roger Stevens, the TV station chief!*

A good thing Meyra and I didn't have our real faces on.

Such a concentration of power must have shone like a star for Gideon Winterbourne and, when the opportunity had come, he would have seized it with both hands. That level of temptation had tipped him over the edge. He had suborned his "Special Projects" department; the other Circle people here were blindly following his orders or had been corrupted by the temptation of virtually limitless money.

I didn't believe for a moment that Gideon Winterbourne was only in it for the money. He was basking in the pomp and the theatricality. He was in his element, a shame that the element was polonium.

All those years. All that aggravation. And now all channelled into this: I thought that at the very least we'd need to re-draft the Special Projects compliance manual. This all went well beyond his scope of work.

No wonder the sly bastard had wanted the Endymion Walker case closed quickly. He would have been incandescent about Walker having nosed around and then fallen foul of Bill.

It was obvious that I would be put on the case. I was even more delighted that I hadn't answered his emails or calls. That would have driven him - more - crazy than he looked now.

It was all about the power that he could grasp, hold and wield. He was top dog here, rather than being merely one more Director at the Magic Circle. He would be glorying in his ability to throw his weight around at his disciples, having always been a bully. Just ask Hilary the Goblin about it, from all those years before.

He addressed them directly, ignoring the five withered bodies. 'Take your assigned places. It is nearly time,' he said, pointing at the central screen. 'The Procedure is on schedule. I expect it to remain so. There is no room for error.'

The countdown would reach Midnight in: **02:10:50**.

How time flies when you're witnessing heinous dark *Ma gic*.

The four spheres had deflated like popped bubble-gum. Two acolytes acting as macabre rag-and-bone men collected a gurney and wheeled it around the circle. They gathered up the remains, stacking the husks of the victims onto the gurney in a muddled, sticky heap, ready for removal and disposal.

I stared at the draped folds of flesh, mere storage jars emptied into the column. And I had done nothing. I would need to come to terms with that. Later.

'I didn't appreciate the *son et lumiere*,' I said.

Glancing at the blonde woman on the slab, Meyra's forehead betrayed a slight crease. Even while she was wearing the thug's body, her self-control was amazing, 'Nor me, Sam Franklin. I found it vulgar,' said Meyra, 'Whatever is planned bodes ill for Olivia Walker.'

'Couldn't bode iller.'

Pagoda played it cool, I sensed that she was mainly relieved that the marble slabs weren't cat-shaped.

62

02:09:41
SAM

Pagoda was at the top of the spiral slope already looking bored: I told her to stay there, not move and act as a look-out. Perfect jobs for a cat.

Meyra and I were just two guys going about their normal business, nothing to see here. We drew up our hoods, walked around the gallery to the alcove opposite the walkway. I couldn't help glancing into the alcove, especially at the odd reflection from the floor. What I saw horrified me.

A section of the floor was covered over with glass, I was able to look down into a large chamber below it, at the pit's ground level. And in it was a nightmare, like a macabre ball-pit for ogre children. Row upon row of the same type of spheres that were at the bottom of the walkway. Dozens. Held under pale blue light, like a night-light, each one filled with a human being, all shapes and sizes, all completely still as if they were waiting to be awoken and join in the activities in the main pit.

No doors, as if the spheres were drawn through the wall into the pit when needed. At the front was a familiar red-haired woman. Vanessa Grant. Brighton's homeless. Off the books.

Nothing we could do now for her or the others. Meyra said nothing. With what felt like a Herculean effort, I turned and both of us walked down the spiral slope. Meyra moved in the other thug's Jumped bodyshell with unhurried ease; I was still getting used to the new me. I perked up at the thought that, when Reynolds woke up, he was in danger of losing track of which body he was

445

supposed to be in. Walker was proving to be more socially active dead than when he was alive.

Pagoda, Meyra and I would use our covers provided by the borrowed bodyshells to somehow delay or stop the "Procedure", whatever that was, and save Olivia Walker from whatever was planned for her. We needed to avoid sharing the fate of the incompetent employees and the victims harvested from the Haven. I didn't want to become an energy source.

For such an exacting series of objectives, we'd have to follow standard Circle protocols in this type of situation: we needed to make it up as we went along.

We reached the bottom of the slope, skirted two spheres, one holding Reynolds's bodyshell, the other holding Asim Hussain. The bodyguards looked on showing total disinterest in us as we passed, about the same amount as for the assorted human debris scattered over the gurney parked next to them. Their only interest was Shevchenko,

and anything that might endanger
Shevchenko. Nothing else.

The single concession from one of them
was a brief nod of acknowledgment in our
direction, conveying something like *I will
probably not shoot you. I am keeping my options
open.*

The first up-close test: nailed it. We had
passed muster as Walker-faced Reynolds
and his tattooed mate.

We were in.

63

02:05:12
SAM

As we approached the mass of acolytes, Winterbourne was speaking to two of them close by.

We circled warily around him.

All of the acolytes had pulled back their cowls and were in animated post-murder clusters of excited chatter. They seemed a mixture of serious and exhausted, and – disturbingly - elated.

Probably a tinge of relief as well: no more power sources seemed to be needed for now, especially after the impromptu top-up from their drained colleague. The atmosphere made me think of a wake with cocktails, punctuated by darting glances towards the coffin to satisfy themselves that there was no room in it for other occupants.

A sharp-nosed acolyte waved to me, 'Hi Reynolds, glad you could join the party.' I gave him a non-committal smile; he nodded to Meyra and she returned his greeting. Not a flicker of concern on the man's face. Around us, Meyra and I recognised Latham and Singh from Winterbourne's Special Projects Group at the Circle. And others. Crafty bastard. He'd used the Circle as a recruiting centre. The Special Projects Group had always thought they were, well, special, egged on by Winterbourne. Now they were trying to live up to that billing.

Meyra and I joined the small group with Latham, close to Olivia's slab. Winterbourne was standing over the other body, the sheet pulled back from her ravaged face. The red and black smudges from her screen reflected in his hair and the edges of his robe, like a bleeding corona.

'What was all that about?' I asked the group, feeling like I was making polite conversation in a torture chamber. 'We were working on an intruder. Missed the briefings.'

'For Christ's sake, Reynolds, pardon my French, keep up…We're making history here.' The man's gaze was rapt and wary rolled into one.

'Give me a break. We've been too busy protecting you lot,' I said, channelling my feelings into my response. 'Some sort of operation, right?'

'Yeah. Operation.' The man looked at me with questioning eyes. 'You're not a details man…Why so interested now?'

'Because we're making history, right?'

Latham glanced across at Winterbourne and the woman and back to us. In a hushed voice, 'If you must know, she's having an

everything transplant from the blonde.' He
was almost breathless with excitement, 'She
got in the way of a radiation leak, they
said...A real mess.'

Another acolyte joined in, eager, 'This'll be
our toughest yet. It's a "closing down sale"
for blondie – everything must go.' A snigger.
'Move over, medical science, here we come.'

'It's sooo cool,' said Latham. He'd always
been a dick.

'Worth all the work,' said another.
'Amazing, right? Plug and play.'

'Better than the last one - that black-haired
bitch was no good.' Latham glanced at the
heap of bodies, 'Never hurts to get rid of
some dead wood'. He sounded like an
investment banker who'd just fired some
analysts, not a serial killer; I noted the fine
distinction. I bit Endymion Walker's lip to
distract myself; it tasted different from mine.

I said nothing.

A full Transfer. Heavier *Ma gic* than I'd thought. From deep in the past; buried. Where it should have stayed; where lots of things should've stayed. Centuries ago, rulers and priests had sustained their lives by transferring – stealing – organs and life energy from the young and healthy: dynasties of parasitic rulers had clung on by feeding on the vulnerable, making themselves immortal. Gods, shape-shifters and ghosts; people returning from the dead. All the legends that were being re-worked down here by Winterbourne and his team of predators.

Winterbourne was blending old and dark *Ma gic* with cutting edge technology, defying – re-defining - the natural order, targeting a new generation of victims: the lost and the homeless.

64

01:50:31
MEYRA

Sam Franklin and I made our excuses and left the group of fools. When would it be their turn, down here where the dwarves lurk, to be fed into the dark? It was *worse* than dwarves: this place was like a mine, with human material as the precious ore, for smelting in the silver furnace.

I edged closer to the slab bearing Olivia Walker, Winterbourne continued to stare at the other woman, composing his thoughts ahead of his Noon deadline.

The red and black patches on the screens cast an ugly glow over the area, polluting the air, creeping over our robes and faces. Olivia Walker would inherit the doomed woman's illnesses. Then a miracle of re-birth on the other slab.

Re-birth. Renewal.

Repugnant.

I would not allow it. Some day they might be able to turn it against my kind.

Olivia Walker had made her way to the coast for a fresh start, a chance to re-evaluate her life. The Haven intended to take that away when she was at her most vulnerable.

They thought that, with Walker out of the way, no-one would come for her.

They were wrong.

65

01:40:12

SAM

This abomination was the opposite of what the Circle had always stood for.

The *Ma gic* Circle had formed once enough people had asserted some control over *Ma gic* – more accurately, *once enough people had learned to harness and manipulate it without killing everyone else in the room, or burn themselves out, or attract and be annihilated by creatures with more tentacles than seemed polite.*

The Circle had evolved by banding
together a motley collection of enthusiastic -
and fortunate – wizards, enchantresses,
coven members, druids and charlatans. Even
hedge wizards. At a stretch, necromancers,
but they're only talked about in low tones
when no-one else is listening, like mentions
of Great-Aunt Mildred at family gatherings,
the one living in the woods with staring
eyes, a moustache and infinite cats.

These days, the organisation is a slick,
virtually invisible to the everyday world,
major corporate body with discreetly - *very*
discreetly - accumulated assets of dizzying
value. So dizzying that it could have been
listed on the stock market if we'd needed the
money – which happily we didn't. And if we
were prepared for the general populace to
have the slightest clue of our existence.
Which we weren't.

One essential fact has held true since the
beginning: if widely known to exist, *Ma gic*
would be a source of fascination closely
followed by absolute terror. Even more
closely followed by pitchforks and the
ducking stools; and, nowadays, automatic

weapons and restraining orders. *Ma gic* needed to be hidden, monitored, controlled, not allowed to run wild in the wider world. Legendary feats and creatures needed to be kept just that: legendary. In a state of routine unbelievability.

Gideon Winterbourne had perverted all of that, and this predation on real world pain had to be stopped. Just as importantly, Meyra needed to see again how we kept order on our home turf.

I sidled over to Olivia's slab; Meyra followed. A thick silvery filament connected it to the one holding Shevchenko. At the mid-point, fat wires met and burrowed into the floor, connecting the silver column and the slabs. A physical and *Ma gic* nexus.

A weakness.

I motioned to Meyra to cast a Burn where the wiring between the slabs met. The abundant *Ma gic* sloshing around this place would amplify it. Burn's a Hex that requires caution and restraint – particularly when barbequing – but, on this occasion, caution and restraint were the exact opposite of what we needed. We needed to unleash our inner pyromaniacs.

I locked together my hands in a complicated double fist that seemed to contain more fingers and thumbs than were strictly required, or normal; Meyra did the same. Flames flickered.

We were ready to rock and roll.

But not the way we'd planned.

Something hit me in the middle of my back. A stinging pain. Followed by 50,000 volts coursing through my system.

I rocked to one side and rolled on the floor as my consciousness was snuffed out quicker than a tea light at a baked beans convention.

66

01:15:03
SAM

I woke up with the sort of headache warranted from necking a bucket of Rioja the night before.

I was floating as if I were in a Zorb ball at the beach, but there was no sand or sea. I span gently in my own personal sphere.

It was peaceful. *Just lie back and relax. It would be so easy.*

Meyra appeared in my line of sight. She was drifting in the middle of her own

sphere, her eyes wide. I tried to wave to her
to say hello, but by doing so I changed the
angle of my body and lost contact with her,
wheeling round to face Asim Hussain, and
Walker's corpse draped in Reynolds's
bodyshell, wearing Reynolds's face.

That was when I remembered:

Winterbourne, creepy cult figures,
necromantic life drain, all that jazz.

I tried to thrash my way out of the sphere
but only succeeded in helplessly coming
round to see silver-robed figures peering
through the surface of my sphere. I spotted
Latham. Then Gideon Winterbourne. Then
the rat-faced man. It felt like it was feeding
time at the zoo, but with me as the food.

'First Walker, then the girl, now *him*',
Winterbourne said. 'I am Really. Not.
Impressed.' The other robed figures fixed
their attention on me or the floor, anywhere
else. Total silence.

Meyra and I were exactly where he needed
us. Restrained, unable to interfere.

'How's your enhanced security been working out for you, Gideon?' I said.

His expression was grim. 'Bearing in mind where you are at this point, ultimately quite well, I think. Dressing up in someone else's face doesn't become you, Franklin. Nor *her*.' He turned to the other onlookers and pointed to one of them, '*You* stay here, the rest of you get back to your work.' The man stood rooted to the spot. The others shuffled away without a murmur, eyes down. Winterbourne's tone brooked no disagreement; they had seen what happened to employees who transgressed. Termination.

'It was a mistake taking on that girl,' said Winterbourne with a nod in Olivia Walker's direction. 'That kind of mistake won't happen again, ask Foden,' he said looking at the gurney. Carelessness with paperwork would result in more than just paper cuts. 'Regrettable sloppiness. We didn't realize who she was until it was too late. No matter. We are where we are.'

'What gave us away?'

'Reynolds. He is useful but weak.
Spineless.' Harsh given that he was wearing
a corpse for Winterbourne. 'He would not
have coped with seeing his face on Walker. I
checked your auras and they didn't match.
Your game of musical faces didn't work,' he
said. 'Who else knows about this place?'

'Just us.'

He shook his head and called to the
acolytes, 'Get ready to do another Infusion
for the column,' he said. No laser beam
hovering over my crotch, no twiddling by
Winterbourne of his spiky moustache, not
even a throaty *MWA-HA-HA-HA.*
Disappointing.

'No point threatening me with that,' I said.
'As you very well know.'

'Not you,' he said. 'Her first. As a practice
run,' One of the acolytes stepped forward
and started to unhook Meyra's sphere. 'Then
your family. You must know they're being
well looked after.'

Emma and the kids. Of course. Their 'guard detail' at the house - Tweedledum and Tweedledee. On Winterbourne's pay roll. Rage swept through me as the acolyte set off with Meyra's sphere to the circle around the column; I thought of Emma, Beth and Jamie at home with the two goons.

'Last chance,' I said. 'Stop all this, pack it all up and walk away.'

He said nothing, turned away and beckoned towards the gallery.

I heard flapping, getting louder, coming closer.

Wings.

Napoleon. Winterbourne's familiar.

He extended his arm and the crow landed on his wrist like a budget falcon. He ruffled some of Napoleon's glossy, dark feathers affectionately. As close as he ever got to affectionate, anyway. Four malevolent eyes fastened onto me.

Necessity is the mother of invention;
desperation is its auntie, the always smiling
one with forearms like a bodybuilder.

'I warned you,' I said.

'Caw,' I wasn't sure which of them that
had been.

67

01:13:14

SAM

Even upside down, I managed to Focus, as if I were lovingly crafting a tiny diamond spider web while balancing on the head of a pin.

I unleashed my improvised Hex.

01:13:12

My body jolted. All of it. As I mentally clawed open a connection between my consciousness, my *being,* and that of the acolyte attending to Meyra. I arrived, didn't ring the doorbell or wipe my feet, just went right in and took up residence in his head and surveyed if he needed any re-wiring or decorating done.

This psyche ain't big enough for both of us.

I evicted him: the soul equivalent of emptying his suitcases onto the street from an upstairs window. His spirit, his essence, passed by me on the way out. I felt a bellowing cry of outrage and protest from him as we passed in transit. And fear. A lot of fear.

I found myself where he'd just been, standing by Meyra's bobbing sphere, the attached line in my hand.

I looked back over my shoulder. Across the cavern I saw Walker's – my! - body still hovering in its sphere at the foot of the spiral slope, containing the acolyte's spirit, essence, whatever. There was a look of complete disorientation on my – Walker's – face. Then he started to panic as he lost touch with where he was, who he was, why he was able to see himself stooped over Meyra's sphere across the cavern. The ultimate split personality.

There was an uncomfortable element of dark *Ma gic* in my Hex. It drew on the rawness saturating this place, but this wasn't a great time for me to be picky.

My Snakeskin victim made some incoherent noises as he battled to overcome his shock.

Winterbourne didn't seem to have noticed the change of occupier and leant down to whisper something in Napoleon's ear. Now I knew why the collective noun is a *murder*. The crow squawked, stretched its wings and settled into a steady rhythm, flapping in the direction of the gallery, and the tunnels and mound beyond. A message to relay to the Tweedles? An order for reinforcements? It didn't matter. The crow didn't have far to go, and I needed to clip its wings permanently.

I plucked three of the smooth, cool, still-glowing, beads from around my neck. So cool, they nearly stuck to my fingers. I aimed

and Fired at the small black shape which by
now had nearly reached the gallery.

A moving target in deepening shadow.
Three shots, shotgun-style. Long distance,
like extreme clay-pigeon shooting in an unlit
tomb.

No chance.

The beads were like tracer bullets,
punching holes into the chalk walls. Not into
the crow. They continued to glow, mocking
my bad shooting. Not as much as that crow,
though: Napoleon flew on unimpeded
radiating amusement and defiance. A cheeky
barrel-roll, then out of sight. Another
countdown seemed to have just begun for
us.

Winterbourne was for the moment still at
the foot of the spiral slope with Asim
Hussain and me – or what he thought was
me. That didn't last long.

He glared at the punctured wall and
traced the origin of the tracers back to me –
that's always struck me as a design flaw in

them. He looked once at the body in the sphere and then back at me. The glowing beads joined the dots for him.

He waved his arms at the acolytes. They had partially re-formed their circle around the column, cowls up, tuning up again, awaiting Meyra's sphere, ready to flay her soul. One particularly cold bastard was tapping his foot impatiently.

Winterbourne pointed at me and drew his finger across his throat.

They stopped chanting: I was delighted. I've never been a fan of choral music; I find it soul-destroying; in this case, literally.

Winterbourne's gesture was very clear: no need for a clarificatory internal advisory memo. None of them wanted to question it, any confusion could be sorted out later.

Winterbourne had given an order.

Kill me and move on.

They had no hesitation in taking me out on Winterbourne's say-so even though, as far as they were concerned, I'd only just worked with them on the earlier ritual. Job security was not high on their list of employee demands here, realistically they just wanted to get this over with and go back to work.

They broke into a run towards me. In the low light, it was reminiscent of simpler times with villagers carrying flaming torches as they jostled for position to be in at the kill.

Winterbourne moved towards me with his angry face on - his marginally angrier than normal face.

Meyra gently drifted around in her sphere directly in their path to me.

68

01:11:44
SAM

I assessed my situation in minute forensic detail: seven hostile luminous fanatics and a seriously pissed off Winterbourne, all homing in on me while I was finishing getting to grips with how my current body worked.

With Meyra out of the way, there was nothing between me and the homicidal cult members. Happy days.

They fanned out as they came, moving fast, deftly re-organising to form a new circle around me. I was about to be brutalised by a line dancing class. Fighting all of them at once would – for me - prove to be short and terminal. Like a gnome in Luton Airport.

Two of the acolytes reached into their robes. So that's where the tasers had gone.

I tossed my necklace straight up above my head, its glowing beads still attached to the chain. When it reached the top of its trajectory, directly above my head, it was like a studded halo lighting up my face. I yelled up into the centre and dragged my hands down and outwards in one swift motion. I pictured each of them as a meteor scything through the Earth's atmosphere to exterminate a herd of dinosaurs.

All the beads hovered in their circle then broke off the chain cleanly with a *snap-snap-snap*. They rained downwards on the incoming soft targets, like designer shrapnel.

Point blank.

Couldn't miss.

The beads ripped through the acolytes, retaining a fading radiance and lending a stylish and sophisticated air to the proceedings. I was like a multi-tasking duellist in a wig and frock coat armed with a bejeweled chainsaw.

The acolytes were scattered at my feet, unmoving.

All the beads had stopped glowing.

The bodyguards pulled large pistols from their shoulder holsters. Ready to act if Natasha Shevchenko needed them. Their body language said *some sort of disciplinary thing. Leave it to Winterbourne.*

For now.

69

01:11:11
SAM

Meyra hates cricket. So does Emma. *Five days. Five days!* Meyra always says as and when it ever comes up. Her – philistine - point was simply that if they could just get cricket down to three shots for each team and then head off for tea and cucumber sandwiches, that might be more acceptable.

I unhitched Meyra's sphere and Focused. With a firm bowling action laced with a bit of backspin, I Pushed the Meyra-sized cricket ball to the top of the spiral slope. I heard the satisfying crash of falling machinery as it landed in the alcove. Felt good. All those Sundays hadn't been wasted. There was no burst of spontaneous applause from my robed spectators (particularly rude on Singh's part - we'd been in the works cricket team together).

Howzat!

70

01:10:35
SAM

I was the only person near the column still standing – a bit of a giveaway. Winterbourne had witnessed my epic display of cricketing prowess with Meyra, not to mention my very own do-it-yourself illuminated St Valentine's Day Massacre.

He put out his arms and leapt towards me and soared through the air, gaining height fast. His Bond. With that bloody crow. Still close enough to lend him its abilities. I hoped that he wouldn't acquire a taste for carrion-eating from Napoleon afterwards. The thought made me shiver.

Six feet off the ground. More gliding than flying. Fast.

He reached into a small pouch on his belt.

Best not to hang about.

Pagoda was also still in range, so I Sprang over to the slabs. I heard a series of cracking sounds as he Fired a volley of bullets at me. They crashed into the floor where I'd been standing. One ricocheted with a whipping sound from the slab holding Olivia, a hint of his increasing desperation, prepared to endanger the prize.

His height gave him an advantage. A big advantage. I saw him grab more bullets and ready himself for another salvo.

I needed to disable the machinery. There was no more time.

I channelled *Ma gic* to protect myself as I ripped out a power cable. It spat and hissed;

I Focused on the filament and grabbed the bare wiring with both hands; it twisted and boiled as I funnelled power from the cable directly into it. Not to be tried at home.

There was a fire at the fireworks factory and the equipment at the head of the slabs fused into slag, the screens went dark.

There was a pleasing scream of rage from above and behind me.

I was not out of the woods yet. In fact, I was so not out of the woods yet that I was more in a clearing in the middle of the woods about to be savaged by a giant warthog.

71

01:09:18
SAM

The bad news:

I'd run out of beads and my new
borrowed body wasn't carrying any other
useful ammunition. Options were thin on the
ground: my head was throbbing from my
over-use of *Ma gic* and from trying to keep
up with where my body *really* was. I couldn't
remember having felt this bad since I guest-
barded at last year's Eisteddfod and drank
random Welsh liqueur at a seventeen-hour
barbecue.

The bodyguards looked impressed at a professional level by Winterbourne's airborne attack. His glide had taken him over Natasha Shevchenko's slab, but there was no present threat to their charge. I clearly represented some sort of problem for Winterbourne, but they wouldn't care as long as he sorted it all out. Easier for them to hold off and let him clear up his own mess. He'd finish me off and then get on with the Procedure. Job done. Their guns were still out, held by their sides, loose but ready.

Winterbourne raised his hand towards me, palm upwards, filled with gleaming bullets all eager to make my acquaintance. *Just passing through.*

Firing position.

The good news:

None came to mind.

More bad news:

I had virtually no cover.

I was a sitting duck, in this case strapped to a chaise longue with a bullseye painted on my bill.

01:08:50:27

Winterbourne tossed six bullets into the air and Fired all of them into me in rapid succession, roaring with triumph. He'd evidently decided to cut short questioning me.

01:08:50:26

The good news (for me):

I had felt the rush of consciousness both ways, and a vestigial trace of terror, despair and overwhelming pain and darkness as six rounds shredded their target.

I had left it late. Really late.

72

01:07:50
SAM

It had been literally a near-death experience – for me - no white light, no choir of angels. I'd had enough of choirs – of angels or anything else. Newsflash: I had no bullet holes in me; they were only to be found in the newly deceased body of the hapless acolyte who'd had an actual-death experience, shot six times by Winterbourne.

Cards on the table, while I don't believe in violence unless there's no other way, just now had been my working definition of *no other way*. If I didn't sort myself out straightaway, I'd join the perforated acolyte. I didn't feel bad about him: he'd been about to siphon out Meyra's soul, so my sympathy and conscience were taking a coffee break right then.

I was numb, the last few moments more intense than I could ever have imagined. It took all that I had to bring myself back, dredging up all my training and willpower to cope with the shock. I cleared my head and wondered why, even though I hadn't been shot, I was on the floor in a sticky puddle. I'd been expecting to find myself nestling back in my sphere, frantically trying to come up with a Plan B.

Instead, back in Walker's bodyshell, I was slumped in tar-like gloop on the floor of the cavern in the dripping remains of my collapsed spherical prison. That was both unnerving and something not to get stuck on my feet. The collapse of the spheres had dumped all of the occupants – including the person in my body at the time - on the floor. He'd landed awkwardly; I could tell because I could now feel a big bruise forming. Careless bastard. He could've at least tried to land on my feet. He should be shot. Oh wait. He had been.

I checked over my reclaimed body and was pleased to note that my Snakeskin victim hadn't had time to do anything rash or stupid with it before his terminal return to base.

I looked around me, scanning for immediate threats.

None in touching distance.

Asim Hussain, poor guy, was on one side of me, also sprawled on the floor, trembling. He was shaking his head to clear it, probably hoping he wouldn't succeed. He made a few unconvincing efforts to sit up, but overwhelming confusion and dread paralysed him. He avoided eye or any other contact with anyone at all. On my other side was Walker's slumped corpse, still wearing Reynolds's Snakeskinned bodyshell, infinity-eyed. Going nowhere, unless Winterbourne had mastered Re-animation.

Close and needing to be watched: the two hulking bodyguards. One monitored Winterbourne and the aftermath of 'my' execution. The other looked in my general direction, checking with disgust our prone, streaked forms. We didn't look like much of a problem, more something not to get on his suit. The tension had slightly ebbed from their shoulders, one chewed gum, their guns hung loose. And why not? I was dead: Winterbourne had killed me. No other problems. Their boss was untouched on her slab, Olivia had not moved from hers, the show could go on. I was bare-footed, seemingly cowering in sludge.

Further afield:

Napoleon the crow was en route to the burial mound. Nothing I could do about that. I had to take advantage of the moments of relative calm created by my recent demise.

Meyra was out of sight and out of harm's way, her sphere presumably also collapsed. I pictured her borrowed body in a puddle of ooze on the floor, looking confused. Then, as she came around, mightily hacked off. Lucky that the goo soaking through her robe wouldn't ruin her own clothes currently adorning the unconscious thug: *for goodness' sake, this top's from Prada,* otherwise her vengeance would have been beyond imagining.

Winterbourne had come back down to earth and was facing away from me, looking down at the shattered and extravagantly dead body at his feet. He was taking time to congratulate himself on a job well done. He prodded the body with his toe as a final check.

His grouping had been exemplary. He looked at each slab in turn, confirming no collateral damage in all the excitement. Satisfied, he turned his attention to the obliterated machinery from which I had created a fine modern sculpture in the cavern.

Then he slowly shook his head. I could feel his concentration burn.

He swivelled on the spot, his robe swirling to catch up.

He stopped dead.

He locked eyes with me as I sat in my puddle.

I'd hoped for longer.

73

01:04:01
SAM

One of my standard rules of combat is never bring just a robe and sticky hands to a gunfight.

I scrambled to my feet, wiped my hands on my robe and looped my arm through Asim's. I pulled him upright, grunting with the effort. Pagoda was close enough to allow me to Spring up the spiral slope clutching Asim, away from Winterbourne, and bypassing the bodyguards just in case.

I was in mid-turn away from Winterbourne when I heard two loud metallic clicks. The bodyguards had evidently decided they'd had enough and it was time for them to join in the fun. Shoot first and resolve issues afterwards. Asim and I were trapped between the Winterbourne rock and the two hard asses. Great.

The bodyguards settled into a crouch, two-handed secure grips, ready to fire. I steadied myself to Spring, but was more likely to Hop given the weight of the two of us. The Easter Bunny would've made a more relevant familiar at that point.

It's an unfortunate fact that scissors always beat paper; and semi-automatic gunfire will always beat Hopping.

Couldn't stop, though. I had to try.

I lurched, trying to create momentum.

Futile.

I started to Spring and it went as well as I'd feared.

On the bright side, no gunfire followed us up the slope, and I just carried on carrying.

Asim and I reached halfway up, lippity lop – more stompety-stomp, in truth - before I looked back from where we'd landed to determine why the Easter Bunny had come through for us.

'Hi Sweetie,' said Emma.

74

01:00:01
EMMA

The huge cave below me opened out, a relief from the mound and the tunnels and the reverberating growl of some sort of animal on the way through. And flapping sounds over my head. I've *never* liked bats. A dark primal shape, sloping past me in the low light. But I had got past them. And I'd found him.

That crouching white-haired old man holding up someone else part way up the slope wasn't Endymion Walker. It was my husband. And further back, was that Gideon Winterbourne? What was *he* doing here?

Apart from looking murderous – somehow, he *always* looks murderous, even in his office. He was stalking through a sea of scattered bodies to the foot of a spiral slope.

More pressingly, Sam and his new friend were about to be shot by two men who would look at home on the door of a down-market club, apart from their ugly-looking guns; Tweedledum and Tweedledee's cousins. The way that Winterbourne was looking at Sam was more disturbing than usual. They had never got on, but this was a whole new level of workplace conflict.

I have always found it difficult to jump off a tall building. But effectively that was what I did.

I stopped myself two-thirds of the way down, floating.

The bouncers did not see me coming. Why would anyone expect a flying witch to appear directly behind them and attack? I Levitated them – using the express version; some might say the *you haven't done your lesson prep, again?* version. They hit the ceiling of the cavern and I heard the snap of a collarbone and a sharp exhalation of pain, I imagine from the same one.

My Friday class hadn't gone well, I'd had a showdown with the Tweedles in my sitting room, breaking one of my favourite vases, and I'd trailed Sam all the way down here to find out WHAT THE HELL HE WAS PLAYING AT.

And my feet ached.

I removed their Levitation.

There were two more thuds as the bouncers re-discovered the ground the natural way. This time no sound from either.

Sam's eyes were wide, 'Glad you dropped in.'

'You're welcome.' I looked Sam up and down, assessing his rather underwhelming new look, 'What have I told you about getting stuff without me being there?'

'I kept the receipt.'

Winterbourne's voice broke in as he came towards both of us, Sam part way up the slope dragging the other man; me still several feet off the floor: 'What is this? A Franklin family outing?'

Sam ushered the other man up the slope and turned to face Winterbourne. With me. Now we were getting somewhere. My questions about corporeal time-share could wait.

75

00:59:09
SAM

Emma's arrival had temporarily tipped the balance in our favour. Until that bloody crow brought back reinforcements. That would only be a matter of time.

A chocolate-coloured shape strutted into view at the top of the slope, padding in that insufferably smug way that cats do. She surveyed her domain and fastened her gaze on me.

76

00:57:27

PAGODA

Can't trust humans to get anything done by themselves. My human's mate had been no use, I just ignored her in the tunnel, she got in my way.

Run a front paw over my face in the eternal quest to be clean. Perfect. Time to strut and preen. A short purr of contentment to treat myself.

Yowr, something was caught in my mouth.

77

00:55:01
SAM

I could see that something was up, even from this distance. Pagoda stopped in mid-sweep of her paw across her face.

I inspected her more closely.

She had missed a bit.

A chewed ugly black feather sticking out of the side of her mouth which she dislodged with a lavish sweep of her tongue. It fluttered to the ground. Even from down here I saw that she was purring, eyes narrowed.

Napoleon had met his Waterloo.

00:50:00

Winterbourne looked up and realized what that black feather meant. That was at around the time the jolt of searing pain caught up with him from his Bond with Napoleon disintegrating.

For a moment, he didn't know his ass from his Elba.

He faltered.

His familiar had been killed; his acolytes skittled over; Shevchenko's bodyguards had been yo-yo'd by Emma into submission.

But Winterbourne was still standing.

A slight shimmer showed that he had a Shield up. I could expect him to have more bullets literally to hand. This was not going to be the time for a gentlemanly *Ma gic* duel between well-behaved senior Casters, like a game of ultimate cage croquet. I needed to bring it down to an altogether more physical encounter. The personal touch.

I Sprang down the slope to finish Winterbourne off.

While I was in mid-air, he reached into his robe. No bullets came out. Instead, he opened his fist and scattered chalk and dirt in my - and Emma's - direction, making a guttural sound as he splayed his arms wide.

His Dig Hex galvanised the rock below me like a beast in torment clawing at the bars of its cage. It tore through the floor, aimed at where I would land. Spot on, despite my frantic attempt to change direction in mid-air. Not good enough.

I reached ground level. Or what had previously been ground level. It had come alive, twisting, clamouring to trap me. The rock became jagged, unforgiving as Winterbourne drove it towards me.

Not just me.

I heard a squeal behind me, then nothing.

I harnessed my forward momentum, Focused on how he was manipulating the rock and, cat-like, dodged – by a whisker - through gaps. Winterbourne's *Ma gic* was crude but effective. I tried to surf the roiling rock, trusting my instincts. WHAT HAD HAPPENED TO EMMA? At that point my concentration and luck ran out. The slashing and grasping rock enveloped my left foot, rapidly forming and reforming around me.

Pain. Crippling pain, as moulded rock gouged into my ankle.

Winterbourne saw his chance. He retrieved a handful of bullets. Reloaded.

Looking round, I saw Emma lying on the floor, blood streaming from her head. A clump of bunched rock loomed over her like a spiked fist, red and glistening. I had to escape, see that she was OK. She had to be OK.

I Focused, ignoring the excruciating pain in my foot, and I Pushed hard. The rock moved.

But not enough.

Winterbourne stood over me.

I could see all six bullets rising out of the palm of his hand, and I just stopped. I had run out of Hexes, no more cat moves, nowhere to go. No escape.

78

00:45:10
SAM

A loud crackle and fizz, snapping and popping, came from behind Winterbourne. He lurched forward but didn't go down.

Whatever it had been, it'd slowed him down. Gave me a chance.

No time to question. Just act.

I screened out everything else in the chamber.

Ma gic is remarkably flexible, it's part of its allure. It grows with the user, Hexes evolve, are refined, ideally like cooking with the contents of a student's fridge and coming up with a Michelin-starred menu; the power of thought made real with combinations of movements, sounds and symbols, all ordered normally in an elegant pattern. A kaleidoscope that crystallises into something wonderful.

I could endure a downturn in elegance here, I needed strong. Right now. This wasn't an experiment in the Circle labs.

I combined a pinpoint Focus with a desperate Push, and some further Spring borrowed from Pagoda. In this place of pumped-up *Ma gic*, I came up with the equivalent of a titanium crowbar. I plunged it into the restraining rock, searching feverishly for leverage. I dragged and scraped my foot out of the entangling rock. Put weight on it. Screamed with pain, transfixed by the ripped flesh that was somehow, unaccountably, part of me.

A tattooed figure stepped out from behind Winterbourne. An acolyte to finish what he had begun?

Meyra. Wearing her borrowed thug-face, set to calm and controlled.

Holding a taser.

She held up the taser, unable to resist the opportunity to show off her diligent cultural research:

'Hasta la vista, baby,'

79

00:42:12

MEYRA

I would have preferred an arrow, but the strange pistol which fired a spear on a wire seemed to work well enough. Sam Franklin was forever talking about back-stabbing colleagues, and there I was doing just that. Sam Franklin should pay attention to that as something that I do well.

My concentration had returned quickly after I had found myself on the floor in the untidy remains of my bubble. I had made my way around the gallery and climbed down behind Gideon Winterbourne, even in this clumsy oaf's skin.

I had seen that Sam Franklin was in mortal peril. The distance weapon was all I could think of, and it worked. Not completely, I noted that Gideon Winterbourne's Shield deflected energy from my shot. My single shot.

Gideon Winterbourne was slowed down not stopped. Sam Franklin needed to get away from him and recuperate. Pagoda was concentrating further up the slope, providing Spring and, in those precious seconds, Sam Franklin Sprang – I suspect the word I would prefer to use would be *Limped* – to his wife. She had been hit by a writhing outcrop of rock from the Dig and let out a low moan. He bundled her up the spiral slope towards the tunnels above.

I retreated and Stealthed into the area around the slabs. The Franklins would be able to fend off Gideon Winterbourne without me. Olivia Walker was breathing evenly and serenely, still unknowingly *waiting*. Her forehead was unnaturally cool to my touch, as if her system had slowed to the bare minimum required to sustain her.

I began to murmur in her ear, incanting to counter the *Ma gic* placed on her. She needed to be on the move, she and I needed to be away from here before Gideon Winterbourne returned.

80

00:39:06
SAM

We needed to regroup in the burial
mound. There, we could figure out how to
tackle Winterbourne: I had a damaged ankle
and a blasting headache from the *Ma gic,* and
Emma, concussed, was reduced to stumbling
along beside me. We looked like we'd just
left the ninth hostelry in a three-legged pub
crawl, six-legged if you counted Pagoda. At
least none of us had been sick yet.

My ankle felt like it was on fire, but I had a
plan. Pagoda needed to stay close, but not
put herself in a position where she might

end up the same as Napoleon. Pagoda was well ahead of me on that thought; she hid near the top of the spiral slope, pupils huge, tail like super-sized candyfloss.

On our way out of the cavern, Pagoda's eyes snaked to Winterbourne, then beyond the gallery to the connecting tunnel, then to me, then back. She had met Bill once in the burial mound at rather too close quarters. The experience had been terrifying, the demon's claws and fangs rather too impressive. At least all her fur and organs were still in their correct alignment. More contact was, to say the least, unwelcome. But Winterbourne was behind us, and our Bond hummed as I insisted that the burial mound was where we needed to be.

Emma and I staggered as quickly as we could along the tunnel, past where we had stashed Reynolds and his sidekick. Into the burial mound.

I heard Winterbourne getting nearer. There was the faint glimmer of a Lantern in the connecting tunnel behind us, mixing with the glow from the floor lights. The

interior of the burial mound remained
unwelcoming, but what would you expect
from a burial mound? Bill was rampaging
around his new home above us where
Pagoda and I had imprisoned him. He didn't
sound like he was putting together a
housewarming party.

I managed to get Emma over to the
pedestal with the skeleton laid out on it.
Only just made it. Limping heavily now.
Emma and I lay down next to the preserved
bones and mimicked the shape. Emma said,
'You really know how to treat a girl, you
silver-tongued devil.' Her voice was faint,
wavering. She moaned with the effort of
saying that, but it meant that she was
hanging in there.

I created an Illusion of the two of us as
skeletons curled up on the pedestal,
superimposed over the real one. Illusions
embellish inanimate objects (Pagoda and my
twins don't count), enhancing what is
already there. They don't stand up to
scrutiny; more camouflage than disguise, a
deferral not a solution. The – I hoped -
artfully arranged tableau gave the

impression of two sets of ancient human remains destined to lay together forever in the burial mound, an eternal threesome with the original and we had never even been properly introduced. Preferably the scrunched up remains amounted to a useful misdirection rather than a prediction of our immediate future.

I examined Emma's head. It was bruised and swollen, the cut was deep but the bleeding had slowed. She let out a pained sigh when I touched it.

I kept her talking, 'The kids?' Bearing in mind that the two of us were here with a vengeful necromancer, that would be awkward for anyone to explain to Social Services if we didn't make it back.

'They're fine,' she said, grimacing with effort. 'I left them with Justin, and it's nearly the full moon,' Justin's a great guy for a practising werewolf, always happy to give hunting lessons and grooming tips to his godchildren. Winterbourne and his team would have to be pretty determined to go after them. And not catch Justin at a mealtime – his table manners at this time of the month were variable, ranging from informal to Splatterfest.

When it came down to it, *we* were the immediate problem. My torn and bloody foot had taken a mauling in the snarling rocks, and Pagoda's recuperative powers through our Bond hadn't done more than let me control the pain. Emma would need to recover the hard way. The usual Bond side effect kicked in and I felt an urgent need to bat around a sparkly ball with a bell in it. I suppressed it. It was not the right time. Patience. Patience.

Despite the hiding and the Healing, Winterbourne knew very well that we wouldn't get very far, and he knew we'd be here. Waiting.

With every step, Winterbourne made screeching noises along the walls of the tunnel as he approached, like birds' claws scraping on steel. 'After I've killed both of you,' he called, 'I'm going to go back and continue with the Procedure. The cheap theatrics with the countdown meant nothing:

it was conjuring to impress the troops. The real power's surging through this place. Through me.'

Even then he didn't let out a maniacal laugh. Cheated again. The expiry of the countdown would have created a spectacular performance, but now Winterbourne just wanted to remove what he thought of as the remaining obstacles: Emma and me. Meyra had escaped his attention, Winterbourne blaming me for the blast of energy hitting him; some cunning Hex on my part. He was solely focused on me, just wanting to finish me off - Emma was helpless - no more tricks. I also wanted to finish this, although the critical steps of my plan for that remained a work-in-progress.

Ever theatrical, Winterbourne had conjured a red Lantern that swamped the area around him, filling the archway with crimson light as he arrived at the entrance to the burial mound, his silhouette sharp and dangerous as he swept inside. I could see a glimmer from his Shield. He was ready, we were waiting.

I remained as quiet and still as possible;
Emma did the same. I prepared a Hex.

Perfect first time would do nicely.

81

00:35:06
SAM

Winterbourne came closer, scanning for movement, Focusing.

He came close enough. I triggered my Burn Hex. It lit up the immediate area with a fierce blue-white beam that cut through his Lantern. Fleeting jagged shadows reared and then immediately retreated into the gloom of the mound. Some got past his Shield and he grunted with pain. Not enough pain. It didn't stop him and, pierced by the beam, it shattered my Illusion, exposing Emma and me, restoring reality.

515

'Was that really the best you can do?' he said, touching his arm, then shutting down the pain. He was almost smiling. I scrambled to my feet from the pedestal. Clumsy, very clumsy, nowhere for Emma and me to run, even if either of us *could* run; Emma tried to rouse herself behind me.

Winterbourne reached for his tried and trusted bullets which gleamed redly under the Lantern, about to be redder still. Difficult to criticise his aesthetics if I ended up lying on the ground in front of him, shot in the head.

He was standing in the centre of the stone sacrificial circle.

Time for some good old-fashioned vengeance and redemption.

I Focused on the Ward over Bill's chamber above us - my old digs, his new prison. I drew the back of my right hand across my eyes, left to right, trailing three fingers, Beth would say it was a tragic Dad-dancing move. The Ward over the entrance dissolved.

One…nearly two.

A piercing scream came from Bill's chamber as he realised that he was free. He injected pure fury and hatred into that scream. I saw his blue, horned visage emerge from the chamber. He saw me and his lips snapped back as he made a low rasping sound that reverberated around all of us.

Then he saw Winterbourne.

That Bastard Gideon Winterbourne.

Outlined against his Lantern, picked out by the lights on the floor.

Although I'd physically imprisoned Bill in the cramped burial chamber, Winterbourne had enslaved his tortured and broken form. His consciousness shaped itself into a series of narrowing tunnels: obey, revenge, rend.

Revenge, rend.

Rend.

Winterbourne stared at his arm; at me, all
in one smooth movement. His protective
bracelet was charred and smoking: the target
of my Burn.

He tried to react, to strengthen his battered
Shield, put up a Ward, do something -
anything - to protect himself.

But Bill was too fast.

Too focused.

Too alive, for the first time since his death.

He dropped from his prison like an
executioner's axe, but sharper. Hi s claws
extended, face folding back until there was
nothing left but row upon row of razor fangs
surrounding expanded nostrils and baleful
slitted eyes. His eyes looked sharper and
more painful than his fangs and talons
combined.

Revenge may be a dish best served cold,
but for Bill it was the sort of cold that *burns*
when you touch it. He landed on

Winterbourne as he was trying to summon a defensive Hex.

Out of time.

Bill reached out to Winterbourne, reached into his flesh, sought his heart.

Found his heart.

Tore it out, his heart still beating; I could almost hear a motorbike revving in the background and a tolling bell in the blazing sun.

Winterbourne's body sagged and collapsed onto Bill's claws. There was a sigh as Winterbourne's life energy left his body, appropriately punctured like a Zeppelin shredded by bullets. A flicker, then eyes forever wide. Life energy poured into the silver of the circle beneath his feet, down into the silver column below.

Bill turned towards me, nostrils widening further, savouring my bouquet, with its tantalising notes of fear and resignation.

I couldn't run; I could barely stand. I was about to become a serving of Sam sashimi.

Bill finished sniffing me and I waited. Couldn't do anything else.

82

00:31:24

SAM

Bill stared at me, looked through Reynolds's face, through my eyes and deep down into my heart – a bad moment – then deeper.

I felt his despair. Without thinking, I reached out towards him. I opened my mind to him, felt a connection, his consciousness clutched at me as if he were drowning. I felt his shuddering desire to be set free, and I shuddered with him. I grasped his wrist, avoiding those claws, and placed my other hand directly onto the silver centre of the floor.

Bill understood and shut his bottomless eyes.

His form wavered.

His claws retracted fully, his features visibly slackened, reforming into the semblance of a human face, Hastings in the photo. The horns were still there, he was scarred and damaged, but I could see for a moment a tiny spark of Hastings once more, exhausted, ravaged. But Hastings.

He was ready.

His essence flowed through me into the column. I was like a lightning conductor, a bridge.

No smart-ass comments from me this time. I observed a quiet few seconds of peace and respect for Kieran Hastings. I went over to his still form. His body was now a husk of spent malevolence. I ignored the fetid smell that rose from his body and carefully picked up his flimsy remains, light enough for me to carry even through my pain. I was not going to leave him here. A proper funeral, I owed that to him and to River. Gideon Winterbourne's remains? He would stay here, I owed him nothing.

I heard a deep rumble, the ground rippled under my feet. Human sacrifices. A powerful wizard. A demon. All passing into the column. Critical mass. Overload. Something had snapped.

A deep bass rumble reverberated around the chamber and down into the depths.

It was time to re-join the others, if we could.

83

00:30:20

I patted Emma on the shoulder, tried to rouse her; she stared at me her eyes like upturned drawing pins without any of the sharpness. Her long fingers gripped me and hung on. I half-stooped to shoulder what felt like a thin leather sack filled with gelatin, all that was left of Hastings.

Somehow, Emma and I reached the archway and carried on down to the gallery of the cavern.

The two bodyguards, hard as Kevlar, even the one with the cracked collarbone, had disappeared, their sense of duty overcome by their immediate desire to get the hell out of there. I sneaked a look up at the ceiling in case Emma had been feeling vindictive.

Asim Hussain was in the alcove at the top of the spiral slope, on the same level as us. I told him that Emma and I were going down to the floor of the cavern for Olivia Walker. He followed me, not arguing, not saying a word, his body language written all over him in bold block capitals, underlined: **I DO NOT WANT TO GO DOWN THERE; I DO NOT WANT TO STAY UP HERE: I DO NOT WANT TO DIE.**

Meyra was attending to Olivia, still trying to revive her.

None of the acolytes was moving; Natasha Shevchenko was still on her slab.

There was a further rumble, much deeper and longer this time. Dust puffed down from cracks in the ceiling. Nature was flexing its oiled and steroid-filled muscles.

84

00:30:00
Thirty minutes to Noon

SAM

Choices.

Emma sitting on the floor enfolding her knees, Meyra busy and alert around the unconscious Olivia Walker, Asim Hussain cowering near us but keeping his distance, trying to make sure he could not be left behind. Pagoda and me scanning the area, what was left of Kieran Hastings propped against the nearest wall, and Endymion Walker's lifeless body wrapped in

Reynolds's bodyshell lying on the ground. All on my list to be saved if we could.

The acolytes were not on that list, their poor lifestyle choices enough to disqualify them. Latham, Singh and the other Circle employees should view the roof falling in on them as a Very Severe Reprimand from Human/Other Resources. Email confirmation to follow, citing their Dark *Ma gic*, moonlighting for competitors. No glass ceiling in their careers, just the cavern's ceiling crushing them. No right of appeal.

Natasha Shevchenko's remaining time seemed borrowed after the derailment of the Procedure but I couldn't face leaving her to be buried alive underground. Bad enough with the sacrificed souls, worse still with Winterbourne and his mates for company.

A fissure opened in the floor and snaked towards us from the side wall with a loud crack. Chips of ceiling pattered down like aggressive snow, the movement of the world around us gathering pace and strength.

'We have no time, Sam Franklin,' said Meyra, looking above her, speaking in the tone she would use if she were ordering a tofu salad and a Perrier. 'It is too far back up to the surface through the burial mound.'

I shook my head, 'We won't need to go that way. Winterbourne will have planned ahead.'

'The two bodyguards ran away when they woke up and saw what was happening,' she said. 'They went up the slope, but I did not see where they went.'

'They didn't pass us. There must be another exit.'

Pagoda was already making her way round the gallery away from the alcove. She scratched at walls as she went, raising her nose and sniffing. I used the Bond to give her some help to see colours better; her eyes narrowed, not with gratitude. She knew she'd pay later when she maybe craved a glass of Merlot and some aged cheddar to go with her cat food.

She reached the corner of the gallery between the treatment alcove and the living quarters. Stopped. Wrinkled her nose and cocked her head to one side. I could see Pagoda's whiskers almost imperceptibly rippling in a faint air movement.

She went over to the wall and worried at it with a single claw when she spotted something among the nuances of colour, then began to work at it with her forepaws.

The Illusion broke down, unravelled by reality. The smooth regular outline of a narrow door cut into the wall behind Pagoda. No *Emergency Exit* sign or *This Way Please*, but good enough: Winterbourne's fast track out. If the bodyguards knew about it, they would be miles away by now.

Pagoda stood by the door composing her body position and demeanour to show how insufferably pleased she was with herself, before dodging some falling debris with a yowl.

Meyra managed to get Olivia Walker moving, one foot trailing uselessly behind

529

her as Meyra half-dragged her along. Asim Hussain ran through some calculations: the door promised salvation, but he needed to stick with us. I gestured towards Natasha Shevchenko and he nodded, understanding. He supported her as best he could, grateful to focus on a mechanical task to take his mind away from all the madness.

Emma gripped onto me and we supported each other, Hastings's body on my other shoulder.

Emma and I led the way up the slope as the cavern shivered again, shedding scales of rock from its pale skin, thudding to earth with a sharp crash around us.

Our bizarre wagon train moved slowly up the spiral slope, but that was okay. No-one was going to be left behind.

The whole of the ceiling shook. Large clumps of rock and concrete rained down like mortar shells on us, one hitting Asim Hussain and making him stagger, blood now pouring from the side of his head, but he kept on going. He made no noise, his mouth closed and thin, resigned.

We all reached the door set in the corner of the gallery. It felt like we had all completed a 10K in Snowdonia during a January blizzard.

The door was tucked snugly into the wall, seamless. I pushed it and it swung back on hidden hinges. No sound, in contrast to the rest of the cavern. More mortar shells thundered to the floor. The roof began to become the cavern's floor and the gallery threatened to join it below.

I looked at Meyra. Time was short. Very short.

I bent down, placed Hastings's body next to Natasha Shevchenko, 'Asim, I want you to take my wife out of here with the rest. I gestured at Hastings's remains and the Russian woman. 'Leave them by the door. Meyra and I will pick them up on our way out. We have a couple of things we need to do.' He gave me a bewildered look. *Why* were we going back in? The rest were too shocked to notice or care.

'Get a move on,' I said.

I kissed Emma on the top of her head. Asim Hussain took up the strain. Behind him, I saw a smooth tunnel, machine-tooled perfect, square in cross-section. More lights were embedded in the walls, the tunnel stretched out flat into the distance towards the side of the hill. Winterbourne had been taking no chances with this Dig if he'd needed to bail out.

And now – oh, boy - *we* needed it.

Meyra and I headed back into the cavern. As I went, I felt a thump on my shoulder and painful pinpricks in my chest and shoulder. Pagoda fastened onto me using all four sets of her claws, ignoring my yelp of pain when she punctured my skin, satisfied that she'd made good purchase.

Pagoda and me. Together. As if the same flesh and blood.

Right then, *my* flesh and *my* blood.

85

11:50 pm
EMMA

Confusion. Dizziness. Pain.

I lurched along a tunnel of rock, leaning on a man I'd never met, holding on to my head to stop it splitting in two, where was Sam?

The man was almost whimpering with effort, this was not the place to rest, but I wanted to rest. I slowed down and the man jabbed me in the side, frustrated and angry, to make me carry on.

There was rumbling all around us.

Where was Sam?

More pain, my legs struggling to support me, the man struggling to support me, pushing Olivia Walker, driving her on, me on.

I squinted, even in the low light, I fought with the juddering images around me and tried to see what lay ahead, surely this must stop sometime. We must reach the end soon. For a few confused seconds, I wondered if we had all died under a hail of falling rock and were making a final journey to wherever was Next, but a sharp squeal from Olivia and an answering grunt from the man brought me back. A door in front of us, a few steps away, none of us knew where it would open, what would lie behind, it could as easily be another section of collapsing cavern, anything.

Olivia struggled to the door, pushed it hard and swung it open. A blast of hot air greeted as it fought with the chill of the tunnel. The opening revealed the side of a hill, a valley below, a small river glistening, dark trees dotting the landscape. It was dark. A blanket of heavy darkness.

'Keep the door open for the others,' I said, the words thick in my mouth like my teeth had been replaced by boulders. Then it was a blur, just a series of staccato lurches as the three of us distanced ourselves from the tunnel.

I felt the earth splintering beneath me, and I dropped onto my knees, the man unable to support me anymore. Figures appeared behind us at the entrance, silhouetted, if I needed to fight them then we were lost. On my knees, I tried to prepare some *Ma gic* to fend off the strangers, but it wouldn't make the right shapes. I collapsed to the ground, I heard a scream from Olivia Walker; I wondered about Sam and Meyra and That Bloody Cat. More blurring.

86

11:55 pm
OLIVIA

The long tunnel was behind me, and behind that the operating theatre run by the grey monks. All of it was collapsing.

A huge crowd burst and stumbled onto the hillside behind us from the tunnel exit like masses of shambling zombies, all dripping with greasy slime, mouths open, eyes wild and staring. Surely no more monsters? They scattered in all directions, pursued by a two-headed giant, deformed and looming, scraping one leg behind, growling with hunger. Another was thin and sinister, cadaverous, although rather stylish for a monster; the third, a ghostlike form floating in the light. Screaming. *Go! Go! Go!*

'Thank the Gods you're all OK,' said the giant taking his gaze from the fleeing zombies and looking at the three of us cowering on the hillside, his features becoming clearer in the moonlight, the deformity resolving into a cat-like figure clamped to his shoulder, his other head the remains of a desiccated corpse.

'It's you,' said the woman lying near me and looking up at the looming figure. Her voice was weak but seemed to gain strength as she focused on the giant. 'I knew you'd make it. I'm glad you got your body back, the other one didn't suit you.'

Was this some sort of trick?

87

Noon
MEYRA

I was pleased to have my own self back from that lumbering oaf, no more *I love Sharon* tattoos in unedifying places.

The floor shook beneath me as I held up Natasha Shevchenko in her white gown. I wanted to drop her. She did not deserve gentleness; I did not understand why Sam Franklin had insisted we bring her out, I would have preferred to leave her down there. Humans are such sentimental, stupid creatures. Mother would have slit the woman's throat to avoid any confusion; I was tempted.

Sam Franklin re-positioned Hastings's body on his shoulder. Both of us knew we were not finished yet, we had to get away from the tunnel. I watched That Feline uncoil itself from around his shoulder where it had been clinging on, a furry grapnel. It dropped down to the grass and ran off. I called out to all the figures that we had retrieved from the sphere chamber, all lying in filth from their disintegrated spherical prisons. 'Please move more quickly, the hillside is about to cave in.'

Sam Franklin was simply yelling in his uncouth manner, 'Go! Get moving! Now!' to all of them that he could reach.

Pagoda observed us, clearly confused by our looking after all the others. To use the time profitably, she started to preen itself in that ludicrously self-indulgent way characteristic of cats.

Grass. In the darkness. Glorious. Like the finest liqueur. I inhaled the sweetness, invigorated and restored, but the moment was spoiled by Olivia Walker screaming like all the others. Hysterical. At least the man was being quiet, 'Stop screaming. Look at us. We are Sam Franklin and his feline and me, Meyra. We have saved you. We have simply returned to our correct bodies. Please compose yourself.'

'Meyra, give her a break: she's in shock, you can't blame her after what they've been through,' said Sam Franklin. 'You've been *trained* for this shit.'

Emma Franklin opened her mouth to join in, but then looked behind us at the burial mound.

We were all looking in the same direction at **00:00:00.**

The hillside imploded with a mournful roar. It collapsed into a sinkhole in a few seconds as the burial mound crashed down through its floor. It sent a tall plume of dust and a groaning sigh of escaping air upwards as a deafening explosion lit up the sky. The blazing midday sun pierced the darkness.

Emma Franklin's voice was clear in the silence that followed:

'My soufflés always turn out like that'.

88

SAM

When we got back to Jezebel, I unlocked the camper van and opened her rock and roll bed. I watched Emma sleep, her head heavily bandaged, her breathing slow and regular. I stroked Pagoda as I fished out a spare mobile from Jezebel's perfectly proportioned glove box. I called River Smith.

'Good *afternoon*, sugar,' River said, her voice more husky than an Antarctic dog-sled team, 'lovely to hear from you.' She made it sound as if she were standing at the foot of the stairs leading up to her boudoir, beckoning.

'River, you can saddle up the troops,' I said. 'I've got something for you,.'

'Just how I like it, sweet cheeks.'

'It's Hastings.' I kept my tone neutral. But she knew what was coming.

I finished the call and left Emma with Pagoda for a bit. I needed a moment to myself.

I sat on the warm ground, basking in the heat of the day, soaking it up.

The record obviously needed to be massaged, history air-brushed: the burial mound and the cavern? What burial mound and cavern? A forgotten end for Winterbourne and his friends. Fitting. Like a well-tailored tomb.

Meyra and I would leave Hastings's body to be found in the grounds of the Clubhouse so that the investigation of the disappearance of Detective Sergeant Kieran Hastings would end heroically. Death in the line of duty as he unearthed the drugs conspiracy. If the regular police saw any of the rest, their helmets would probably all fall off. Case closed.

Not so straightforward for the others.

The incoming Circle Dark Arts clean-up team would take care of the immediate area and turn the victims' memories mostly into fuddled half-dreams. Natasha Shevchenko would remain gravely ill; Asim Hussain might end up back on the streets if the authorities failed again, another rescue mission for Sarah Grantham and Beattie. Olivia Walker might follow in her father's footsteps if resilient enough. Time would tell, perhaps with a nudge from me.

Meyra came over, looking ready to go, as if she were about to put on a stylish hat and go out for brunch at the Ritz.

Now *that's Ma gic.*

PART FIVE

MONDAY, AUGUST 9TH

89

Late evening
A STRANGER

The man bristled in the corner of the Brighton bar. He nursed a golden malt and peered around him at the tourists who had wandered in and stayed for a quick beer in this out-of-the-way dive.

Where? He didn't quite know. He had dust on his black suit that he had brushed as best he could with his former partner's jacket sleeve. They had parted ways soon after emerging from the emergency exit, the man to this dingy hole, the other to an unmarked resting place in the Downs. It had been a short struggle: the element of surprise, his doomed partner's broken shoulder. No witnesses.

He sipped at his drink and felt its heat.

This body was bruised but serviceable, younger, in many ways an improvement, still exuding spikiness as he started to adapt to its contours. He pulled back sharply as a young woman in torn jeans pushed past him, and then slouched, exhausted, grimly clutching his drink. He automatically felt his chest for the umpteenth time to check that it was whole. The Franklins had a great deal to answer for, but not now. Later.

When he was ready.

PART SIX

SUNDAY, AUGUST 15TH

90

Evening
SAM

I approached my hotel room door, it opened and there she was, renewed.

Emma wore a beaming smile over a huge glass of Chablis for each of us.

''Evening,' she said cocking her head towards me and motioning Pagoda to come in too. She passed me my glass and raised hers. We clinked them together and savoured the wine. 'Here's to lost companions and battles won,' she said. Pagoda made herself scarce.

Emma smiled at me and said slowly, 'The kids are fine; they're with Justin until tomorrow.'

'Splendid.'

I put on some Ella Fitzgerald. The curtains were closed and the lights down low. Emma had made a roaring fire in the grate. Pagoda was nearby but far enough away. I poured some more wine from the bottle nestling in the large ice bucket.

'An open fire in August. How decadent,' I said.

She went and sat on the bed and stretched out, 'Better turn up the air con, then,' she purred daintily.

'I love it when you speak Feline,' I said.

'Did you remember to bring the catnip?'

I didn't answer, just dimmed the lights a fraction more.

Printed in Great Britain
by Amazon

36314765R00326